About the Author

Pier Simone Marrocchesi was born in Siena (Italy). A particle physicist and university professor, he worked at CERN and on cosmic-ray research with balloon launches from Antarctica. At present, he is co-PI of an experiment aboard the International Space Station. A fan of hard science fiction, this is his first novel under the pen name of Pier Marr.

Through the Wall of Time

PIER MARR

Through the Wall of Time

Vanguard Press

VANGUARD PAPERBACK

© Copyright 2024
Pier Simone Marrocchesi

The right of Pier Simone Marrocchesi to be identified as author of
this work has been asserted by him in accordance with the
Copyright, Designs and Patents Act 1988.

All Rights Reserved

No reproduction, copy or transmission of this publication
may be made without written permission.
No paragraph of this publication may be reproduced,
copied or transmitted save with the written permission of the
publisher, or in accordance with the provisions
of the Copyright Act 1956 (as amended).

Any person who commits any unauthorised act in relation to
this publication may be liable to criminal
prosecution and civil claims for damages.

A CIP catalogue record for this title is
available from the British Library.

ISBN 978 1 80016 749 0

This is a work of fiction. Names, characters, businesses, places, events and
incidents are either the product of the author's imagination or used in a
fictitious manner. Any resemblance to actual persons, living or dead, or actual
events is purely coincidental.

Vanguard Press is an imprint of
Pegasus Elliot Mackenzie Publishers Ltd.
www.pegasuspublishers.com

First Published in 2024

Vanguard Press
Sheraton House Castle Park
Cambridge England

Printed & Bound in Great Britain

*To the wisdom of all females of my life
including, but not limited to,
my daughter, wife, and mum.
And our cat Mimi, of course.*

*Live as if you were to die tomorrow.
Learn as if you were to live forever.*
- Mahatma Gandhi

Nubes — incertum procul intuentibus ex quo monte (Vesuvium fuisse postea cognitum est) —oriebatur, cuius similitudinem et formam non alia magis arbor quam pinus expresserit.

Nam longissimo velut trunco elata in altum quibusdam ramis diffundebatur, credo quia recenti spiritu evecta, dein senescente eo destituta aut etiam pondere suo victa in latitudinem vanescebat, candida interdum, interdum sordida et maculosa prout terram cineremve sustulerat.

[For those who were observing from afar, it was not clear from which mountain (later it became clear that it was the Vesuvius) arose a large cloud, whose form can be represented by none other than the pine tree. In fact, forcibly elevated as on a high trunk, it spread out in branches, I guess because of the strong push from the first breath of air and then collapsing when it subsided, or even defeated by its own weight, it dissolved in a horizontal spread; sometimes white, sometimes dirty and blotchy, depending on what had been raised along with it, earth or ash.]

- Pliny the Younger, Letters, Book VI, Lett. 16
Herculaneum, 79 A.D.

The villa was now deserted.

Everybody had left in terror, desperately seeking an escape to the harbor. Instinct pushed them toward the water like a herd hounded by the flames of a fire. But the sea looked very bad: it had withdrawn several meters from the shore and was inflated by waves the size of a two-story house.

Black and deadly.

"That's not the way to salvation," thought Setis. "Those unfortunates will never be able to face the fury of the waves. The more daring of them are going to fall into the water and surely be drowned while the others probably will try to take refuge inside the *fornici*, the port warehouses crammed with beached boats."

The town was slowly being covered by layers of ashes and pumice of increasing thickness. Although it was still broad daylight, the sky dimmed and a shower of fiery stones had begun to fall. People were running away trying to protect their heads with garments drenched in water. All around, the screams of pain from those who had been hit, the laments of frightened animals, women in panic, babies crying desperately.

The villa jutted into the sea with an elegant circular-shaped belvedere that dominated a cliff from where Setis could cast a last look at the menacing waters beneath him. Shaking his head, he turned onto the road that ran all along the wall of a rugged embankment on the north side of the villa bordered by a long pergola terrace facing South, a peaceful place where they used to stroll after dinner.

Barely repressing the urge to run, he moved with long strides at his usual morning pace when he walked miles and miles along a dirt path near the coastline. A habit he had developed as a boy and had allowed him to keep his body in excellent shape despite being in his fifties.

He still could not face the crude reality, the terrible calamity that had struck suddenly, anticipated only by weak precursor signs like the small earthquakes of the previous days or the incessant barking of dogs through the whole night. Behind the town, the flat top of the Vesuvius covered with forests, vineyards and lush vegetation – a place beloved by Bacchus and Venus and consecrated to Hercules – had been wiped out and projected at dizzying heights in a cloud that had gradually branched, spreading out like an umbrella and assuming the familiar form of a Mediterranean pine with its variegated foliage in colored stripes of bright colors ranging from dark-red to brown, from gray to black, and fringed with pure white plumes of steam.

The fate of that magnificent villa built on a low promontory overlooking the sea and belonging to Lucius Calpurnius Piso Caesoninus, father-in-law of Julius Caesar, was already given. As indeed was that of nearby Herculaneum, a fashionable seaside resort situated on an incredibly beautiful coastline stretching from Sorrento to Baia, Pozzuoli and Cuma: a small Mediterranean paradise where the patrician villas of many wealthy members of the Roman aristocracy had been built over the years.

With a flash of insight, Setis correlated the devastating phenomenon around him with the strong earthquake that had struck the same area about seventeen years earlier, severely damaging many buildings of the city. At that time no one had suspected that the event had been nothing else than the first sign of the awakening of a giant who had been asleep for centuries under a peaceful-looking mountain covered with rich and fertile soil, a kind of Garden of Eden.

Setis reached a long peristyle surrounding a magnificent garden adorned with bronze statues. An elegant ornamental pool stretched the entire length of the peristyle. Many years ago, in the shadow of those columns, scholars and philosophers of the Epicurean school had meditated in a *cenaculum* gathered around Philodemus, a Greek poet and philosopher native of Syria.

During his years at the villa, Filodemo had collected an impressive number of writings on papyrus scrolls that constituted his personal library. Setis, who had been educated in Greece by one of Filodemo's disciples, had become the curator of the library after his master's death, as well as the superintendent of the villa of the powerful Pisoni family.

He felt his heart tighten at the thought that the library would be destroyed, the papyrus scrolls burned out. Some pieces were unique and all traces of what they contained would be wiped out forever. He *had* to try to save as much of it as possible, even at the risk of his own life. It was just unacceptable that the brainchild of brilliant minds who lived centuries before him would fall into oblivion and their works be lost as if they had never been written. There remained a single possibility: only a supernatural intervention could reverse the fate that now marked the villa and the treasures it contained. Setis clung to this faint hope with the faith of those who are truly desperate.

He knew exactly what to do.

A flow of adrenaline ran all along his spine from head to foot and urged him to move in the direction of the eastern side of the villa where the library was located. He moved quickly along a second smaller square peristyle. Then he passed through a few rooms that were normally used for accommodation in the main body of the villa and finally crossed the entrance of a room of modest size entirely filled with by wooden shelves from floor to ceiling.

Windowless, the room contained hundreds of papyrus scrolls arranged on different shelves fitting into a logical scheme developed by Filodemo. The organization of the library had been extended and improved by Setis himself who knew by heart the location of each section in which the scrolls were stored. Most of the papyri were written in Greek, with the exception of a few shelves that contained works in Latin.

Setis walked to the north side wall and, with the confidence of someone who repeats a familiar gesture, placed both hands on a shelf apparently identical to all others and pushed firmly to one side. A portion of the shelf spun around revealing a cleverly disguised niche in the wall. It contained a dozen hidden scrolls whose existence was known only to him. They were kept inside a leather bag closed at one end with leather straps. Setis felt relieved after checking that the seal was still intact. He took a golden ring from the hide and slipped it on his left ring finger. In the dim light through the door, the ring large dark stone looked as if lined with bluish veins.

Setis closed the hiding place and cast a last look around to check that everything was in perfect order. Then, with a sigh, he quit the library. The footprints left by his sandals warned him that the layer of ashes on the floor of the peristyle was growing quickly thicker. Wasting no more time he headed for the stairs and descended to the lower level. He entered a large room decorated with magnificent polychrome mosaics and quickly scanned it all around. His choice fell on a finely chiseled votive cup placed under a statue of the demigod Hercules. Setis seized the exquisite artifact and, holding it under his arm together with the leather bag containing the precious papyri, he descended two floors below where a steep staircase lead to the cellar. He crossed spacious rooms topped with brick vaults and crammed with large earthenware jars filled with fine wines, oil amphorae, reserves of grain and dried foods. A long series of warehouses ended in a room smaller than the others: a storage room full of wooden crates stacked to the gills.

Setis lit a torch and made his way slowly through the junk. He pushed aside a heavy crate leaning against the wall and uncovered a trap door on the floor. Holding the torch high above his head, he pried it open and carefully stepped down a stone staircase. Finally he slipped into a narrow tunnel dug into a compact layer of lava rock. After a few meters he stopped, overcome by a sense of oppression that weighed on his stomach like a stone. Gritting his teeth, he forced himself to move forward, step by step. He remembered quite well when he had first explored the tunnel. It departed a few hundred meters from the body of the villa leading into a large room with a barrel vault supported by massive arches and brick walls. It had been dug in an area devoid of groundwater seepage and kept completely dry thanks to an ingenious ventilation system that eliminated all traces of moisture. Originally used as a storage room during the construction of the villa, it had fallen into disuse until Setis had rediscovered it. A perfect place to store a part of his large collection of precious antiques, some of which had belonged to his father.

Over the years spent at the villa, Setis had accumulated artistic artifacts from various regions of the Middle East. They reached him by sea thanks to a profitable – but expensive – collaboration with a shipowner from the nearby Neapolis and via his countless contacts, both in Egypt and in various ports in the Mediterranean, with art dealers, brokers of all kinds, people of ill repute and even tomb robbers. A passion he had inherited from his father who had left him the most extraordinary piece of his collection: an object in which now Setis placed his last hopes of salvation.

The history of the artifact was lost in the mists of time and surrounded by an aura of legend and superstition. Changing hands from one owner to the next, it had followed a tortuous journey that could be traced back to a distant region of Mesopotamia. Though it carried no inscriptions, the artifact was certainly very old. It had been found accidentally by a farmer while digging a well in an area that according to the local tradition hosted the remains of a very ancient city that had been buried by a violent cataclysm. Fragments of clay tablets had been found not far away. They were inscribed with cuneiform characters whose meaning was totally unknown at the time of their discovery. From the excavation of the well emerged a metal plate bent into the shape of a somewhat flattened cylinder and adorned with small studs of dark metal forming a complex geometric pattern. The plate would have aroused no interest if not for the extraordinary fact that the metal – of an unknown alloy – showed no signs of rust or corrosion, a fact which was totally incomprehensible at that time. While popular legends abounded with references to otherworldly metals and invincible swords forged by some mythological divinity, people with a practical mind knew very well that the only metal known to be incorruptible was gold. If not for the valuable ring that the farmer had found nearby, the plate would probably have been thrown away together with the debris of the excavation pit. Instead, the two objects passed from hand to hand through various owners until Setis' father saw them in the bazaar of a Phoenician merchant. The latter turned out to be quite eager to get rid of them because he held the popular belief that they definitely brought back luck.

The mystery of the incorruptible metal fascinated both father and son for many years. They carried out extensive research, dusted off old legends, followed faint tracks that seemed promising, but never got to the bottom of anything. And neither of them had bothered to give into the silly superstitions that the artifacts would bring, sooner or later, considerable misfortune to their owner. Actually, that was precisely what had happened to Setis' father, who drowned in the sinking of a merchant ship on his way home from Egypt. Now it was not difficult to guess who would be the next victim.

Setis wondered if the sudden cataclysm that would very likely kill him might have a link with his recent findings about the metal plate. Perhaps the gods were angry with him and had decided he deserved severe punishment. He went back to the memories of a few months earlier when, after his usual long walk in the morning, he found refreshment in the swimming pool of the villa. Stretching lazily in the sun after a reinvigorating swim he had fallen asleep in the sunshine. It was unusual for him to indulge in a such idleness, but he really felt very tired from the hard work of the previous days. He had to organize a sumptuous bacchanal offered by the owner of the villa in honor of a group of wealthy guests who occupied important positions in the aristocracy. Now Setis was happy that it was all over and the bunch of depraved had finally returned to Rome. He was wearing the ring that his father had bought at a good price together with the metal plate. The black stone – after a long exposure to the scorching sun's rays – was now hot to the touch.

With a sudden decision, Setis dressed and descended into the cellar. He slipped into the slim passage and reached the underground room. There he spent some time dusting and tidying his collection. While holding the plate to polish it, the stone mounted on the ring happened to touch the surface of the metal. Setis did not pay attention to it, but he was dumbfounded when suddenly his vision blurred and his field of vision filled with colored blobs. Frightened, he leaned toward the plate with the palm of his hand. He wondered if the abundant libations of the night before had played a trick on him. He closed his eyes, but the colored spots did not disappear at all. Instead they began to merge together until they slowly formed a sharper image.

It looked like the face of a man.

Instinctively, Setis withdrew his hand from the plate and immediately the image disappeared.

After recovering from the shock, he decided to try again and reached out, cautiously, until he touched the plate again with his fingertips. The colored spots reappeared instantly. Setis tried hard to focus the image, until he recognized a familiar face staring at him.

"Yes, it's me. Setis, my beloved disciple…"

With a lump in his throat, Setis slowly stretched out his hand to make sure it was all real. Eyes closed, how could he see his hand reaching out his old master and touching his robe? How could he *feel* the touch of his fingers on the soft fabric?

"But… how is it possible? You were… "

"Dead for many years. Is that what you mean?"

"Yes. Who are you, then?"

"Listen, Setis. You're not really talking to your old master, but to his representation."

"…representation?"

"I'm drawing it from your memories," said the old man "from the images of the elderly teacher you have stored in your memory. Stitching them all together I've built a representation of myself. That's it."

"And to whom I'm talking then, if you are nothing more than a mere simulacrum?"

"It is not so easy to explain, dear Setis. What you're experiencing right now is not reality, but only a mere projection of your mind. I will just vanish if you break contact between your hand and this plate."

"So you are just an illusion. Perhaps the work of a god? By the same deity who forged this metal which does not suffer from the ravages of time?"

The face of my old master took on an enigmatic expression, lips pursed in a faint smile, vaguely ironic.

"No. At least none of the gods you've heard of."

"And who else, then?"

"Put it this way, Setis. This plate should not be here. It came up to you many centuries after it was swallowed into the ground by a cataclysm no one could have predicted. It remained dormant for a long time, but now the tiny amount of energy absorbed by your ring was large enough to awaken it. And its owners have already been notified of the circumstance and want it back. For the sake of simplicity, you can think of them as superhuman, as semi-gods, a bit like the myth of Hercules to whom this city is dedicated."

"Master, you know very well that I have never been content with childish fairy tales."

"I know, Setis. I know. But remember that I am not your master but only a means to communicate with you. I cannot answer any of the questions that are currently crowding your mind. I received precise instructions about that. I can only tell you that they will soon be here."

"*They* will be... here? Who?"

"Two of them. Soon everything will be ready and eventually they will recover the plate."

"How will *they* manage to access this underground cellar?"

"Setis, believe me. It is not a problem for them. Accept them as if they were gods. In fact they are not, but for you it is as if they were because they can do things that people of your time are not yet able to do. Follow my advice. I'll tell you what you must do."

When the images and the voice in his head disappeared, Setis remained motionless for a long time.

Finally, he opened his eyes again and recognized the brick vaults of the underground room. He stood looking at them for quite a while, puzzled, under the flickering light of the brazier that was still burning in the corner.

Setis thought he might have been the victim of a hallucination. But the metal plate was still there, in front of him, so real, reflecting the light of the flame tinged in a bluish color. Slowly, Setis spread the palm of one hand and what he saw came as a blow to the stomach. Between his fingers he was holding a gold pendant adorned with a sort of small black pearl.

"So it was no dream," he thought. He remembered the last words of his master: "Take this necklace and these earrings. They will make it easier to communicate with me even with no direct contact with the plate."

"It doesn't make any sense," Setis told to himself," I have to find out what is going on here and if someone is cleverly making fun of me."

There remained nothing else to do but play the game.

During the following days, he followed the instructions and led two slaves into the tunnel to do the job. He did not like the idea that somebody could spread the news about the location of the underground vault and its content. Therefore he carefully kept the two slaves isolated from the others until the end of the work and then sold them to a Greek merchant whose ship was about to sail from Neapolis. Following the instructions of his teacher to the letter, Setis built a sturdy wooden crate, ten feet long and six feet wide, equipped with a lid. He fixed the metal plate at the center of the lid with the concave surface face down. Then he emptied all the display cases containing the artifacts from his collection and placed them close to the walls, leaving an open space at the center of the room where he located the crate. He also built a small votive altar on which he lined up some of the most valuable objects: a locket with a finely worked chain, bracelets decorated with lapis lazuli, and a ring with a large ruby. He had not been asked to arrange either drinks or food for two guests: on this point his teacher had been quite clear. Instead, he had to prepare a copy of a complete list of the papyri scrolls contained in the library which were mostly written in Greek. Setis compiled the list, omitting the scrolls he had hidden inside the library and whose existence was known to him alone. Once the preparations were completed he was forbidden to cross the sturdy wooden door that separated the room from the tunnel.

A few days later, he learned from his old master that the two guests had come and they had already left the villa. They would, however, came back at a later time.

When Setis was finally allowed to enter the room, he immediately noticed that all the offerings were gone.

"A sign of appreciation," he thought "or someone is cleverly robbing me." Suspicious, he looked around and meticulously inspected the premises. The case had been moved slightly aside and there was a strange smell in the air. At first he could not tell what it was, but eventually he remembered when, as a boy, he had taken shelter from a storm under a large oak tree with his father. A lightning had hit nearby and the air was filled with the same smell of "burnt air," as he had named it. And it was the same smell that now permeated the room down the tunnel.

Puzzled, and more and more convinced that it was a plot against him, Setis decided to await the outcome of events and gave orders to double the surveillance around the villa. The visits of the two mysterious guests went on for almost three months at irregular intervals, usually a few days apart, but sometimes even after a whole week. Setis was never allowed to see them. He was burning with curiosity and therefore he felt frustrated for not being admitted to their presence. He was also annoyed with the routine imposed on him of replacing the papyri that had already been examined by the distinguished guests with those of a new list that was regularly left on the votive altar at the end of each visit. In the past few days, the activity had intensified as if the two were anxious to finish their survey of the contents of the library. The gateway to the tunnel remained barred at all times, a sign that the two were at the villa.

On the day of the eruption, Setis felt a trickle of cold sweat running down his spine as he entered the narrow tunnel. He was afraid that the two had already gone. What would become of him and of the precious papyri he carried along if he had found the door ajar and no one inside? Maybe they had not yet realized what was happening on the surface. He had to warn them of the danger immediately and persuade them to take him away with them.

Or, at least, to save the papyri.

He sorely regretted not having included them in the first batch.

Setis had nearly reached the first half of the tunnel, when he started running in fear of being too late. He did not know he was racing against an opponent faster than him, in a race he would never win. In fact, at that moment, a glowing cloud of gas and debris was sliding down along the side of the Vesuvius at an impressive speed. The powerful pyroclastic flow hit Herculaneum in full, vaporizing instantly those who were outside. With a devastating force, the cloud invaded the houses, the streets, the elegant plazas, wrapping as if in a shroud the unfortunates who had sought refuge indoors.

The villa was hit in a full blow and, in an instant, all the light structures were plucked, plasters burst out loudly, clusters of tiles broke off from the magnificent mosaics. All furnishings, curtains, precious fabrics, embroidered linens were charred. Inside the library the high shelves leaned forward and the papyri folded onto themselves.

Setis never knew that the door at the end of the tunnel remained closed. Whoever was inside was unaware of the danger coming down at the speed of a galloping horse or realized it only when it was too late. The destructive fury of the glowing cloud tore the flimsy door and swept everything along its path, transforming that cul-de-sac into a death trap.

Later, when no trace of life remained in Herculaneum, a huge semi-liquid mass of debris and mud slid – at a slower pace than the glowing cloud, but equally relentless – along the side of the volcano. It covered everything and slowly solidified, sealing off what was left of the city. The "Villa of the Papyri," as it would be called many centuries later, was buried under a thick layer of mud lava, not less than twenty meters deep.

The distinction between the past, present and future is only a stubbornly persistent illusion.
- Albert Einstein

Vienna, 1840 A.D.

Yellow flowers, red flowers.

Standing on a line, over my head, on a balcony I was quite familiar with.

A sequence of alternating colors, a bit unusual perhaps, but totally meaningless for the casual observer. Obviously they had been arranged in a hurry and for the only purpose to block my way.

Yellow flowers, red flowers.

They were shouting a silent message to warn me of a serious danger.

I had to stay clear for a while.

My guess was that something unexpected had screwed up the – usually predictable – daily activity of the husband: an enterprising banker, always busy, always-somewhere-else. He had ended up neglecting his wife, a very attractive woman much younger than him and for sure no less enterprising. On my side, I had adapted easily to the husband's schedule and with regular attendance – not less than twice a week – I paid homage to the austere elegance of my beloved Vienna and to the generous beauty of the lady.

While waiting for the all-clear, I began to wander along the streets of the neighborhood and ended up standing at the window of Mr. Stahl's shop.

Yellow flowers, red flowers.

Sometimes, flowers can speak loud and clear.

"Buzz off," they sneered, in silence. Or, worse: "No fish for cats today. Right?"

And they started laughing out loud at me. Again and again.

C*ertain* flowers are definitely like *that*. Just a matter of poor education.

I pretended to hear nothing, but was really mad at them. I returned my hardest look dreaming of incinerating them all. Unscathed, they kept mirroring their colorful heads on the shop window and making fun of me.

Enough. I guessed that from inside of the shop I could monitor the balcony with greater discretion. I was also in a mood to have a chat with the owner, so I decided to step in.

At first glance, Mr. Stahl could have been easily mistaken for an elderly rabbi, maybe for the impressive gray beard and for his bushy, white eyebrows curled on a pair of round glasses riding on a big nose. His sly expression and the way he smiled through his pale blue eyes, glittering, small and cunning, behind the thickness of the lenses gave him the look of an old fox.

I had purchased several ancient books from him and a few beautiful engravings, plus an unknown number of objects of little account that I decided to buy if only for the purpose of gaining his good graces. And every time that nice rascal was able to amaze me with his inventiveness and the magician's skill with which he could turn any obvious imperfection and opacity of the form into something that he was able to sell you as being as transparent as a crystal, for the feline instinct to sniff in the trap, for the patience of the spider in weaving elaborate webs. More often than not, at the end of exhausting negotiations, he managed to sell me some unworthy piece of junk.

It may seem strange, but all in all, this kind of competition amused me and I gladly played into the game. I still remember with pleasure the hours spent with him negotiating the price of some new recent acquisition that intrigued me for one reason or another.

As a matter of fact, one could easily find dozens of strange objects in Stahl's lair. In no particular order, they accumulated slowly, layer by layer, like grains of dust blown there by a herd of loyal suppliers always busy rummaging through attics all around Vienna, or personally unearthed by the old man, an avid frequenter of auctions.

That day I pretended not to notice a couple of recent acquisitions that stood out in plain sight in the shop window and I stepped inside. As soon as he saw me, he took his leave from a customer who had already pulled out his wallet, leaving him to the unctuous attentions of an apprentice. He met me, jovial.

"What a pleasure, Herr Mayer!" He bowed, returning my greetings.

"This time I put aside for you something *really* special, something... *unusual*." He vaguely gestured toward an indistinct mass of objects that overflowed from the back room.

"Let's see, old rogue," I thought to myself wearing an ambiguous smile, while fingering in my hands a bronze statuette of uncertain Eastern origin and pretending to inspect it with interest.

"You see," he continued, flaunting some excitement, "I managed to get my hands on some really unique items that belonged to an extraordinary individual…"

I looked at him with curiosity, returning the statue to its original place.

"Who lived here in Vienna and who *vanished*, so to speak, a few years ago. It was a chance, really just a lucky strike that allowed me to get my hands on some of his personal effects. You know, with all the debts he left behind, it is just a miracle that something survived the fury of the creditors. "

"It was perhaps his most successful magic," he continued in a tone of admiration, "to disappear so suddenly, in spite of so many nagging creditors: an artist's trick, a true artist. Do you happen to remember that Russian magician?" – he narrowed his eyes in an effort to recall his name – "What was his name? Oleg, I think, or something like that. His disappearance made a sensation a few years ago. He had become famous throughout Europe, tickets for his shows were snapped up in Paris and other European capitals and here in Vienna he performed even at the Emperor's. I am sure you must remember him, Herr Mayer."

I nodded, trying to remember. The name was not new to me. At last, I remembered the chitchat of two ladies, great friends of my wife, who had attended the magician's show. They remained enraptured by the charismatic charm of the Russian magician and had fueled a series of passionate drawing-room discussions, during which many noble minds tried hard to figure out the trick. In the end, they had concluded that it was magic for real.

"But maybe you are getting bored with my gossip," said the old man with a twinkle in his eyes and he changed subject.

"Let's talk about you, Herr Mayer. How about your business here in Vienna? Recently, I have been seeing you a bit more often and it is of course a great pleasure for me."

"You are right, in fact. My affairs drive me into this part of the city more and more frequently, at least once or twice a week, I would guess." I thanked him, confirming that my business had recently taken an interesting turn.

"And, as you know, I am always unable to resist the urge and the pleasure to visit you. But, tell me: personal effects, did you say? What sort of?" I asked, steering the conversation where he wanted.

"Well, the tools of the trade, I suppose..." the old man said with a wry smile.

I burst into laughter.

"Do you mean the alembics, the retorts with magic potions and what else... ah yes, the crystal ball, of course."

"No, nothing like that," he protested, serious. "Please do not neglect to notice, Herr Mayer, that we are talking of a professional who had achieved a considerable celebrity through a large part of Europe. He performed some incredible displays and, for all I know, no one has ever managed to unveil his tricks."

"He must have been a skilled illusionist," I ventured.

"I don't think so. He performed several times in front of first-class colleagues and famous illusionists, leaving everyone stunned."

"And nobody knows what happened to him?" I asked, intrigued.

"Dis-ap-pea-red," he articulated, accompanying the word with a grand gesture of the hand.

"And then, Herr Mayer, the world is large and when lenders keep breathing down your neck…"

"Of course, I understand," I cut short, "but weren't you about to show me something?"

"Well, yes. Please follow me…"

He showed me to the back room.

"Please take a look. These two remarkable instruments were used by the master in his famous show." He smiled, showing two wooden travel trunks covered with a canvas worn out in several places.

"A volunteer in the audience was locked into one of two boxes," he explained, pointing to an impressive double lock, "to reappear at the right moment in the other case that, of course, was locked, too."

"A fake bottom, I suppose."

"No, I'm sure it wasn't," he denied emphatically. "Each of the two cases has an armor of metal on all the four sides and there are no openings in the bottom. I examined the crates, carefully, in person. They are in excellent conditions, would you like to see 'em?"

"Well…" I muttered, "he could have used a fake volunteer from the audience and a sibling in the other case."

"I don't think so," replied the old man, sternly. "As far as I remember, the volunteer was selected at random at the beginning of the show and the case was shown to be empty and people from the audience were asked to check its integrity."

"Have you seen the show yourself?" I asked, unconvinced.

"Yes, a few years ago in Paris. At that time he was not yet so famous. Most probably at the beginning of his career. I was very impressed, and not just because of the show."

"What do you mean?"

"He was no ordinary man: tall, very thin, a hollow face, a magnetic gaze. All the eyes from the audience were irresistibly attracted by his long fingers moving fast and with a surprising skill. Everybody followed, stunned, those nimble spiders that seemed to climb in the air, the flurry of colorful scarves and white doves, the flutter of multicolored fans opening, intertwining and then, all of a sudden, disappearing into as many decks of cards. He was extraordinary."

"And why, then, did he get ruined?" I ventured.

"He led a strange life. Traveled a lot and collected paintings, old books, objects of art. Expensive stuff. He was a regular visitor to galleries, museums and libraries and a well-known customer for the antiques in the many towns where he performed. It seems that he spent a lot of money, much more than he could earn from his impresarios who, so to speak, were not known as pearls of honesty. Then, it seems he suddenly cancelled all commitments and returned to Vienna. There, he disappeared without a trace. The house where he lived was auctioned after the court…"

"And the paintings, the objects of art?" I interrupted.

"Gone," chuckled the old man.

"Wait a moment, I beg you, Herr Mayer," he added, realizing that I had extracted my watch from my waistcoat pocket. "I have not yet shown you the most interesting part."

He walked towards the store entrance and with his index finger pointed at the shop window. Between an African tribal mask and a stuffed parrot with multicolored feathers, a top hat was proudly displayed on the slightly faded red velvet that covered the floor of the display case. The light of an early afternoon sun was pounding on the black felt, which scattered the sunlight all around with bluish reflections. Next to it, an ivory wand glistened, dazzling white.

The old man stopped suddenly and stood speechless. Then he started bending his head from side to side, scanning the objects displayed in the shop window. Not finding what he was looking for, he began to remove them one by one, feverishly, until he raised the cylinder and began to curse loudly at the apprentice.

Under the magician's hat, a beautiful crystal egg lit up the penumbra of the shop with a shower of colors.

"You animal..." cursed the old man, pointing to the boy. "*Never* again shall you dare to touch what I put in the shop window!"

Fascinated, I kept staring at the crystal egg.

Instead of restoring the hat into its original position on the shop window, the old man gently laid the ivory wand on a low, dusty, wooden table.

"Forget the egg," he said. "It is not worth much. The crystal is no good. Please look at the wand instead. It is with that wand that our man performed his miracles."

I touched the wand: it was still hot to the touch after a long exposure to the sunlight in the display case. It was finely chiseled and, on top of the upper tapered part, I noticed a small sphere, bluish and dull as of rusted metal, ending in a microscopic cone-shaped tip. The metal ball almost burned at the touch.

"Yeah... it really looks like a magic wand," I stammered.

The old man walked away, heading with a firm step into the back room to teach a good lesson to the unfortunate boy.

For a long while I studied the symbols engraved on the wand and finally placed it on the table near the crystal egg. I turned my head to peek into the animated discussion between Mr. Stahl and his subordinate in the back room. Then I turned back to examine the egg.

It had disappeared.

The ivory wand was in the same position where I had left it, but the crystal was gone. Startled, I stood for a moment, staring in disbelief at the table surface. I began to inspect the floor, certain that the egg must, of course, had rolled down under the table.

But there was nothing there.

I stood dumbfounded staring at the ivory wand on the table, until I noticed that someone had come up behind me. Stahl was looking at me, perplexed.

"Are... you... all right?" he asked politely.

"Yes, I think so..." I stammered, eyes wide open.

He continued to stare at me, unconvinced. Finally he examined the table and realized that the crystal was gone.

He burst out in laughter.

"I understand. You too. Who else is playing tricks against this poor old man?"

Then, with a flash of insight into his eyes, he added, "I would bet that..."

I remember, as in a dream, seeing him stretch his hand and quickly plunge it into the shop window, lifting up the top hat and showing me, triumphant, the crystal egg that – according to him – I had maliciously concealed into its original location under the magician's hat, taking advantage of his absence.

From the color of my face he concluded that I must not be well and urged me to sit down. After all, he said, he did care about my health even though I enjoyed making fun of him a bit too often. I have a vague memory of what he was saying because I felt my knees weak and my temples were pounding.

I kept trying to find an explanation, unable to give any to what I had seen.

Then I slowly regained control of myself. I thanked him for his concern and reassured him by saying that I was feeling better now and that probably I had been a victim of the first sun of March. I begged him to arrange for the delivery of the two cases to my home as soon as possible and I declared that I was willing to buy them together with the wand, the hat and, for that matter, why not the crystal egg, too?

I paid in cash without discussing the price, a circumstance that more than anything else left him stunned and disappointed. Finally I stepped out the shop with a conspicuous package under my arm.

The old man remained at the doorway watching me as I walked away, shaking his head. I rushed out looking for a coach with the air of one who had just bumped into the devil. I stopped a coach and ordered the driver to take me home immediately.

In haste, I neglected to notice that the arrangement of a long line of flowerpots on a certain balcony had in the meantime changed to a neutral pattern.

***

I got home three hours earlier than usual.

Ulrike stared at me with the unmistakable look of a wife in bewilderment. Why her husband – usually a late comer – had suddenly decided to show up so much ahead of time for dinner, was something she expected me to clarify. So I decided to tell her that I forgot some important documents at home and I was planning to work on them before dinner. She noticed that I was pale and nervous and asked me if I was all right. I replied that, yes, I was just tired and the only thing I needed was to stay for a while alone, taking care of my paperwork.

I kissed her forehead and locked myself in the studio. As always, she let me go without complaining. I continued to feel her resigned look, veiled with sadness, even after I got safely on the other side of the door. I wondered for how long she had been aware that I was lying to her.

It was the end of the winter. Daytime was still short and the sun was already low on the horizon. The delicate grid of one of the checkered windows projected a thin elongated shadow on the floor where the sunset light bounced up at an acute angle, painting in red the white and blue ceramic tiles of an enormous *stube* that occupied a large fraction of one of the walls. A pleasant warmth enveloped me and I hurried to warm my hands, numb from the cold, on the hot surface of the stove.

I loved that room. It was in that room that I could read my books in peace and smoke my cigars.

The stillness of the study had a beneficial effect on my nerves. I poured something strong and opened the package to inspect the crystal egg with a magnifying glass. As the old man had pointed out, the crystal was imperfect and the quality of the cut was inaccurate. It was just a paperweight of little value.

Without hesitation, I started to study the wand. Some of the symbols carved in the ivory stick were somehow familiar to me. I guessed I must have seen them in a book about magic, one of the many I had a small collection of.

Nothing new, I thought.

I noticed that the little metal sphere, stained with purplish blotches on a bluish metallic background, had been fixed to the top of the wand carelessly without much regard for the symbols carved in the ivory. Some symbols were scratched, others were incomplete as if the end of the wand had been cut or machined out with a primitive tool.

The metal sphere had a diameter of about one quarter of an inch and, invisible to the naked eye, I discovered two small holes arranged symmetrically on the two opposite hemispheres, as if to hold the thread of a necklace. I wondered what they could be for. Then, I began to study the small conical tip protruding from the surface of the sphere. It seemed to be cast from the same kind of metal and was extremely sharp and hard, to the point of being able to scratch the blade of my knife.

Then I turned my attention to the hat. It looked normal: just a cylinder of black felt with a white satin lining. Pretty confident that some secret must be hidden inside, I started to inspect the interior of the cylinder. But I was wrong. I could not find anything unusual inside.

Then I took the wand and placed it gently on the egg crystal, trying to imitate what I had previously done in Stahl's workshop. I held my breath expecting that the phenomenon I had witnessed a few hours earlier would repeat itself.

Several seconds elapsed, then minutes.

But the egg remained quiet in its place.

I tried to change the relative positions of the egg and the wand: above, below, forward, backward. I tried several times to touch the glass with the tip of the wand… but the egg stubbornly remained where it was.

Disappointed, I considered breaking the egg with a heavy bronze pestle that was at hand in a mortar on the desk. I was beginning to believe that I had been the victim of a hallucination in the old man's shop.

I continued with my futile attempts, until a timid knock at the door brought me back to reality. I jumped up from the desk with the intention of hiding those strange objects at the sight of Frau Peisert, our servant, who had come to announce that dinner was being served. I hurried to the closet holding the hat, the wand and the crystal egg in my hands. I quickly opened the closet, hiding the hat inside. Then I placed the wand and the egg, close to each other, on top of the hot stove. A second polite knock, propelled me to the door. With the air of an urchin being caught while stealing jam in the pantry, I opened the door and I found myself in front of my wife who had come, in person, to call me.

I endured the dinner in silence, elaborating on the possible causes of my failure and rewinding the events of the afternoon. After dinner, I accompanied Ulrike upstairs, telling her not to wait for me because I had to finish my paperwork and would probably go to sleep quite late.

Finally I returned to the study, laid the oil lamp on the table and unlocked the closet. The magician's hat was where I left it.

I slowly lifted up the hat and… I let out a strangled groan.

The crystal egg was there, at the exact center of a circle that was previously occupied by the base of the top hat.

In the flickering light of the oil lamp, I realized that the ivory wand was still standing on the stove, exactly where I left it, while the egg had taken the opportunity for a trip to the closet!

The circumstance was even more far-fetched as the cabinet – I was damned sure of it – had been locked.

My hands were slightly shaking when I removed my wedding band from my ring-finger and placed it on the desk. Then I took the wand, still warm after its long stay on the stove, and carefully placed it onto the ring.

As soon as the small sphere came in contact with it, the ring disappeared before my eyes!

Breathless, I reached the cabinet, eagerly lifted the cylinder, and…

For a long while I kept staring, happy, at the flickering flame of the oil lamp being reflected by the golden ring that had reappeared on the wooden shelf of the cabinet.

I was amazed. How could this miracle happen at all? The simple contact with the wand seemed to be able to move an object from one place to another, passing through solid obstacles.

Seeking a confirmation, I figured out a new experiment. From my waistcoat pocket, I extracted my watch and laid it on the table. Then I gently touched it with the wand, expecting that it would immediately disappear.

Instead, the hands turned on and on for a couple of minutes, but the clock was still there.

I was baffled.

I tried again and again. Without success.

After many failed attempts, I touched the metal sphere with my fingers and I realized that it was cold, much colder than the ivory stick. At last, the solution occurred to me and I knew what I should have figured out a long time before.

I took the wand and shoved it inside the oil lamp, taking care to keep it far from the burning flame. In this way, I was able to heat the sphere without warming the wand too much. When the ivory stick began to heat up to the point of burning my fingers, the watch disappeared!

This time I had the impression that it took a little more time than in the case of the ring, but the result was the same: I found the clock inside the closet in the same position formerly occupied by the egg and then by the ring!

I clearly remember running to the kitchen to get a bucket of cold water. Then I repeated the experiment several times, heating and cooling the little sphere. And each time successfully.

At last, I understood what had happened, unwitnessed, in the warmth of the afternoon sun in the shop window at Stahl's, triggering the old man to unfairly reproach the poor boy. It was the same incredible phenomenon I had been able to reproduce at home, at least a dozen times so far.

The sun was already creeping up in a radiant dawn when, tired from the emotions of the day and happy to have unveiled at least part of the mystery, I decided to go to sleep. But just before doing that, I erased any trace of my night work, carefully hiding everything inside the closet.

In bed, I could not sleep and I kept rewinding again and again what had happened. I turned to one side and the other without falling asleep, my mind wide awake and busy designing new experiments for the next day.

***

In the following days, I started looking for a quiet place where I could work undisturbed. It was quite clear that I could not continue my activity locked in my office without arousing the suspicions of my wife or servants.

I eventually managed to find a semi-abandoned hunting lodge, about a half hour from town. It belonged to a gentleman infatuated by gambling who had fallen at the time on serious financial straits. He was happy to sell it at much less than a fair price.

Entirely of wood, it consisted of a single long and narrow room, lit by two tall windows and heated by a huge stone fireplace. Blackened and sooty, it occupied one of the two longer walls almost entirely.

I got a carpenter fixing the roof and windows and before long the lodge became habitable again. I also installed a wooden workbench and some second-hand furniture that I bought from a junk shop including a large and comfortable chair, a small wall bookcase, and an iron bed.

One evening, during the three weeks it took to restore the pavilion, I made an interesting discovery at home. I had decided to inspect the hat more closely, so I locked myself in my office and I began to examine the inside.

I noticed that the seams on the liner satin on the bottom of the cylinder were more irregular than those on the inner side surface. It looked like a handmade work of mending. Touching the padding on the bottom with my fingertips, I realized that there was a small boss at the center. I took courage and with a penknife I began to unpick the lining. Under the padding, I found a small bluish metal ball stuck to the bottom of the cylinder. I studied it with a magnifying glass: it was identical to the one attached to the ivory wand, except for the small conical tip. Of the same diameter and with the two small side holes, it had – unlike the other one – a small conical cavity instead of the tip. It matched perfectly with the small pointed cone of the other sphere.

Disregarding the hat, I took the small sphere and laid it on the shelf inside the closet with the conical cavity facing down. This done, I warmed the other sphere and, not without a certain theatricality, I made my pocket watch disappear again. Needless to say, inside the closet I found my watch with the small sphere on top of it. It was positioned right in the middle of the dial and was reflecting an eerie cold bluish light.

***

When the hunting lodge restoration was over, Mr. Stahl came in person to deliver the two cases he had shown me in his shop. He arrived on a carriage, escorted by two of his young attendants. It was late morning and a strong spring sun had come out, bright in a pastel-colored sky after the brief shower of a few hours before.

"Great place to get a bit of intimacy away from the prying eyes of the city," began the old man, smiling and holding out his hand, mischievously. "I am happy to see you in much better shape than the last time, Herr Mayer."

"Thank you, Herr Stahl. But intimacy has nothing to do with it," I replied, winking and shaking his hand. "I would rather say that I am seeking a bit of innocent tranquility, some time to devote to myself, to my studies.

At my age one feels the need of it and it's difficult to achieve that at home… especially when you are married. I am sure you know what I mean."

"Of course, I do understand perfectly." He nodded, entering the pavilion and looking around. "I have been married for much longer than you and when you have children then the time left for yourself is reduced virtually to zero."

"This place is actually quite rustic." He cut short after a quick look at the pavilion and realizing that, as a matter of fact, it offered little comfort.

"It does not look at all like a *garçonnière*," he said, while the two boys were moving the first one of the two boxes.

"I hope you were not too disappointed with your purchases," he added, handing me a small package carefully wrapped. "this is a small present for you, Herr Mayer."

I unfolded it to find a beautiful crystal paperweight inside.

Before I could protest, Stahl added with a good-natured tone, "You see, Herr Mayer. This one is a real crystal. A good one, I mean."

The good man would never have intended to charge me a price so exorbitant for the objects that belonged to the magician. My apparent illness and my sudden rush off his shop must have impressed him and now he was trying to fix it.

"It's really a beautiful thing," I said admiringly, while watching the multicolored reflections coming off the facets of the crystal. I thanked him, asking if I could ask him a few more questions about the magician.

He nodded.

"Did you see any of his performances in public?"

"Only once, unfortunately. Tickets for his shows were snapped up and I could make it just once because an old friend of my father offered one ticket to me as a present."

"What was his repertoire during the show?"

"Amazing stuff. He made any kind of object disappear and reappear at will using the wand... but, unlike the average charlatan who covers them with a cloth, he made them disappear just in front of your eyes. And then he made them reappear a little farther, sometimes into the hat, sometimes above the table, but always in open positions. I never understood the trick."

"What kind of objects did he transfer?" I asked carelessly.

"Transfer? You mean what kind of objects did he make disappear? Well, usually belongings from someone in the audience: rings, bracelets, necklaces..."

"Did he ever made animals or people disappear?"

"Sure. I saw doves and rabbits disappear in a wink of an eye, in short, all the classic magician's repertoire, with a remarkable difference – and here's the rub – that all seemed to be done with a simple touch of the wand, no need to hide the animal or object from the view of the public before disappearance."

"Did he do the same with people?"

"No, in this case he asked a volunteer to lay down at the bottom of one of the two boxes. He locked him in, then touched the lid with the ring and... zap: gone!"

"Ring, which ring?" I asked, my heart pounding of expectation.

"Oh yes. Did I ever tell you about this? It was a spectacular ingredient, though. When he touched the lid, a glow emanated from it, like a flash of blue light, which was probably part of the staging. Then, the magician showed to the audience that the second box was empty, except for a black magician's hat he had placed on the bottom. After a minute or two, he reopened the box and the guy who had disappeared from the first case came out of the second unscathed, though pale."

"And the magician's hat?"

"Placed on the belly of the volunteer. When he reopened the case, the poor man was lying on the bottom, the hat sitting at about the height of his navel. And then there was the trick of the two hourglasses..."

"Which hourglasses?"

"In this performance he used again the two crates. He overturned two large hourglasses at the same time, the first remaining on the stage in full view to the public, while the second was locked into one of the two cases and then made to disappear. Then the public was asked to make sure that both cases were actually empty. Meanwhile the first hourglass exhausted all the sand. At this point, the magician closed the lid of the second trunk and reopened it after a short time, recovering from the inside the hourglass that had disappeared. The extraordinary thing is that the second hourglass was still more than half full and the sand continued to fall down at that very moment! "

"A nice trick indeed. But what about the ring?"

"The ring was never found. I'm sure it has followed the same fate of the magician and the artworks. "

"But have you ever actually met him?"

"Yes, after the show I once had the privilege of being introduced to the magician and to shake hands with him. In fact, I remember noticing a bulky ring on his finger, a golden one, too showy, too ostentatious, with a bluish stone, perhaps an imitation. An object of bad taste. On the other hand, I remember very well the elegance and the charming graces of his young assistant. She was a wonderful creature."

"Ah!" I said biting my lips. "I would have liked to see the ring. It is unfortunate that it has been lost."

"Well, this is something to be expected. You see, when the magician did, so to speak, disappear, he was being hunted not only by the many creditors, but also by the Austrian police who had been keeping an eye on him for some time. They were going to charge him for the theft of some famous paintings that had disappeared two months before here in Vienna. There was the legitimate suspicion that the magician was not new to this kind of business, at least if you trust a report by the *gendarmerie* of Paris, according to which Oleg was seen in that town during the same period in which the thefts of important artworks had occurred."

He winked.

"Do you know who was charged instead of him?"

"Here is the answer: his beautiful assistant."

"Really? And what happened to her?"

"She was accused of complicity in the theft and sentenced to a severe punishment after a questionable trial that provoked much discussion. They needed a scapegoat, obviously."

"I don't remember hearing anything of that."

"Perhaps you are not aware of these facts because they date back to a few years ago."

"You are right: now I remember! Probably that was while I was a medical officer on a ship sailing to Indochina."

"That's the explanation. But let me in my turn ask you why are you so interested in this guy?"

"Well, as you know I always try to give a rational arrangement to facts that seem pretty inexplicable…"

"I know, I know. I heard about your scientific work, but I can assure you that in this case if there was a trick, it was well hidden."

"No doubt about it. Are there any other items that belonged to him?"

"Not here in Vienna, as far as I know. I made myself a small survey among his creditors. Apart from the two wooden trunks, the cylinder and the wand, I have found nothing else. Maybe some other personal items have been kept by his young assistant."

"How about her now?"

"I don't know. She may still be in prison. But I'm not sure, because I guess that the penalty might well have been reduced under some mitigating circumstances. With good behavior, she may be already out."

As we talked, the two boys had finished arranging the two cases and were waiting for us outside the building. I thanked the old man again, and he took his leave, shaking my hand and wishing me good luck for my studies.

The carriage departed with a slow teetering motion on the dirt road splashing rainwater from deep puddles. Still wet after the recent rainfall, the first leaves of the season were now glittering on the trees under the rays of a bright midday sun.

***

Before receiving Mr. Stahl's visit at the hunting lodge, I had started a series of small experiments with the two little spheres: the one that I found hidden under the cylinder lining and the second one fixed on the tip of the ivory wand. It was now clear to me that the magician's hat and wand were nothing else than ingenious disguises of a simpler reality, though of a completely incomprehensible nature. So, I devoted all my energies to study the bluish spheres.

In a first series of tests, I began to relocate small lead cylinders, of the kind of those normally used as counterweights of a two-pan balance, from one sphere to the other. With my pocket chronometer I measured the time necessary to heat the sphere on the pointed tip before the cylinder disappeared.

I realized that the heat that had to be delivered to the sphere before the transfer could start was increasing in proportion to the weight of the object to be moved. But this was not the whole story: as the weight increased, the transfer time became longer and longer and, in practice, I failed to move objects heavier than the crystal egg.

I knew that, during his performances, the magician used to transfer 'objects' that could reach to the respectable size of a rabbit or a human being. Moreover, it seemed really unlikely to me that, during a public performance, the magician would have been forced to heat again the sphere on the tip of the wand after each transfer. I wandered if it was the magician's ring that provided instead, in some unknown way, the energy needed to recharge the spheres.

On the same day of Stahl's visit, I began to carefully examine the two cases. They were two solid travel wooden crates covered with a worn cloth and reinforced by a metal casing that formed a sort of skeleton. On the middle of one of the two longer sides of each case was a heavy metal lock blotted with patches of rust here and there.

In one of the two cases, I noticed that the inner wall of the lid was lined with a metal plate. Its presence inside, rather than on the outer surface of the lid, puzzled me and even the shape of the plate aroused my suspicions. In fact, unlike the external surface of the lid, that had the usual shape of a cylinder cut in half along its axis, the inner metal surface had a different curvature and resembled a flattened paraboloid.

The plate was mounted from the inside on the wooden lid with many large nails, dark and a round headed, that formed a geometric pattern over the entire length of the plate. After being cleaned and polished, it did not take me long to recognize the bluish-purple color I was now familiar with. Touching them with the tip of my finger, I had the confirmation that they were not just ordinary nails, but rather small spheres with a single tiny sharp point, identical to the one of the magician's wand. They were set into the wood and arranged at regular distances from each other.

I counted sixty-four of them.

At this point, I was expecting to find a second metal plate very similar to this one inside the other trunk, maybe decorated with small spheres of the second type, i.e. with a small hollow replacing the tiny conical tip. Instead, the second trunk had just the appearance of an ordinary wooden crate. It had a lid reinforced by metal strips nailed into the wood, but inside I couldn't find any metal plate. Despite a long meticulous search, I found no trace of spheres.

With some trepidation, I placed a terracotta flower pot on the bottom of the first case and began to heat the metal plate of the lid with the flame of a candle. I sat staring at the empty bottom of the second box, expecting to see the pot moving from the first into the second case.

I remained watching motionless for a few long minutes.

The flower pot remained obstinately where it was.

What had gone wrong?

I tried again with a smaller object that I had already previously 'transferred' successfully using the wand and the cylinder, but also in this case the experiment failed. I tried to heat the plate more and more, but to no avail. I even tried to exchange the role of the two cases, but all my efforts were in vain.

Annoyed by the failure of what I considered an experiment with a guaranteed result, I decided to remove the wooden coating on which the first of the two plates was fixed. I worked very carefully with a carpenter's tool, removing the wood from the outside of the lid to extract the bluish spheres embedded in as many holes in the plate. Each sphere was indeed identical to the one I had found on the ivory wand. I managed with great difficulty to extract one from the plate and I decided to test if it worked in the same way as its sibling on the ivory wand.

Using the new sphere and my pocket watch, I repeated the well-established experiments I had performed earlier at home and got the same results. As expected, the spheres were all identical and functioned in the same way. Then, why on earth had I failed with the flower pot? What had to be done to make many spheres work together instead of just one? Maybe, I thought, the heat supplied from the candle was not sufficient.

The ring might be the clue.

A bluish stone cast in a ring, as Stahl had described it... another one of those spheres? Perhaps, unlike all the others, it had the property to enable them to work together?

But how to find the ring?

I suspected that the magician, as Stahl claimed, had taken the ring with him. Why then had he abandoned the two cases, the hat, and the wand as well?

I wondered where Oleg had gone. Had he fled in haste, spurred by events to the point of abandoning his valuable work tools and his beautiful assistant?

Maybe she knew something.

My head was still teeming with a thousand questions when I arrived at home. Overcome by the emotions of the day I soon fell into a deep sleep.

***

That night I had a strange dream.

I was in a long and narrow room that looked like a museum. The walls of the gallery were covered with paintings and long rows of display cases alternated with shelves crammed with books. Artifacts from all over the world could be seen lined up behind the dusty windows and apparently arranged without an obvious criterion of classification. Some were small masterpieces of local handicrafts, others were simply everyday objects, tools, curious gadgets made of wood or metal, some of them looked ancient, some more modern. Under the vault in the back, I noticed a display shelf larger than the others. Inside I recognized a wooden case that looked familiar to me.

Behind my back I heard a soft sound of footsteps.

I barely had time to hide behind a book shelf, when I saw a shadow moving along the tunnel. Tall and thin, the shape paused for a while in front of a picture hanging on the wall, then slowly moved to the back of the room.

After some time, the shadow pulled out the wooden case from the shelf and set it on the floor. Then it took one of the paintings off the wall, opened the lid and bent down. A faint blue glow lit up the semi-darkness of the room for a short while.

Then the shape retraced his steps along the gallery and started tinkering around the wooden case again, then slipped into it, folding down on the bottom and slowly closed the lid. Again a faint blue glow.

Then, darkness.

But now... the scene had changed. The gallery was gone. In front of me a nice fire was crackling inside the big stone fireplace at the hunting lodge. I watched, fascinated, the tongues of fire and enjoyed the warmth radiated by the flames. Behind me, the two crates were covered with a worn travel canvas.

Suddenly I felt a presence.

I spun around and saw with horror a long slender hand that clung from the inside to the edge of the wooden crate, trying to stand up.

With a cry, I woke up from the nightmare, drenched in sweat.

Quickly I got dressed and ran to the hunting lodge fearing that something dramatic had happened.

***

Inside I found the usual mess, but everything was exactly as I had left it.

Just a bad dream.

I breathed a sigh of relief and went straight to work, spending the rest of the day in vain attempts to transfer some small object from one crate to another by heating the plate at dangerously increasing temperatures.

In the end I decided it was not worth it to continue along that road. Disappointed and tired, I sat in the armchair staring for a long time with hatred at the two crates. In a fit of anger, I jumped up and I made a clumsy attempt to cut one of the spheres in half to see what was inside. The bluish metal turned out to be of exceptional hardness and after much effort I began to realize that I would never be able to cut it with the tools I had available. However, I continued stubbornly in my pointless attempts and it was already dusk when I decided to go home, frustrated by all those failed attempts. My head ruminated dangerous contraptions for the dissection of the sphere.

The next day, early in the morning, I took with me one of the small specimens and rode to town. I went straight to Friedrich's laboratory, a dear college friend, a clever fellow who got quickly tired of school and had become a skilled carver of stones and a respected jeweler.

"How are you, Mayer? Old unrepentant..." Fred always used to greet me with a series of epithets that would have made a trooper blush, but between the two of us they were usually taken as a polite demonstration of esteem and affection.

"Still enjoy yourself with your experiments at the University or are you full-time chasing any nice skirt passing close by?"

"Of course I do. Both."

"By the way, do you know that we went short of setting the Institute on fire? One of my machines got overheated and ignited a small fire. Luckily, Hans realized it immediately and saved my ass just with a few buckets of water. You had to see the poor guy soaking wet, his glasses smeared with soot, coughing and cursing as he tried to open the windows."

"You are the usual two crazy fellows." Fred laughed heartily, imagining the scene.

"And all this for the sake of... what's the name?"

"Forget it. The science of heat. Someone calls it thermodynamics."

"And what is there to be understood? Don't you know that heat is a kind of light syrupy fluid passing from a warm body to a cold one. What's wrong with it?"

"It is not *that* simple. If so, a warmer ball should weigh more than a cooler, right?"

"Yes, but the heat could also be something very light, lighter than silk."

"Or it could be that the explanation is completely different. Look, there's a guy in England who has shown that…"

"Hey, gentleman, please hold on. You have in front of you a crude carver of stones. And if I can cut them, it means that my head is harder. So take it easy."

"All right then. I'll spare you a nice headache."

"Rather, tell me of your experiments with the truly and only source of warmth. I bet you have in your hands some nice bird. Or have you lost your good habits?"

"I keep exercising, that's all."

We laughed and kept talking about women, our favorite subject since college. He pulled out a special bottle that he held for a special guest and we started chatting about town gossip as in the good old days.

"I have something to show you," I said, getting back to serious and pulling out from my vest a silver box where I had placed one of the spheres.

"I tried to cut it, but I could not do it. I would like you to try. I want to see what it looks like inside."

He was taken aback by my unusual request but in the end he agreed to try the dissection. He then set up the operating table and it was not long after that he started to apply his cutting tools against the hard bluish surface.

It turned out to be a long and laborious process.

In the end, a special tool with a pointed diamond tip was able to cut the hard metal and the sphere was sectioned into two halves. The thin but strong metal outer casing was followed by an internal layer with a blackish color. This, in turn, surrounded a gray material that, to the naked eye, seemed tinged with small dark spots arranged in a periodic, but not entirely regular, pattern. Equipped with a high magnification eyepiece, Fred began to inspect one of the two sections of the half sphere, scrupulously professional as if dealing with a precious stone. But he could not hold an exclamation of surprise:

"Unbelievable!" he muttered. "Never seen anything like that!"

Then, after a stroke of time long enough to seem endless, he raised his head and looked at me quizzically. Now he looked very serious.

"What is this stuff?"

From the expression on my face, he realized that I had not the faintest idea and invited me with a gesture to get closer to the eyepiece:

"See for yourself…"

I went over to the eyepiece and, when the picture came into focus, I could not believe my eyes.

The portion I was looking at corresponded to one of the darker spots scattered in the gray mass that formed the core of the sphere. It looked like in some way to a small town seen from the top of a nearby mountain. On the dark background matching the spot, I could clearly see the geometric profiles of small rectangular objects that looked like microscopic 'buildings' almost everywhere uniform in size, overlooking what seemed to me 'streets' intersecting at right angles.

The 'buildings' formed groups according to a geometrical pattern that repeated itself here and there, again and again. The light illuminating the scenery reflected the colors of the rainbow on a delicate web of 'channels' or 'roads' that flowed into 'main streets,' changing hue as I inclined my head slightly from one side to the other. The incredible network wound on multiple levels and the strange 'buildings,' in turn, seemed to possess a finer structure that the instrument could not resolve. A fly-by over this well-ordered universe showed a repetition of hundreds of small transparent objects in the shape of regular polyhedrons, grouped into larger blocks and connected by tiny 'channels,' also transparent, running along parallel rows of high-rise buildings, even more microscopic structures in the gray mass of the core of the sphere getting blurred in the distance.

A rectangular black building, much larger than the others, stood in the area closer to the sharp metallic point placed on the outer surface of the sphere. From its basement, surrounded by a kind of 'ditch,' thin transparent filaments spread out radially connecting to the small arteries that converged at that point.

I looked up raising my head from the fascinating landscape, trying to focus my friend's face. We stared at each other for a while without saying anything.

"It looks like a miniature town," I ventured.

"Yes. But with such a degree of finesse in the details… I have never seen an engraving of this precision. Where on earth did you find this masterpiece? Who has made it?"

At this point, I decided to tell him everything about the workshop of Stahl and the ivory wand that had belonged to the magician, but I decided not to reveal the existence of the other spheres and not to tell him about the outcome of the strange experiments I performed first in my house and later at the hunting lodge.

We discussed at length, trying to imagine what kind of miniature chisel could have been used to carve so finely the crystalline material which formed the core of the sphere. We studied the second half, which turned out to be very similar, although not identical, to the first one.

Fred overwhelmed me with questions. Who could have made something so complex and for what purpose? And using which kind of technology?

I refrained from telling him everything I knew and we went on and on speculating. At last, after having extorted from him a promise not to tell anyone about what he had seen, I thanked him with affection. I swore that he would be kept informed of any development and that I would not hesitate to call him if needed.

Then I left, but before returning to the hunting lodge, where I intended to spend the next few days exploring with a microscope the two sections of the sphere and mapping them on paper, I still had a pending matter to be settled once and for all in town.

***

This time those damned flowers would not stop me.

I entered the garden from a side entrance, through a small iron gate, and carefully approached the *limonaia*. Originally conceived as a side porch attached to the back of the house, the lemon green-house was a huge, elongated hall with a long row of arches running along the side facing the garden and many large checkered windows painted in white.

The door was ajar.

I stepped in.

The shutters were closed and the inside wrapped in gloom. The wooden trusses of the high ceiling were barely visible. Patches of light rained oblique from a small aperture in the roof and wet the floor. Everywhere a smell of rotten leaves, of damp, of moss.

I waited until my eyes adjusted to the dim light and I could make out the dark shapes of the plants standing up in their giant earthenware jars.

I started moving slowly along the room, near the wall.

Stealth as a cat.

An eerie silence surrounded me. Time was asleep, only to be awaken abruptly when a drop of rain water fell over with a splash into the tank from the roof.

I felt myself growing in wild excitement.

I knew she was there, hidden in the midst of those plants, sheltered by the shadow. And it was there that I wanted to take her. In front of the rhododendrons, the azaleas, the jasmine, the bougainvillea, the dwarf palms, the broad-leafed banana trees, in front of everyone, but especially in front of those red and yellow flowers I had an old question to settle with.

A metallic click, dry.

Someone had locked the front door from the inside.

I went in that direction. Slow and stealth.

I was doing well until I happened to trip over something: a small vase, perhaps.

A sudden and horrible crash of broken shards echoed loud along the room.

A chuckle on the other side.

I moved quickly in that direction.

Then I slowed down taking a long detour.

The only sound now was the rustling of leaves that I gently touched as I passed.

She was there, hidden behind a pillar.

I approached her slowly from behind.

She saw me, but it was too late.

With a single cat-like movement, I lifted her skirt, pushed her against the column and nibbled her at the base of the neck. I felt her tingle of pleasure as I filled my nostrils with her scent. She tried to pull away, but I held her firmly. I had already sunk my hands in the complicated maze of her petticoats, working my way quickly in the midst of those fragile barriers.

I knew very well where I wanted to reach.

I felt the warmth of her skin on my lips, my fingers running up and down a sea of dunes, silky smooth and then hard as her nipples, amid the valleys and the ridges rounded by the wind, following up and down the soft undulations, caressing the secret folds, and then diving into an oasis of lush where the soil is moist and where the spring of life is concealed.

Now I was inside her.

I heard her moaning with pleasure, clinging to the edge of a large trunk, bent forward, legs spread, her head stuck into the leaves of a jasmine. And the broken branches, the raped leaves protested in an overwhelming noise that grew in my ears at the same rhythm of the pounding blood that now engulfed my arteries, and I heard her screaming as her sap and mine climbed up along the trunk, along the main branches, along the secondary branches and even higher, up to the highest leaf, driven by a pressure that was building up from the inside of us, wildly making its way to its outburst.

In the end, among the leaves, we shouted her relief and mine.

My legs were shaking from the effort and the excitement.

I remained planted where I was and when my vision cleared, I looked around me.

Slowly focusing on something vaguely familiar.

Hidden in the gloom.

It looked like a row of small flowering little heads peeking in the middle of the foliage.

Spying on us.
Yellow and red, all giggled in my direction.
And winked at me.

***

After a few days spent at the hunting lodge in unsuccessful attempts to get some insight into the puzzle hidden inside the sphere that had been dissected by Fred, I realized that it was unlikely that I could make any progress at all in that direction. So I decided that I might perhaps learn more from Irina, the magician's assistant. Sometime later I found myself in a long and narrow corridor dimly lit by a row of small windows with iron railings which led me to the parlor. The visit had been granted under very exceptional circumstances thanks to the intercession of a distant relative of mine who held a prestigious role in the administration of justice.

The director of the prison received me in his office showing a formal, but kind and respectful, attitude that was obviously bogus and presumably just focused to obtain some benefit. In fact he did not fail to remind me of his devotion to my relative who was at present in a position more favorable than ever to get him a promotion or, who knows, an honorable mention. While never losing sight of his true objectives, the director tried tactfully to find out why I had decided to visit to one of their 'guests' who had already completed about three quarters of her sentence.

I had expected such questioning. Therefore I had elaborated in advance a nice little phony story, stuffed with a bunch of vague explanations that nevertheless implied, not openly but clearly enough, that I had been prompted to do so for reasons of state well above his pay-grade and of no concern to him.

To my great relief, my strategy was successful and our conversation soon came to an end. I was escorted by two guards into a room with a heavy gray door with a peephole and a metal grate. They left me standing alone in front of an empty cage with a wooden chair inside.

About half an hour later, a prison guard entered the cage warning me with little grace that the interview that was about to begin could in no way last more than fifteen minutes.

At last, the gray door slowly opened and Irina entered the room.

Her eyes met mine for a long moment: pale blue eyes with a delicate almond cut. A fascinating glance shining with intelligence. Sweet, yet proud.

From that very moment I started drowning in those eyes.

Her blonde hair, gathered behind the neck, showed off the delicate features of her face. No matter how sorely tired and with deep hollows under her eyes, she was surrounded by an aura of elegance and beauty. Even though bundled in gray canvas and wearing a rough prison uniform, Irina moved with a grace and poise that made me imagine a figure far leaner than it appeared in that dress deliberately designed to be impersonal.

She stared at me for a long time, holding my gaze and studying me carefully. Then she sat down, resting her hands on her knees and lowering her head, in silence.

I took courage and began. "We do not yet know each other, mademoiselle, but with your permission I would like to ask you just a few…"

She did not allow me to finish the sentence. Instead she raised her head and looking straight into my eyes, told me, "If you are one of those folks, sir, please go away and leave me alone. I'm not going to answer any more questions."

Her voice was tired, but firm.

"Please… I do not know whom you're referring to. Let me explain, if you please," I said as gently as I could, when I saw her ready to get up and leave.

"Who are you? We have never met before, as far as I know," said Irina.

"My name is Heinrich. Heinrich Mayer. I am a doctor and I am also teaching natural philosophy at the University. I do not know what you meant before with 'one of them,' but I assure you that I managed to get involved in this story just by myself. "

"What do you want from me, then, Herr Mayer?"

"Let me first tell you what happened to me, please."

I looked around. I saw the prison guard watching us through the peephole. Lowering my voice, I began to tell her about Stahl, about the tiny bluish spheres and the disturbing discoveries I had made. As I spoke, I saw that her interest was growing and I realized that she was studying me, curious and worried at the same time.

I tried to be as honest as possible and explained to her that Stahl had been talking to me about her and about Oleg, the magician. When I saw her bowing her head to hide the tears that ran down her cheeks, I stopped talking and waited in silence, respectfully.

"So... you decided to come to see me," she finally said, slowly raising her head and wiping away the tears with the back of her hand.

She stared at me with moist gray-blue eyes, now even brighter and more beautiful than ever.

"I just hoped you could help me understand," I said.

"I'm not sure I understand any of that myself. Oleg is gone long ago. I do not know where he is and I would not be able to find him even if I were free. I have been waiting for a long time, expecting him to come back and take me away from this awful place. But he will not come back, I am sure of it now, and I'll never know what happened to him."

"I'm sorry to see you suffering, believe me" – I said it my way, as sweet as I could – "but I hope to convince you that I'm telling you the truth and that no other reason prompted me to come here."

"I would like to believe you. First I thought you had come to ask me questions about Oleg on behalf of someone who is still trying to recover the paintings. Until now I was sure that no one else but Oleg and I knew about the magic spheres. Herr Mayer, I would like to believe you... indeed... but even in this case, I cannot give you explanations that... please hold on, let me... I need more time to think about it."

"As you wish. I'd love to help you but at the moment I don't see how I could. If I may, I would like to come and visit you again in the future."

Irina got up and took her leave with a faint smile. "Go now please, Herr Mayer. Come back again if you wish. Your eyes are clear and you look sincere. But, for too long I have learned not to trust anyone."

The interview was over.

I was escorted back along the endless corridors and through the courtyard. There, I raised my head and glanced at those gray walls, up there, along a row of railings. It was probably just my imagination, but I had the impression to catch a glimpse of a small blonde head leaning against the bars and looking down in my direction.

***

Thanks perhaps to the good offices of the Director, the treatment of the prisoner must have undergone a marked improvement because, when I saw Irina again, I found her in better physical condition. I managed to get permission for a visit, but under the agreement that the interview had to be very short.

She looked more serene and the air of grim resignation was gone from her pretty face that now looked more relaxed. She greeted me with a smile of gratitude and thanked me for the few things that I had managed to get for her.

"Tell me, Mayer. Is it just by sheer coincidence that you appeared just before they started to treat me better? I hope you did not make a deal with the director to extract information from me."

"No, Irina, believe me," I said, looking straight into her eyes.

"On the contrary, I think I can help you. My lawyer read the record of the trial: your conviction is based only upon weak pieces of evidence. He told me that you can request a review of the process."

"Maybe, but I do not care much. No one will be able to give me back the days I was locked in here. And no one can give me back Oleg, too. I have been thinking about it for so long… and life in this place leaves you so much time to think, unfortunately."

"Tell me about him, if you will."

"Not much to say. He's gone. He could not or maybe he did not want to return. Who knows? I do not know if I will ever know the truth."

"It all started by using the spheres that are on the case, right?"

"Yes, those damned spheres that have been his obsession for so many years."

"An obsession that now has become mine, too. But when did all this start?"

She still looked doubtful.

"Mayer, I think you have been honest with me and I want to satisfy your curiosity, at least up to a certain point. The history of the spheres goes back many years ago when Oleg began to follow his father in his excavations."

"Excavations?"

"Yes, Oleg's father is an archaeologist. He devoted much of his life to Roman archeology and directed a number of excavations mostly in Italy. It's a long story, Mayer. I cannot tell you all of it now in this short visit."

"You are denying a drink to a thirsty man. Now I burn to know the connection between the spheres and archeology. Are you telling me that they are archaeological findings?"

"That's precisely what they are. Listen to me, Mayer: we do not have enough time to talk about it now. But there are diaries, or perhaps I should call them workbooks, that Oleg wrote during the excavations. They are accurate in every detail as required by our profession. There you will find all the details of the discovery of the spheres, or rather, the beginning of the story."

"Diaries? And would you be willing to let me know about them?"

"I think I will run this risk. But first you have to swear that, at the appropriate time, you will help me find Oleg and the only way to do that, I fear, is to face his father."

"I've already offered my help, but if you want a promise, I am ready to swear on what is dearest to me, that I will help you find Oleg. But what does his father have to do with it?"

"You will understand everything after reading the diaries. And do not forget that Oleg's father would be willing to do anything to get them back. "

"Why?"

"Oleg left home and his father has always blamed me for that. I think he hates me. Oleg brought along with him the diaries, the spheres and…"

Two raps at the door interrupted our conversation. The expressionless face of the prison guard showed up behind the peephole.

"You have to go now. Ask Frau Kraft. You will find her at 8, Rot-Gaβe. Tell her I sent you and that… *the cat jumped off the mirror*. She will give you the diaries. "

The interview was over, but this time I left the gloomy courtyard behind me with a lighter heart. It was too late to rush to the address Irina had given me, so I went back home. That night I slept very little, looking forward to paying my respects to Frau Kraft on the next day.

***

The address led to a small two-story stone house with a balcony full of flowers and pretty white curtains at the checkered windows. The entrance and the small sitting room were pervaded with a pleasant perfume coming from the kitchen.

Frau Kraft, a plump and good-natured lady, was evidently a good cook who enjoyed eating. I showed up on behalf of Irina with a box of *chocolaten kugeln* as a welcome pass.

When I started talking about her, the joyful eyes of Frau Kraft immediately became veiled with sadness. She told me that she had visited Irina in prison and found her in a poor condition. I tried to reassure her explaining that I had seen Irina the day before and that she gave me a much better impression than during my previous visit. When I reported the message and pronounced the secret sentence that Irina had arranged with her for the custody of the diaries, the good woman gave me a long stare, as if inspecting me over from head to foot.

"And you would be the cat, right? I guess that Irina knows you well enough and has full confidence in you if she asked me to entrust the diaries." She smiled, trying to read in my face what kind of relationship I had with Irina.

"I have known Irina since she was a little girl," she continued. "At that time her parents lived in Vienna and I was the housekeeper in their home for many years. I raised the children. Irina was fond of me in a very special way and she considered me as almost as a second mother. When the police came to question her for the first time, Irina handed me the diaries because she was afraid, as it indeed happened later, that she would be arrested. I have carefully hidden them not uttering a single word with the police nor with the other gentlemen who came later."

"Which gentlemen?" I asked.

"I don't know who they were. They came twice after Irina was sentenced. Not from the police, for sure. They said they were lawyers seeking evidence to make a request for a revision of the trial. They went to see Irina in prison and asked her questions too, but she kept her mouth shut. She did not trust them. Perhaps they were just after the paintings… or perhaps they had been hired by someone of Oleg's many creditors. I do not know. However, eventually they gave up."

She took one last inquisitive look, but more benign then before. Then she drew a long sigh. "If this is what Irina wants… I will give you the diaries," and she disappeared up the stairs.

I stood for several minutes alone in the room immersed in a silence broken only by the ticking of a wall clock. I considered what I had just heard and I wondered want sort of folks could have an interest in getting their hands on the diaries and how they had managed to locate Frau Kraft.

I was interrupted in my thoughts by the sound of footsteps coming down the wooden staircase from the top floor.

"Here are the diaries, Herr Mayer. I really hope that you will make use of them for the good of Irina," she said in a tone almost of prayer, looking straight into my eyes and smiling with her jovial manner.

"Trust me. I care about the fate of Irina as well as you do."

She made a sign of assent and returned a look of approval, but at the same time it was clear that she was full of curiosity. She could not help a question that tormented her since the beginning of our conversation.

"You... and Irina... I mean..." she said, slightly blushing and lowering her eyes to the floor.

"We're just good friends, Frau Kraft. But fear not: I do care for Irina and I will do everything I can so that she can get out of prison as soon as possible."

"I want to believe you, Herr Mayer. You look like a good guy."

"Thank you, Frau Kraft. You will not be disappointed," I smiled with a hint of a move in the direction of the front door. I was afraid that if our conversation would continue for too long, I would end up betraying myself. I knew so little about Irina that I had no hope of being able to evade the natural curiosity of Frau Kraft who, as I imagined, would have wished to know details about how we met and get a better understanding of the nature of our friendship.

"Are you leaving so early? My husband is about to return. I am sure he would like to meet you."

"Same for me, but unfortunately I have to go right now."

After taking my leave, I walked through the front door with a sigh of relief, but not without first inhaling for one last time, and with pleasure, the inviting aroma of good home cooking that permeated the entire house.

***

The diaries, three large leather-bound volumes, covered a two-year period during a campaign of excavations at Herculaneum led by Oleg's father. They were workbooks, containing the daily account of the operations at the archeological site, written by the young scientist who had joined his father in Italy. The notebooks were extremely accurate and rich with technicalities including the detailed description of each archaeological finding and its exact location with respect to given reference landmarks. The data were continuously updated as the excavation proceeded. For someone like me, oblivious to the meticulous procedures of archaeologists, the reading was extremely laborious, often dark, sometimes cryptic. I felt a sense of frustration and boredom after reading not more than forty pages and I began to skim entire pages at first and entire sections later while searching for something interesting like a few lines highlighted by the author. My eyes were feverishly flying over the pages in search of an underline or a portion of text written in capital letters or laid with a calligraphy altered by emotion. Instead, the manuscript proceeded orderly with disciplined and smooth writing, interspersed with a number of pencil drawings. My research then proceeded haphazardly, the eye indulging only on the magnificent pictures. Whoever had made them had an exceptional talent, that was for sure.

The excavations had started from a point that, at the time of the disaster, corresponded to the first row of houses nearest to the sea front. A staircase was brought to light that descended steeply toward the shoreline and led to a series of large brick vaults that were used as shelter for the boats.

In that tragic August 79 A.D., a glowing cloud rolled down relentlessly from the top of Vesuvius and killed all the people that were desperately running towards the beach in the vain hope of escaping their fate by boarding a boat or taking their chance diving into the dreadful waves. Some of them drowned, swept away by the tsunami generated by the eruption, others tried to take refuge under the vaults. But the glowing cloud did not give them a chance and the wave of mud that later engulfed the whole town, found them already dead.

Under the large brick vaults were found at least thirty skeletons, perfectly preserved and carrying evidence of the anguish of those last moments. Those who entered the vaults first were found near the inner wall sitting on the floor, some of them locked forever in an embrace. Those instead who were left standing in the crowd had eventually fallen down onto one another when they lost consciousness. Judging by their white teeth carrying virtually no caries, most of them must have been very young, perhaps the children of wealthy families on holidays at Herculaneum, a fashionable seaside resort. The emperor himself spent the summer not too far away, at Baia.

During the excavation, they found many pieces of jewelry: almost all of the bodies carried some. Pages and pages of the diary reported long lists of personal objects and pencil sketches gave a more precise idea of the most interesting ones: pinkie rings in gold with a small encased stone, band bracelets, snake-shaped teardrop earrings, gold medallions fastened at the center of the chest with a long golden chain to a large mesh that was passed around the waist and then as a double bandoleer across the chest and back.

About a hundred meters away, they discovered the remains of a magnificent villa, later known as the "Villa dei Papiri," that belonged to the noble Lucius Calpurnius Pisone and probably had been a meeting place for scholars of the time, a kind of academy. The excavations proceeded in that direction.

It all had begun in the early eighteenth century. In those years, an Austrian garrison was stationed in Naples and one of the young officers was Prince Maurice d'Elboeuf. The young man happened to notice a large quantity of ancient marble in the workshop of a stonemason. He asked about its origin and was told that it had been found by a farmer who, in an attempt to revive a well that had gone dry, had dug deep and found a veritable marble quarry.

The prince bought the farmer's field and started a campaign of excavations. He soon found a statue of Hercules in Parian marble and later three magnificent feminine statues that were immediately sent to Vienna. There, they aroused enormous enthusiasm at court and were later put on public display. Prince d'Elboeuf never knew he had discovered Herculaneum and that the excavations had stopped close to the wall of the theater, full of statues. The King of Naples resumed the excavations in 1734 and found an inscription providing the evidence that the archaeological site indeed corresponded to the theater of ancient Herculaneum.

Oleg's diaries described the finding of a very extensive and multi-layered walkway during an excavation that proceeded in the direction of the "Villa dei Papiri." In the third volume he described the discovery of a room of modest size, with brick vaults, located in one of the lower levels of the excavation. It had been found by following a tunnel, approximately a hundred meter long, that lead to the basement of the villa. The room had no other access than the underground tunnel that connected to the main building.

Inside the vaulted room, they found three skeletons positioned as shown in one of the sketches. The first one was the skeleton of an adult male, aged between fifty and sixty, who was found along the tunnel at the end nearest the villa. He had with him an object of great value: a cup depicting hunting scenes, engraved in gold, exquisitely crafted and of great artistic value. What he was doing in the tunnel, why he was carrying that precious object and what were his intentions was not clear at all. The position of the body indicated that the pyroclastic cloud had caught him on his way to the room at the end of the tunnel. The situation seemed quite odd because the only way to safety was in fact in the opposite direction, toward the villa.

Later, they discovered two skeletons inside the room at the end of the tunnel.

Why, wondered Oleg, had the three of them sought refuge in the wrong direction? Were they in a blind panic, or perhaps the man in the tunnel did not know that it ended in a cul-de-sac?

The drawing on the next page made me shudder.

It showed the skull of one of the skeletons that had been found in the room at the end of the tunnel.

I could not believe my eyes.

A very high forehead was divided into two well-separated lobes with an overall cranial volume that was at least twice as large as average. The nasal septum was completely absent and in its place was a strange and complex lamellar structure that developed horizontally. The eye sockets, too small and of unusual elliptical shape, were widely spaced on either side of the upper blade bone. At the base of the skull there were no traces either of jaw or teeth.

The structure of the 'cervical vertebrae,' of which another drawing depicted a detail, was totally different from what I had learned during the anatomy lessons I attended as a student at the university. On the contrary, the rest of the skeleton – at least for what I could judge from the sketch on the following page – had a morphology not very far from a humanoid, with the exception of the arms that were too short. The hands were small with an opposable thumb and with very long phalanges. But I could count only four fingers in both hands!

The size of each skeleton was of a giant, seven feet tall at least, when at that time the average height did not reach much more than five.

Viewed as a whole, it was not human.

Not a bit.

The first hypothesis that came to my mind was that it was the case of an individual affected by a rare disease (such as the syndrome later known by the name of Reiner's) or congenital malformation. This was also the opinion of Oleg at the time of the discovery. However, the continuation of the excavation brought to light, a few meters ahead in the same room, a second skeleton almost identical to the first one. Enlarged details of the second finding were reported in pencil sketches on the following pages of the diary and in a series of dense notes where Oleg carefully compared the strange characteristics of the two skeletons.

Were they affected by the same syndrome, he asked himself, or were they members of the same peculiar genetic *filum*?

On the next page, my eyes fell on two drawings that depicted a ring and an earring with a pendant. Both had been found in the tunnel close to the first skeleton. The ring carried a stone of considerable dimensions in a golden mount. Oleg described it as: "[…] of spherical shape with a diameter of about a quarter of an inch and with a black-bluish look as if of metal. I am not able to figure out of what material it is made: certainly not a mineral or a metal that I know. It conducts heat well and I think it could be a metal alloy unknown to me. But an alloy of very heavy metals, because I could verify that its weight exceeds that of a lead sphere of equal volume..."

On the golden pendant was mounted a "pearl" seemingly made of the same bluish material, but smaller than the one on the ring. Near one of the two abnormal skeletons they also had found a second ring identical to the first and a very similar pendant. There were also the remains of a necklace scattered all around: many identical beads of the same size. I studied a sketch that showed a zoomed view of one of the them and, to my bewilderment, I realized that it had two small holes one on each side and a small conical recess in the center. Which reminded me of something I had seen.

I read avidly, again and again, the records written by Oleg. I hoped that at least one of the two rings had belonged to him as I was told by Stahl, and wondered if the 'metal spheres' resembled those I already knew.

The diary reported the records of the excavation until the discovery of the tunnel and of the room at its end. Oleg suggested that both had been built prior to the construction of the villa. The function of the vaulted room was unclear, as was the reason it was built so far and detached from the body of the villa. Perhaps it was originally intended as a warehouse at the time of construction.

In the room was found an artifact that Oleg did not hesitate to define 'impossible'. The excavation brought to light a metal frame completely corroded by rust. Fixed to the rotten frame, or rather to what was left of it, a 'metal plate' appeared instead to have withstood the offense of time. After having cleaned it, Oleg realized with astonishment that it was in excellent conditions. Made of an alloy with a bluish-black metallic look and entirely similar to that of the two rings, the heavy plate showed no signs of corrosion. In Oleg's drawing I could easily recognize the shape of the flattened paraboloid that I was already familiar with. Embedded on the plate, Oleg had counted 64 spheres of the same 'metal'.

I exulted with joy.

No doubt about it: it was the plate I had found fixed to the interior of the lid of one of the trunks that belonged to the magician: thanks to Irina, I was on the right track!

I continued eagerly reading the diary. In the following pages Oleg had tried, unsuccessfully, to connect the geometrical arrangement of the spheres on the plate with some kind of ornamental motif or functional purpose. What astonished him most was the absolute absence of rust on the metal and its extraordinary density. It could hardly match the available metallurgical know-how of that time.

Oleg decided that the excavations had to be extended to the areas surrounding the room and the tunnel. The entire work went on for a few months without producing any new result. Eventually Oleg was forced to stop the excavations in that area and to focus on the sector relative to the main body of the villa.

The last part of the diaries reported news of the most important discovery of all during the campaign, a discovery of such a magnitude that it had totally focused the interest of the archaeologists and ended up diverting Oleg from the mystery of the strange skeletons. In fact, in the eastern part of the villa, a new site was identified where a large number of papyrus scrolls were discovered. There were rumors that this could be the long-sought library of the villa, an important archaeological treasure that might lead to the recovery of long-lost literary works in Greek and Latin. But this possibility was thwarted by the technical difficulty of unrolling, without destroying their precious content, the papyri from their 'cocoons' created by immersion in the mud from the eruption.

At the time of the discovery of the strange metal plate, many speculations were formulated about its origin and the unusual state of preservation of the metal. Experts of Roman and Greek metallurgy were consulted, but their investigations led nowhere.

In the meantime, the archaeologists' attention was all taken by the papyrus scrolls found in the villa and the mysterious artifact remained a small piece of secondary importance, difficult to be placed in the overall jigsaw puzzle and soon forgotten.

***

Irina's health improved rapidly and I was allowed to meet her in the private garden of the director of the penitentiary. She was happy to be outdoors and not forced to see me in that squalid parlor. She told me she had witnessed events that any sane person would have defined as 'impossible.'

Irina spoke and her eyes sparkled with excitement. My eyes could not break away from her delicate neck and the thin blue vein swollen in the heat of the story.

Irina's neck.

Her pale blue eyes, now in plain daylight, were luminous as if the light itself was springing out. Her glance captured mine.

Irina's eyes.

From week to week, she became more relaxed and regained much of her natural good mood and open, sunny nature. All this thanks to the good offices of the Director and in spite of the ironclad prison regulations.

"It goes without saying," the director had made it clear, "that such special treatment is not at all usual and therefore cannot last long, you understand, Herr Mayer... I try to do what I can."

I understood. So I worked through my uncle and quite soon the director was gratified with a modest promotion to a slightly higher salary class. It was not much, but from that day on we were granted a full hour of conversation every week in the garden and a much more discreet surveillance than in the past.

Following the course of events, Irina told me about the strange experiments of Oleg. She was glad to be able to share with someone the heavy burden of memories and secrets she had concealed for so long. She became less suspicious of me and finally the day came when I was able to make her laugh for the first time.

Irina's smile.

Irina's lips.

She told me that they had met at the University of Geneva where Oleg had a teaching assignment on his return from the excavation in Herculaneum. The fact that his father was a professor of Roman archeology in the same university was of course a pure coincidence.

Irina was enrolled in a course that introduced the basics of the techniques of archaeological excavations. During the lectures, Oleg had often indulged in telling his recent experiences in Italy and Irina had been fascinated by the tall young man with dark curly hair and a magnetic glance. She literally hung on his every word. The images so sharp that Oleg evoked of those days in Herculaneum spoke of a world that she was eager to know first-hand. They spoke of a real world, sunbaked, blanched by the dust, drenched in sweat, where imagination, impatience and the anxiety of discovery were galloping at full speed, though harnessed and governed by a ritual of gestures that were repeated always the same, methodically, with a slow cadence, sometimes to the point of sheer exasperation.

The stories on which Oleg occasionally lingered were definitely much better than a formal lecture. She could see clearly that Oleg was not ready for the drabness of an academic career: he still burned with the fire of enthusiasm and of the impatience for discovery.

Irina's passion for archeology came from her grandfather and had manifested itself already when she was a girl. There were not many women at that time who could afford to be so unconventional to attend the university, but Irina's father was a wealthy bourgeois of liberal ideas, so he decided to let her choose.

She was now the only woman attending the first year, surrounded by a dozen of young men of her age who were totally unattractive to her. She was more than pretty and Oleg could not help noticing her. They had exchanged just a few words during the lessons. Although the age difference between them was only nine years, Irina was intimidated by the rigid formal relationship between the teacher and the student that was the practice at the time and which was difficult to ignore, at least inside the walls the university.

It was to be expected that everything would follow its natural course: the end of the lessons, a brilliant exam, the congratulations of the Committee for the diligence of the student and nothing more, if not for the casual circumstance that made them meet (or to be more precise, collide) more or less at about ten o' clock in the morning of a Wednesday like any other, at the corner between Rue de la Fusterie and the Quarrefour.

Oleg, an early bird as usual, had spent a couple of hours in his office at the university and was proceeding briskly in the direction of the Cafe de la Paix on the south side of the square, determined to sit outdoors and to enjoy the sun that was shining strong, after the morning fog had cleared the lake.

Irina, late as usual, was almost running to the university trying to make up for a few minutes of delay and avoid missing a valuable lesson that began at ten o' clock sharp.

In the collision, the body of smaller mass bounced back from the one of greater mass and Irina would have certainly fallen head over heels if Oleg had not caught her by the waist with the reflex movement of a tango dancer.

Irina, overcome with surprise and emotion, could barely stammer, "Please forgive me, Professor... I didn't see you coming."

"But, I don't mind it at all, mademoiselle..." Oleg smiled, amused. "it's my fault, I got into your way. Are you in a hurry?"

"Yes. I'm late for the lesson of Ancient Greek class," said Irina, blushing.

"If I'm not mistaken, let me see... and if my memory serves me correctly, it is probably not the first time that you happen to be late at a lecture. I'm just kidding, don't worry... whatever time you decide to show up, it is always a pleasure to have you with us."

Oleg, extracted his watch from his vest.

"But frankly, I fear that for today you have no hope. It's already ten and you can't make it even if you run."

"You are right, Professor. I guess I have to give up... I'll go right back home. "

"Wait... just a moment, please. Since, after all, it is entirely my fault that you were not able to get to your class, I would be honored if you allow me to invite you for a cup of coffee. How about it?"

"I don't know…" Irina mumbled, in embarrassment. She bowed her head, looking down at her feet.

"Please. You don't not wish me to live with this remorse all day, do you?"

So they sat outdoors in the beautiful spring sunshine that lit up with dazzling colors the immaculate white tablecloth, the blue china cups and the yellow forsythia bouquet in a centerpiece.

First they chatted of this and that. Then Oleg began to tell her what he was doing in the laboratory at the university. Of course he was very careful not to reveal anything, but simply told her about the discovery of the tunnel below the villa at Herculaneum and the finding of some jewelry and of a metal case. He did not mention the skeletons.

Irina was extremely interested and studied him with her eyes of the same color as the sky, reflecting the sunlight that caressed her face.

"I examined the pendants and the ring, but I found it difficult to date them. They seem to be of Roman age, but some details leave me in doubt. Would you care to have a look at them?" asked Oleg with a vein of shameless impudence.

Irina was puzzled. The proposal had every appearance of being a trivial pretext for an affair, but her curiosity prevailed. She recalled that the archeology laboratory was close to the classrooms and therefore not in a particularly dangerous location. She first pretended to refuse, then relented, hesitated, and finally agreed to follow Oleg to his laboratory.

They left the café. Shortly after they passed by the classrooms and, through a narrow corridor, entered a small study that was connected to a wider room lit by enormous arched windows, paneled on three sides by heavy wooden shelves full of drawers and glass cases. A long bench in the center and two smaller ones in a corner were literally covered with fragments of vases, amphoras and craters patiently reconstructed from a myriad of small fragments. She saw artifacts of stone and metal, spatulas, brushes, drills, chisels and work tools to scrape, clean, smooth, polish, glue. And dust, dust everywhere. The only exception was a corner of the room occupied by a desk meticulously kept neat and clean, protected from behind by a small bookshelf that was also well taken care of. Alongside, a frosted-glass door opened into an adjacent room. They could hear muffled voices coming from inside, a sign that there was someone at work.

That's better, thought Irina, realizing that in the large hall they were alone.

"And here they are!" said Oleg "Have a look on the table. Those are the findings from the excavation at the villa."

He pointed at a crater of Greek origin currently under reconstruction and a series of numbered fragments. Next to them, a bust carved in stone its nose broken off, as usual.

"We found a lot of golden brooches and rings, bracelets, necklaces and earrings. Many of those unfortunate people were young and of rich families. You can notice some very beautiful jewelry in the glass case over there, in the corner. Unfortunately, most of the findings remained in Naples."

They slowly moved around the room. Oleg described the most important objects and, since Irina did not seem bored at all, he went on describing the various activities going on at the tables around .

"But… it seems that you do not keep any papyrus from the villa here, is that right?" asked Irina.

"Not many. In total we have only three and they are religiously preserved in the next room. We are studying, without success, a method to unroll them without damaging the interior. This is the work of Schinzel. Please look here, on this table. This metal structure is what remains of a kind of chest or case that we found in the tunnel."

"Interesting, but if I'm not mistaken, you told me about some jewelry found in the same passage."

"Yes, of course… they are in the next room. I'll show you. Just wait a moment. I will get them. "

Oleg disappeared beyond the glass door.

Left alone, Irina began to inspect the case. The iron framework was completely devoured by the rust and there remained only a few fragments embedded in the solidified mud from the eruption. The metal cover, however, was perfectly preserved, with no trace of corrosion. It reflected a sort of black-bluish color. Irina fingered the geometric pattern that adorned the internal surface, wondering if it had any meaning. Small beads of the same metal, in relief, formed a complex design with a geometric symmetry, but they did not reminded her anything that she had previously seen. She stood pensively for a long while staring at the strange pattern, when she heard Oleg coming back from the other room.

"But, Professor... this cover..."

"It looks brand new, right?"

"Yes. But what kind of metal is it made of? There is no trace of rust. "

"I wish I knew. It is probably a metal alloy, very hard and stiff, but we could not find out what it is. It is as strong as the steel swords of Damascus, but much heavier. It is a real mystery. Nobody has ever seen anything like it, to my knowledge, in an archaeological excavation of that period and, indeed, even of a later epoch..."

"But how is it possible then?"

"It's strange, I know. But, this is not the whole story. There is more: look at these earrings and the ring."

From Oleg's palm, Irina took a large golden ring holding what looked like a dark bluish pearl.

"It looks like a black pearl... but... it is metal. I would say it looks like... "

"Like what?"

"... like one of the nails on the big heads forming the ornamental motif on the cover..."

"... of the case. Brava! I see that you have a great sense of observation. And what about these? Do they remind you of anything else?" asked Oleg, handing her one of the two earrings.

"It seems again a sort of small metal sphere, a bit smaller though, but similar to that of the ring. Even the color looks pretty much the same, bluish-black... I would guess that they are of the same metal."

"That's also what I think. You see, there is something in common among these objects that were found within walking distance of each other along the tunnel. In that room on your right there is a second ring, a necklace and a fragment belonging to another pair of earrings exactly identical to these."

"And nothing else?"

"No other jewel, if that's what you mean. Nothing else."

And he was not lying to her. Simply, he thought, it was not the right moment to mention those other "things".

"I am very surprised. The mounting ring and the type of earring, that's my guess, do not belong to the first Roman period."

"There is no doubt about that. Indeed, this kind of necklace is quite common in the first century."

"The problem is those strange 'pearls' of metal. And there is more. Would you mind trying on the earrings?"

"But... really, I do not..."

"It's a just little experiment, no trouble at all. Trust me, if you please."

Irina, reluctantly, put the earrings on and, contrary to what she expected, without any difficulty.

"Here you are!" she said, smiling at Oleg.

"That's good... yes, I would dare say that you look even prettier with them on. But, come here, please, near the wooden case. Would you mind resting your hand on the cover... on the ornamental motif, wherever you prefer... just like that. That's perfect!"

"Are you making fun of me, Professor?"

Oleg shook his head and smiled reassuringly, the big ring on his finger.

He looked around: there were only the two of them.

From the next room came the sound of a muffled conversation and laughter. Oleg touched the larger sphere encased at the center of the lid with the ring.

A small blue glow flashed between the two small spheres.

"But what's that...?"

Irina could not finish the sentence. A colored image blurred her vision and completely covered Oleg's face in front of her.

Instinctively, Irina withdrew her hand and the image immediately vanished.

"Did you see anything, Irina? Please put your hand back on the lid, there's nothing to be afraid of. I've tried it myself, several times."

Without saying a word, Irina put her hand back on the lid. She was frightened.

Again, colored shapes, indistinct and in slow motion, overlapped the images of Oleg and of the room.

"I'm scared," stammered Irina," I do see… strange colors… but what is it going on?"

"Ah, well. You do see something. Don't be afraid: at the beginning you cannot see much, then slowly the images will focus. If you feel tired, though, it is better that you stop. Just remove your hand."

"No, I want to continue. But… may I have a seat, please?"

A few moments later, Irina was able to resume the experiment.

"Now, I can see some kind of shapes, maybe a little more distinct than before, superimposed on your image."

"Close your eyes, it will be easier."

Irina obeyed and, slowly, behind her closed eyelids the images stabilized and she began to see something.

"It looks like… a big house, or maybe… a castle or… rather a monastery?… I see a massive door in front of me. Yes, now everything is clearer, I see a door."

"Very well, continue. You are much better than I am. It's your very first time, yet you are able to get a clear picture. If you feel fine, you can go ahead. Try to knock at the door."

"To knock?"

"Yes, at the door. As if you were actually in front of a door. "

Irina, more and more amazed and frightened, followed Oleg's advice and raised a hand to grab the knocker. With amazement – because she knew and felt that her eyelids were shut – she saw her hand rising and knocking at the door."

"But… that's amazing. How can I see it with my eyes shut?"

"I don't know. But I did that too and, believe me, it is not dangerous. As soon as you get used to it… it is also fun, believe me."

"I knocked… did you hear it too? Hey, the door is opening…"

She gave out a sharp cry, frightened, and withdrew her hand.

The image faded and disappeared.

"You got scared. Sorry. What did you see last?"

"The door opened and I saw…" Irina trembled.

Oleg put a hand on her shoulder.

"Calm down, it's just an illusion. It is just like in a dream when it seems so real, yet it is just a fragment of your memories. You always remained here, in front of me. Nothing real happened to you and nothing can happen. So, did you see something bad?"

"No, I saw him just for a moment, then I got scared. He looked… "

"He looked… like what?"

"Like… a friar."

"A friar?" asked Oleg, barely stifling a giggle. "someone perhaps you know well?"

"I do not know any friar. But, now that you make me think about it… yes, he looked somehow familiar to me."

"Please come with me, that's enough for today. We're going to talk about it outside. I think I owe you an explanation and certainly you need something to pull yourself together. I'll be back in a moment. I apologize."

He disappeared with the jewels into the next room and reappeared a few minutes later. Irina was overwhelmed by the recent events: she felt her legs weak and looked all around trying to make sense of what had happened.

Oleg smiled. He took her hand and ushered her out of the University.

Irina followed him obediently.

***

Irina realized that the dish in front of her was almost empty and the delicious *filet de canard* was now just a pleasant memory for the palate. She did not expect that the surprise and violent emotions experienced in Oleg's laboratory would unleash such a formidable appetite. She wondered if an experience that totally overwhelmed her both physically and mentally, like a storm striking suddenly on the calm waters of a lake, could produce these effects.

She smiled to herself and wondered once again whether it had been a good idea to taste that delicious white wine that Oleg had recommended so much. Now, filled by a cozy warmth that flowed in her veins, Irina felt comfortable and safe. She did not know how long she had been sitting face to face with her teacher in the Bistrot des

Philosophes (a discreet restaurant at a safe distance from the University) to listen, as if hypnotized, at Oleg's story.

"I owe you an explanation," he said.

And kept his word.

While speaking, Oleg kept his eyes on the rim of the glass in front of him and his index finger moved slowly on the gilt surface. He cleared his throat with a sip of Muscadet, cold at the right temperature, and went on telling his story to Irina.

***

The first time I noticed something strange was when I accidentally touched the plate with the ring. Something had happened, I was sure, but I thought it was just a feeling, nothing real. I tried again and this time I noticed a small blue spark flaring silently between the sphere set in the ring and the metal plate as soon as they came close. When I touched one of the spheres of the plate with my finger, I saw blurred colored spots crowding my field of vision… just like patches of color. That's what they looked like. After a little practice, I noticed that after a while, the colored spots disappeared. At that point however, if I touched the plate again with the ring, they reappeared. As if the plate had been… *recharged*."

I took care to say nothing to my staff. In those days we were working on a reconstruction of the site where we had found the plate, helping us with the notes taken during the excavation. We had partially reconstituted a necklace putting together the beads we had found scattered not far from the place where we had found the ring and the earrings. I was wearing the ring on my finger and, while discussing the work, I casually laid my hand on the plate. Immediately I saw some colored shape overlapping the image I had before my eyes. It was blurred, but the contours were slowly taking shape, much better than before. Fortunately at that moment, Schinzel was monopolizing the attention of the others, so no one noticed my stunned expression. I walked away as fast as I could from the case, pretending that nothing had happened.

I remember that I had to wait impatiently for my staff to leave the room.

As soon as the laboratory was empty, I touched the sphere at the center of the metal plate with the ring. My vision immediately became sharper and the colors more intense. I put my hand again on the plate and immediately the previous colored image reappeared.

After a bit of practice, I discovered that if I was wearing either one of the two earrings the image became more intense, as if the earring was able to amplify that strange visual phenomenon.

I closed my eyes and began to distinguish the contours, first confused, but soon getting more and more focused, of a square courtyard surrounded by a large colonnade. Now I was in one of the four corners of a cloister where, facing ahead, two huge portals – not less than four meters tall – towered over me. The door to my right was closed and a reddish-yellow light filtered under it. Instinctively I reached out and… you've tried yourself Irina… I saw my hand moving toward the door and touching the rough surface of the wood. And I felt in my nostrils a sweet and oily scent, similar to the one you can smell when you walk into a church, a scent that smells of wood, of oil and incense that have soaked the wood day after day.

I looked down at my feet. I saw them move forward, slowly. I opened the door a crack and peeked inside…

Books, it was full of books!

In neat rows, they extended up to the ceiling crowding the shelves of a huge library that occupied the four walls. In front of me, in the middle of the vast room, I saw a number of wooden lecterns holding large sized books with their leather bindings. Most of them were closed, but I saw a pair with pages wide open. So I headed toward the nearest for a look.

It was a strange book.

But was there anything normal in that world which seemed to have been extracted from my dreams, a world I was part of and where I could touch and feel, sweat and breathe?

It was a strange book: the figures were clear, the colors beautiful.

And they moved!

The first one of the two large books was opened to a page where I could see a blue globe illuminated by the sun. The opposite page instead was completely black except for small bright dots of light here and there. I concentrated on the first colored page: a water world streaked with white and blue. Among those streaks, the profile of the continents. There was no doubt that it is was the Earth.

But it was not a static image: that Earth revolved slowly around its axis!

It made a complete revolution in a quarter of an hour or so. Even the clouds were moving imperceptibly and there was a nice anticyclonic system in the northern hemisphere rotating clockwise. The line that marked the boundary between day and night was clearly visible. It divided the globe more or less into two halves. I thought that it was showing the current time because we were at the end of April and therefore close to the equinox. Fascinated, I remained standing near the lectern for a long while, looking into the book like a child peeping into a magic sphere.

Then I began to examine the opposite page and, straining my eyes, I realized that it represented a starry sky. The stars twinkled feebly on a dark and cold background, the blackest of imaginable blacks, darker than any ink I had ever seen on a printed book. I easily recognized some constellations I was familiar with. It looked like the sky of the northern hemisphere. I studied it for a long time: nothing moved and the stars seemed small holes pierced in a dark vault.

Eventually I got tired of it and went back to admire the enchanted land that revolved undisturbed on the left page. The Mediterranean basin was clearly visible, encumbered by that strange anatomical appendage that corresponds to the Italian peninsula, happily surrounded by a high-pressure zone where the sun was shining and the sky was cloudless.

Suddenly, I noticed a red dot.

Quite clear. Not far from the Gulf of Naples.

I pulled my nose closer to the page to see better.

Zoom!

The image zoomed in as if someone had read my mind. Now the book showed me a magnified view of the peninsula that filled the entire page. Just focusing my sight on the red dot, I was able to get three magnifications in quick succession, the red spot increasing its radius each time. First the southern part of Italy, then the Gulf of Naples and then the surrounding areas. Finally a detailed view of the area around Herculaneum. I could distinguish a finer structure inside the red area and, at the final magnification, the dot turned out to be actually not a dot but a small equilateral triangle with red sides shining bright. It occupied a large part of the archaeological site near the coastline. The intersection of the three medians identified the location of an area not wider than thirty feet.

Now I understood what I was looking at. I recognized some landmarks that I had mapped during the excavation. A kind of three-fold crosswire was indicating the exact position in which we had found the skeletons and the case.

I was impressed.

Suddenly I became aware of a presence behind me. I spun around and I recognized a face that was familiar to me.

Anselmo.

Father Anselmo, my tutor at the Jesuit college.

What was my good old teacher doing in this strange world, in this dreamlike reality that a metal plate, dozens of centuries old and unscathed by the time, had drawn from my memories?

" Father Anselmo, what are you doing here? "

" Take it easy, son." He smiled sweetly.

" I will explain. I am not Father Anselmo in flesh and bones as you met him at the college. I'm just a product of your memories, extracted from your mind. I am of the same material dreams are made of: shreds of your memories sewn here and there in a consistent, seamless, realistic pattern. I am a well-done dream, that's all I am."

" Maybe, but how can you? I know very well I'm awake. I am fully conscious and yet... you really look exactly the same as Father Anselmo."

" Do you remember what you were doing before you got here, do you? "

" Yes, sure. The plate, the ring, the earring..."

" And you are still wearing the earring, aren't you? "

I reached my ear, and I felt the cold touch of the metal.

" It is through the earring that I can access your mind, your deepest memories, your thoughts, even your conscience."

" Do you? " I shuddered.

" Not me. I told you. I'm just a representation, you may call it *virtual* if you want, set up for the sole purpose of communicating with you. It is the *machine* that actually reads your mind."

" Which machine? "

" The one hidden in the case, or to be more precise, in the plate attached to the lid. It is not really a *machine*. It is something more than that. Machines do not have self-awareness."

" I would like to believe that. Is there a sentient creature hidden in the plate? "

" Call it what you will. In the plate there is something actually very small in size, and inanimate according to the way your folk define a living being, but perfectly able to think, to take decisions and equipped with self-consciousness. I'm just a simulacrum: remember that you're not arguing with Father Anselmo, but with a *machine,* if you prefer to call it that way."

" That's crazy…" I laughed. " Sorry, but it seems so funny to hear Father Anselmo talking about a machine endowed with free will."

The outburst of laughter made me feel better and helped me to release a bit of the tension I had accumulated.

" Well, do you remember our endless discussions about free will? "

" Yes, I do. It really sounds like you are Father Anselmo in person "

" If I'm not mistaken, one day you put me in trouble with the paradox of a guy who manages to split himself into two perfectly identical beings. Do you remember that? "

" Of course I remember. After all, they are my own memories. "

" Good. I see that you begin to understand. The problem was... correct me if I'm wrong: what decision will either copy take about what to do? Will they take the same decisions? Or will each use his own free will? "

" Yes, that was precisely it. All right, Father, you have convinced me. You can also read my deepest thoughts. But if you are a machine or sort of, who are those people who built you? "

" Aha! Here we go. About this point, I am afraid that you will find Father Anselmo quite reticent."

" You do not want me to believe that a machine can build itself? "

" Here the discussion would become too long. But, tell me, what do you think about people. After all, are they not just intelligent *automata*? "

" Uhm... Father Anselmo would never have admitted such a thing. Now I believe you. You are definitely *not* Father Anselmo. Who are you then?"

" Actually... you have a point here. Examining more carefully your memories of Father Anselmo, I can only agree with you. He would never have given you the satisfaction of admitting such a thing. He might, perhaps... have thought that, but not openly."

" That's unbelievable! Father Anselmo, or whoever you are, please give me a proof that I'm not dreaming, that I'm not fooling my own brain! "

"The proof is out there, dear Oleg. The plate and the ring together can make certain things happen. And I can give you a proof."

" Things? What are you talking about? "

" I will tell you what I can. But I must warn you right now that there is some information that I cannot give you. There is a block in this direction built inside me. You cannot get around it in any way. So please, as of now, do not insist when you come to ask me questions that I cannot answer. Do you see this library?"

" I do see it… it's huge!"

" It contains a body of knowledge that is unlike anything you can imagine. You can read many of these books and they will be for you an almost inexhaustible source of knowledge. But there are other books that you will never be able to open. They will remain closed in their binding, inviolable, indifferent to your efforts. Maybe you will be able to read just some titles. This will make you suffer even more and burn of curiosity, but I won't be able to help you."

" This is…"

" Hard to believe, I know. I cannot blame you. But you'll get used to it after a while. Now listen to me: I'll explain to you how to use the ring and the plate."

***

While Oleg was telling her of his first meeting with Anselmo, Irina remained silent, sitting in front of him, her eyes lost in the eyes of the young professor. Through the tone of voice that now felt quite familiar, she had the impression of witnessing the scene firsthand.

An atmosphere of intimacy had built around them in the small bistro and the waiters did not dare to disturb them even after the other customers were long gone and it was now time to close. Oleg finally noticed a waiter who was pretending to be busy checking the cutlery on the nearby tables while the owner was once again patiently recalculating their bill.

"Time to go, I think. They are going to close."

So they left the bistro and walked toward the lake in the crisp spring air. They continued to talk paying no attention to whatever happened around them: the pounding of hooves on the road as horses passed by, the deafening clatter of the wheels of the carriages along the *Quai*, noises coming and going, growing and decreasing in intensity, fading away unnoticed, all along their way downhill to the lake.

They sat on the dock watching the boats that looked as if suspended in midair in the motionless water of the lake, stripes of bright colors swinging lazily in pairs, each in perfect synchronism with its reflected twin image.

"I want to show you something… a sort of magician's game." Oleg smiled, looking all around him and making sure no one was close by. He could not see anybody, except a couple of young lovers on the front dock who were tightly embraced and too busy to care about what was happening around them, a blonde head with a long pony tail and a curly dark-haired man. They kissed passionately and Irina looked at them with envy, smiling to herself inwardly.

Oleg reached into his pocket and pulled out two small bluish spheres. He handed one to Irina.

"Would you hold it in the palm of your hand? Please do not tighten your fingers…"

"Is it dangerous? Are they one of those spheres…"

"Sure. But don't worry. I know what I am doing. I've tried it before. Will you give me your necklace for a moment?"

"Why not?" replied Irina, removing a pendant from her graceful neck: a drop-shaped aquamarine hanging on a thin gold chain.

Oleg took the pendant and laid it on the well-honed stone of the pier. He took from his pocket a second sphere and placed it close to the pendant, so that they touched.

"Wait and see…"

Oleg gently touched the small bluish ball with the ring on his finger.

"My necklace!" shouted Irina "It's gone!"

"Don't worry… here it is. Please open your hand…"

Irina obeyed and remained in disbelief staring, mouth opened, at the palm of her hand where her aquamarine with its slender thread of gold had just reappeared, as if by magic, next to the little metal sphere.

"For a moment I was afraid that…"

"It would be a shame," whispered Oleg looking straight into her eyes. Irina's hand was still hanging in mid-air when he took the necklace from it and gently fastened the pendant around her neck. Irina slightly bowed to help him. When she raised her head, she met his eyes – those eyes that now she could recognize among thousands – gazing at her in a special way.

She closed her eyes, waiting...

A kiss. Sweet and passionate. Timeless.

When she opened her eyes again, time suddenly restarted its pace at an accelerated rate. Many different noises coming all together: voices from the distance of people walking on the lake shore, the lapping of the boats, the cries of the seagulls – sounds that had been turned off and now suddenly had been awakened, the caress of Oleg's glance on her cheeks aflame, the boats rocking lazily on the water, the dark outline of the Jura at the horizon, the couple on the pier in front. They had taken a break from their effusions and were looking at them, smiling.

She felt confused, a mixture of feelings. It was not the first time she had kissed a man. And yet... she felt there was something special this time.

Her eyes sparkled with a new light. Beautiful as ever.

"If I'm not mistaken, dear professor, you were talking about one game of magic, not two."

"You are right. But one of them was much more challenging than a sleight of hand."

"Which one?"

"The second one."

And he kissed her again. With passion, this time.

"Not bad," said Irina, catching her breath.

"The kiss?"

"The sleight of hand. You learnt it from Anselmo, am I right, professor?"

"Under the circumstances, I think you may drop the academic title…"

"I bet these are the pearls from the plate, right?"

"No. They are two of the pearls from the necklace we found at Herculaneum."

"From the necklace? I thought the necklace was only an ornament and did not matter for anything else."

"I thought that too, but Anselmo taught me that…" Oleg took the sphere that had been left on the pavement of the pier.

"Can you see this little tip, mademoiselle?"

"Under the circumstances, I think we could drop the formality…"

"Good. Can you see it?" he repeated, smiling.

"Yes, I do see a sort of small tip."

"Please look at the other sphere instead. It has a small cavity instead of the tip."

"I do see it. But what does it mean?"

"Anselmo told me that with the spiky sphere you can make an object disappear, provided it is of small size. Then you can make it reappear near the other sphere."

"Had I not seen all this with my own eyes, I could never believe you."

"I did not believe my eyes too when I first tried. The trick, however, works only if one has the ring that I am wearing. It is the ring that makes everything work, which allows one to 'see' Anselmo and is able to activate the small spheres for the transfer."

"But this is all…"

"Unbelievable, I know. But it works. I have tried it I don't remember how many times. It seems that it is the ring which provides the necessary energy to start the whole process."

"But how can you make something disappear *here* and make it appear over *there*? In this way you could make objects travel from one place to another…"

"Brava. That's precisely what it does. The problem is that the trick with the two spheres works only with small objects. However…"

"Please, continue. I beg you."

"Anselmo told me that to move larger objects, one must use the plate."

"How much larger?"

"As large as a man, for example."

"But then… the two skeletons that you found in Herculaneum near the case…"

"That's what I thought too. But about this subject Anselmo is a tombstone. I could not extract a word from his mouth. I suspect that those two strange guys were using the case to enter and exit the tunnel or perhaps to send and receive, who knows… some kind of objects?"

"But, did Anselmo tell you how to?"

"Yes, in part he explained it to me. But there are still points that are unclear. Needless to say, I did some tests."

"And did it work?" Irina asked, excited.

"Yes, it did. If you place an object in front of the plate and activate it with the ring, the object disappears. But it can be dangerous. Anselmo warned me. "

"And where does the object move to?"

"It's up to you to decide... Anselmo is the one who tells the plate where the object has to end up."

"You mean that it is Anselmo who somehow instructs the plate?"

"Anselmo, as you know, is just a representation of the *machine* that communicates with us."

"So, by means of Anselmo, you can send the item where you want?"

"Yes. More or less. But the machine is not able to 'center' exactly the desired location. I mean that the object does not land exactly in the desired place, but nearby. Say, within a certain radius of uncertainty. For example, if you ask to move the object miles away, then the error can be less than about ten feet or so."

"In other words, the object may end up where you want or within ten feet."

"Exactly. And sometimes with disastrous consequences because if the object happens to land in the position occupied by a solid body..."

"There is a kind of explosion?"

"You guessed right."

"Have you tried?"

"Yes. Anselmo recommended that I try with a very small and light object. So I sent a small coin crashing into the wall of a barn that I wished to demolish."

"And what happened?"

"A hole of half a meter diameter in a brick wall."

"But you could have hurt someone…"

"Not quite. I was there when it happened and I had checked that nobody was around."

"Did you make an agreement with Anselmo on the time of the transfer?"

"Yes I did. When you use the plate, the transfer cannot be instantaneous. The object disappears and reappears, but at a later time."

"How much later?"

"It depends. If you want, you can instruct the plate to make the object reappear in the desired place after many hours, days, or even years."

"More and more cumbersome," said Irina.

"I agree. There are basically two ways to move an object. If you want to move it around with great precision and therefore with no risk, you can use one of those blue balls with the notch. The position of the 'receiving sphere' defines the exact position where the object will appear again. In other words, the sphere helps the plate to locate the target. God knows how. This method, however, works only for small distances."

"It's like the trick with the two spheres that you used to impress me before: the one with the tip *transmits* while the one with the notch *receives*."

"Exactly. This system works only with small objects and in this case the transfer is practically instantaneous. For larger items, you must use the plate as a transmitter instead of the pointed sphere. In this case there is always a time delay for the arrival."

"Let me check my partial understanding of these amazing facts: you could for instance play a sort of wizard trick by making a whole person disappear in front of the plate and then make him appear again at a distance in a safe place."

"That's what I want to do."

"But are you sure it works also with living beings? Have you tried?"

"It does work with animals. With humans I do not know, but I'm willing to bet it does."

"You mean... you've already tried it with a..." stammered Irina.

"With a cat."

"Oh my... poor little kitty: it could have ended badly. Professor, you are a true monster."

"But everything went well, Irina. That cute ball of fur arrived without a scratch.

"One night I locked myself in the lab and started a series of experiments. First, I tried with a flower pot that I placed in front of the plate. It reappeared into the next room, right in the middle of the carpet – you remember that round rug in the lab? – where I had placed the receiver. Then, I tried with a book, next with a paperweight, the flower pot, and then I started doing it with everything that came to hand. Addicted by my successful attempts, my eye fell on the cat that roamed the laboratory..."

"Poor little kitty..."

"That damned beast did not want to keep still in front of the plate, so I had to get it immobilized..."

"Spare me the cruelest details. You are definitely a monster, dear professor..."

"Nothing cruel, believe me. I just closed the cat in a box with many generous holes for the air. The cat was fine. Just a bit annoyed, that's all."

"Just a little bit... he says. And then?"

"Then, the cat disappeared and arrived safe and sound inside the little box on the table of the laboratory."

"Well done. Now I begin to understand: wishing to move on to experiments on human beings, the eye of the professor fell on this poor student who was passing by..."

"Come on, Irina... my eye fell on the same student for other reasons. In any case, it is me who will play the cat."

"You don't mean... to try... yourself?"

"I shall be the guinea pig. But I need your help."

"Don't even think about it. I'm too scared..."

"Come on, Irina. With the cat everything went well. We can try first with a larger animal, for instance, a monkey if we find one. But if it works well with the monkey, there's no reason why..."

"And if instead it ends up like the coin?"

"One professor less..."

"And a student in tears..." said Irina, jumping to Oleg's neck and kissing him as a soldier leaving for the front.

"I'm afraid it's time to go," said Irina after a long, long kiss. "At home they will be wondering where I am. If it were up to me, I could stay here forever." She sighed, embraced Oleg tenderly, her glance lost over the lake.

"Me too," sighed Oleg.

They walked slowly along the *Quai*, hands in hands.

"It's not that late. Look... we may spend a moment at my place... It's is a small study, but it's cute..." suggested Oleg.

"I guess the professor has in mind some other trick of magic?"

"No more tricks for today." Oleg smiled.

"But I think that we are indeed a bit late and that the good Irina better go home. They have not seen me since this morning. It is already a scandal, so our neighbors say, that my parents allowed me to attend the University. Women must look after the house and raise children, so they say. Therefore, as you can understand, I have to behave myself because I do not want to be exposed to further criticism from those bigots. I will dream of you and what has happened today. It is a memorable day and..."

Oleg pulled her toward him and kissed her again and again.

They hugged once more before separating, no less than two blocks away from the cottage where her parents lived: a safe distance, so Irina had decided.

***

Fred was sitting in front of me deep asleep, head turned backwards, mouth wide open. The train jolted in perfect sync with the poor guy who was shaken from all sides. How he could sleep in those conditions, I did not know. For sure, I could not.

Beyond the window, the green landscape was slowly receding against the motion of the train, small patches of bright sky peeping among white puffs of steam, a few houses here and there, pastures, cattle, white mountains, snow glistening in the sun.

Besides Fred and I, in the elegant first-class compartment of the Österreichische Bundesbahnen, sat a distinguished gentleman, white-haired and dressed soberly in a dark gray double. He was reading and quietly smoking a pleasant-smelling tobacco. Wisps of fragrant smoke enveloped us with a sweet scent at regular intervals.

I had stuck in my head the memories of my last meeting with Irina and the sweet expression on her face when she told me about her first weeks with Oleg.

They had decided that it was not possible to continue working together in the laboratory of the University. Too many people coming and going. Sooner or later someone would have become suspicious. So, Oleg decided to move the plate to his studio where he could work away from prying eyes. After replacing it with a copy, the original was hidden at the bottom of a wooden trunk filled with books and personal items that he usually carried with him during the excavations. Then, he sealed the trunk and arranged for its delivery at home.

The copy of the plate was very similar to the original. It was made of a heavy metal alloy that had undergone a special surface treatment to look bluish. The craftsman to whom Oleg had commissioned it was someone who knew his business and Oleg was well aware of it. In any case, no one at the Institute noticed the exchange.

Oleg was eager to experience firsthand a body transfer and Anselmo had assured him that there was no risk as long as he would use a sphere as receiving target and that he would pay attention to leave enough space around it to accommodate the whole body size.

Following his instructions, Oleg purchased a travel trunk of considerable size, reinforced all around with a metal frame. After some practice, he learned how to fold himself at the bottom of the case, grasping his legs.

The original plate was then fixed to the lid. Anselmo explained that the process could begin only if the object was entirely contained in the case. In other words, there was no danger, for example, that dangling out an arm, the bumbling traveler would find himself at the destination but with just one arm left behind. Indeed, in this case, the transfer was automatically blocked until the full body fitted into the visual field of the plate.

Oleg was ready for the final proof, but Irina persuaded him to perform a final check.

One day they happened to notice a cute little monkey in a Lebanese shop that traded in exotic animals and they decided to take it at home. She was pretty, smart and restless and Irina loved her at first sight. When Oleg tried to convince her to put the little animal into the case, Irina shook her head, looking worried.

"Don't kill this poor animal. It's so cute…"

"But there is no reason why it shouldn't work. Nothing will happen, you'll see."

The monkey was stirring and screaming and did not want to hear any reason to stay still inside the case.

"Come on, come on. Help me to hold this little devil."

"I can't, Oleg. I'm too scared for her."

The job turned out not to be easy, but they eventually managed to close the lid of the case, although the screams from inside did not diminish in intensity.

"Come on, quickly. Touch the lid with the ring! That's it…"

"She's gone, look!"

The case was now empty. Irina felt her heart pounding.

"We must wait a bit."

"Yes, the transfer will take some time. But not so much, right? Let's hope that everything goes well. Maybe we should have tried outdoors. It is risky here at home."

"Everything will be fine, Irina. Let's see. Now it's time."

They moved toward the living room and were just midway when an unmistakable shriek, beyond the door, startled them.

They rushed into the next room.

The large living room was empty except for a few paintings on the walls. On the floor at the center of the room, there was a wooden case, a travel trunk they had found in a junk shop and that looked quite similar to the other case. Of course it had no plate mounted on it, but just an ordinary wooden lid. Inside, on the bottom, Oleg had positioned one of those bluish pearls with a small cavity on the surface.

Together they carefully lifted the lid, but had not time to look inside. The little hairy quadrumanous creature shot out and immediately started to jump around the room as if nothing had happened, screaming as it was her habit. She seemed in good shape and not at all impressed by being the first of her species to have made *the leap*. Not from the branch of a tree, but a leap through space and time, slipping off as if by magic from a case hermetically closed and landing unharmed a few meters away in a nearby future.

"She is alive! Thank God, she is alive!" shouted Irina, running to hug her.

"I told you. Anselmo had assured me that…"

"You always make it all too easy."

They both laughed and the tension loosened.

"Look! Fantastic… look how well she jumps!"

They watched the unleashed animal for a long time. It looked all right.

For some days they studied her habits and reactions and eventually concluded that everything was perfectly normal with her.

Now the time was ripe for another species to try the leap. A human should be the next. Oleg was determined and ready to do it, but Irina was still afraid though she was now almost convinced that there was no major risk.

The decisive moment had arrived, but Irina used all her feminine weapons to postpone the experiment. One afternoon she awoke suddenly from the pleasant torpor in which they had fallen and lazily slid her hand on the silk sheet searching for Oleg's body next to her.

The bed was empty.

"Oleg, where are you?" She jumped up with an accurate premonition.

No reply.

"Oleg! I bet that crazy..." She rushed into the study and, exactly as she feared, she saw the box with the plate installed below the lid. Sealed.

"He did it! Son of his good mother, he did it!"

She rushed into the next room, screaming, and opened the lid of the second case.

Oleg was there, completely naked, curled up on the bottom. Motionless.

"He is dead! Oh God, no!"

Irina, in panic, shook the still body, hugged him, tears streaming down her cheeks. Suddenly two strong arms encircled her waist.

"Come on, come on… There is no need to take it so seriously."

"You…" she stammered, incredulous.

"I'm still in one piece, as you see."

"You, son of… Did you want me to die of fear?"

"No, darling. I'm sorry. It was an idiotic joke. I just wanted to see if you…"

"If I, what?" Irina, annoyed, pulled herself together trying to look indifferent. She hurried to dry her tears with the back of one hand. Oleg took her face tenderly in his hands and kissed her.

"Stupid, stupid fool." She hugged him tight.

"Everything went fine. Look, nothing is missing," he gestured toward the inside.

Irina glanced inside the box and smiled mischievously.

"It is has still to be seen if everything works as before." She poked him with a bold look, biting her lips, openly provocative.

"Right! Let's try it right now!"

He struggled to get out of the crate and to embrace her. But Irina easily escaped his grasp with a burst of laughter. Oleg failed to maintain his balance and collapsed heavily on the carpet, hitting his knee hard on the edge of the box.

Gritting his teeth against the pain, Oleg tried to stand up.

"Serves you right, professor. Lesson learned. Be more clever next time."

Irina barely had time to finish the sentence. With a squeal, she started running around the room, chased by Oleg who was limping noticeably. Irina shouted and laughed, excited by the pursuit and the humor of the situation. They went like that for quite a while.

Eventually, the prey decided it was time to end that game and let another one to start.

As old as the world, a game that game is not.

***

Their clandestine affair went on for several months in Oleg's small apartment on the top floor of a decorous building of unpretentious architecture. A gray façade at 18 Rue Vauvillard in the heart of the part of the city that is now known as the Vielle Ville.

Usually they met in the early afternoon. After the classes at the University, Irina joined him after a long vicious circle, taking care that no one was following her. She did not want to run the risk of being seen accidentally by someone who knew her, fearing that her parents would sooner or later discover her relationship with Oleg. For them, Irina was studying at Claire's and indeed this was what happened almost every day of the week, except for a few special afternoons. And sometimes it was Claire who stayed at their house to prepare her exams for most of the day until a carriage sent by her father came to take to take her back to their beautiful villa in Cologny.

A blonde with regular features, though not really beautiful and with a few extra pounds, Claire was a girl of open character, cheerful, a bit naïve perhaps, but with a golden heart. She was enrolled at the University and studied the Classics against the advice of the whole family. The only exception was her father, a wealthy banker of Bavarian origin, who had eyes only for her and believed himself rich enough to afford the privilege of completely ignoring the other people's opinions. "After all," he thought, "since I do not have a son, I can well allow my daughter to develop interests and ambitions that are usually the prerogative of the opposite sex."

Claire and Irina had met at the University, the only two women enrolled in the same faculty, and they had immediately become good friends. They studied some common subjects together, like ancient Greek and Latin literature, and Claire lent herself willingly to prop up Irina's fragile castle of lies with her parents. These were kind of favors that a young woman could pay to a good friend.

Sometimes Irina met Oleg twice during the same day. In the morning, sitting quietly in the relative safety of her desk at the University, she had all the time she wanted to study him at a distance in his official role of teacher. And sometimes, when she was quite sure that no one would notice, she amused herself fixing her gaze on him with a provocative look, trying to embarrass him.

One afternoon, in the privacy of their small den overlooking the rooftops of Geneva, Oleg was pacing headlong around the table with long strides, furious.

"The old bastard! He says you're too young. That we have to wait. That I should be more responsible!"

Irina stared at the floor in silence.

"That's all crap. The truth is that he can *not* stand it. He just does *not*. God only knows what he has in mind. I disappointed him, he says!"

He continued back and forth like a wild animal in a cage, stumbling over everything that happened to cross his way in the happy little mess of their lair: a book, an empty bottle, an unpaired shoe.

"We can't go on like this, Oleg. My parents will eventually know. Even our neighbors look at me in a strange way."

"And what did you expect? They are formal people, keen on the form. People are mediocre, bigoted. They are all like that, you know."

"Do you think your father might change his mind?"

"No. Of course not. He wants me to marry a woman with Russian blood in her veins, maybe someone from the community here, someone I should marry under the golden domes of the Orthodox Church. He was born in Petersburg. That's important for him, while the mere accident that I was born here instead and that I speak, write and think in French, just as well as in the language of our ancestors, has no meaning for him."

"I understand, Oleg. I do understand... but calm down, *please*."

"There's only one little thing that the old goat disregarded. My character: rebellious, like my mother's. She was from Sverdlovsk, poor woman. A small village. But tough people. They are all hard-headed over there."

"And what will you do then?"

"Let's get out of here, Irina. I'm sick of this embalmed town. When I am at the University, I feel the cobwebs sticking onto my skin and sooner or later I will finish cocooned like those mummies of my respectful senior colleagues. Let's leave, let's go to Paris! Let's get a breath of life. Here I feel... suffocating."

"And ?"

"Meanwhile, we get married."

"We get married, he says. Easy to say. And my parents?"

"With them we can talk. I'm sure they will understand. They will give their blessing."

"Maybe. But I cannot stand the idea of not seeing them anymore."

"Come on, Irina. Paris is not the end of the world."

"Yes, but..."

"Listen. I have some ideas of what we could do in Paris."

"And that is?"

"You know the trick with the wooden case? The one with the monkey. How about doing the same with someone from the public? In a theater."

"You're *really* crazy. Want to go along this nonsense and become a magician?"

"*The* magician, not a magician. We have something unique here, Irina. Think about it. Something fantastic that has never been done before. It will be a triumph, you'll see, in Paris."

"It might well be. But what would we do exactly?"

"Let me explain."

They began to talk about it.

Irina, with that innate common sense that the vast majority of women possess from birth, believed in her heart that it was really crazy to go along with that kind of insanity. But, little by little, she began to change her mind.

In addition to the performance with the two cases, the highlight of the show, they developed together a series of impressive numbers that for the two of them, now quite familiar with the potentiality of the spheres, were a breeze.

So the magician's hat took its shape and it was Irina who sewed the lining at the bottom of the interior to hide one of the small bluish spheres.

And then came the ivory wand.

Oleg practiced several hours a day to master the techniques of magicians. Certain skills, such as handling a deck of cards or a strand of knotted scarves, which were a must in a show of that kind, were based on a manual dexterity foreign to Oleg and he had to struggle for a long time until he could master it. But he learned quickly and, after the first failures (Irina enjoyed herself a lot teasing him whenever she caught him making a mistake), she became confident in his new abilities. He worked hard and within a year he had learned a new profession. And he had learned it well. Now Irina was sure that they would have some success.

She was wrong.

Their success was resounding.

***

The train approached the platform of Gare Cornavin and slowed down, enveloped in a cloud of white steam. The long and squeaky lament of the brakes overcame the background noise that had accompanied us all along the journey, a rhythmic rattling we had eventually become accustomed to and that was now slowly fading away. A long final whistle and the train stopped on the quay.

It was a beautiful day. The air was clear, the sky deep blue without a single cloud. The sun was already strong and I could feel the warmth of its rays on my skin in the crisp morning. I filled my nostrils with a gentle breeze carrying the characteristic smell of the lake and mixed with the scents of the flowers and of the trees in bloom in an already mature spring.

A cabbie offered to take us to our hotel, but despite the fatigue of the trip, I felt in good shape and I wished to stretch my legs. We entrusted our luggage to the driver of the cab and we set off on foot along Rue du Mont Blanc, downhill towards the lake.

Sitting outdoors at a table of a bistro on the long lake under the shade of a large acacia tree, Fred and I enjoyed a sumptuous breakfast, actually the second of the morning after the one consumed a few hours before in the dining car of the train. Freshly baked white bread, butter, orange marmalade, croissants, fresh berries, all washed down with a jug of strong and well-toasted black coffee. We leisurely discussed an action plan for the day and then, reluctantly, we resumed our journey.

After crossing the Pont de la Machine, we split into different paths. Fred disappeared inside a bank holding a heavy leather bag. I walked with a lighter burden under my arm in the direction of the University, through the square of the Grand Theatre, and then on a cool tree-shaded path inside the park that ran along the walls of the Vielle Ville. Finally, I reached an austere building in neo-classical style.

I climbed a long flight of stairs leading to a wide peristyle at the main entrance of the University. Stepping inside, I felt immediately at ease in surroundings that looked familiar to me, while totally alien to that sense of awe that in the mind of the architect the pomposity of the building intended to impose on the visitor.

I asked to be announced to Oleg's father, the director of the Institute of Archaeology. The janitor respectfully reminded me that the old professor had long ago retired and now had the title of senior director. A purely symbolic role, I thought.

Oleg's father received me in his study, a cramped, messy room cluttered with books, not far from the much more spacious and airy room that for many years had been his and was now occupied by Rufus, his former assistant, in the role of new director. It seems that the latter had not lost any occasion to inflict the worst humiliations on the old professor, now effectively ousted from his academic powers, as a personal revenge for the many years during which he had been his humble 'servant,' as many people remembered all too well.

Oleg's father had a decidedly gruff look, but overall he gave the impression of a good person with his long but well-trimmed mustache and deep blue eyes. He towered over me from a dizzying height stretching out his hand, slender and with very long fingers, inspecting me from head to foot.

"I am pleased to make your acquaintance, Dr. Mayer."

Of course I had been preceded by my title as it is customary to do on these circumstances.

"My pleasure, professor. I owe you an explanation for the reason of my visit."

"Please, make yourself comfortable."

I sat down, a bit uncomfortable and worried about the words I was going to say, on a chair in front of his desk entirely cluttered with papers. I mentally rehearsed the introduction I had prepared.

"I realize that what I'm about to tell you will reopen an old wound and frankly I regret, but I cannot do otherwise. I'm here to tell you about your son Oleg."

The last part of the sentence struck him as if by a whip and his eyes darkened. The whole body stiffened against the back of the chair and a wave of heat colored his cheeks.

"Who are you? How *dare* you?"

"I beg your pardon, professor. Please let me explain. I understand your reaction. I came here to deliver this."

I held out the leather-bound volume that I kept under my arm.

"It belonged to your son and I consider my duty to give it to you."

He looked hostile, but reached out and immediately began to turn the pages of Oleg's diary as if in search of something specific. I let him, and we remained both silent for a time so long that it seemed to me forever.

"It is one of Oleg's diaries written during the excavations at Herculaneum. But where are the other diaries? And who gave them to you? Wait… maybe I can guess. It must have been that young bitch. Who else? Maybe you are here for the money, eh? Or maybe… *they* sent you here."

"Please, professor," I gasped, struggling to remain afloat," I did not come here for any kind of money but just to deliver spontaneously what I received from Irina, that is, all the diaries of the period of the excavation. I do not think I deserve and I will not accept a judgment so superficial, at least not before you've listened to my story."

"All the diaries, you say?"

He looked at me with a hard look, but I understood that he was interested.

"And do you have news of my son?"

"No. Unfortunately, nothing that you don't know already."

He gestured in midair with his hand – a tired look of disappointment and disgust on his face – letting me understand that he would consent to listen to me, although reluctantly.

"It's a long story, it will take time," I warned him.

As I had decided earlier, my best weapon was sincerity. So I started from the very beginning, from Stahl's workshop. Then I described my domestic experiments with the magic spheres until the time I met Irina. I did not omit any detail from her story, but I decided not to talk to him about Anselmo for the moment.

As my story unfolded, I could see that his interest increased and his severe blue eyes, that kept darting on me all the time, did not reflect any more an openly hostile attitude like at the beginning of our conversation. Instead they now gave me the impression of a new state of mind, of a more conciliatory mood. Our conversation paused for a long moment of silence. Long, but much lighter than the previous one.

"I appreciate your honesty, Mayer," he said at last with a sigh, standing up and starting to walk back and forth as far as the room size could allow. He spoke slowly, measuring his words and staring at the floor.

"What you have told me – in good faith, I believe – is a largely implausible story. I imagine that you realize very well that no sensible person would be willing to believe a single word of what you have just said about the improbable properties of those spheres. However, I have myself been a witness of an 'equally implausible' archaeological finding that shook me deeply at the time and that fills me with doubts and fears even now. I think you know what I mean, since I imagine you have read the diary in its entirety."

I nodded.

"Well, a fact you are certainly *not* aware of is that the tangible evidence of that finding does not exist anymore."

He said it bitterly, reading on my face the confirmation that I knew nothing about it.

"After the disappearance of my son and the judicial facts that you know…" He paused, his voice suddenly broken. "You know, Mayer, my son was a good guy. We have raised him as we should. It is that woman who ruined him!"

"However," he cleared his throat and continued, "when Oleg left the Institute taking with him some archaeological findings owned by this university in the most shameful and unworthy way, he had at least the decency not to touch what seemed to be the most important of all and which was being studied by a group of anthropologists and specialists from various disciplines who cooperated with us. Needless to say, everything was kept strictly confidential. We believed to have in our hands a sensational discovery.

"Oleg's disappearance deeply grieved me. I was very attached to him. But more than anything, I was heartbroken when I realized he had voluntarily taken with him objects that were property of the state. When one of my assistants realized it, I decided to protect the honor of my son and not to allow any leak of these facts. It was not so difficult because in the end they were just a handful of jewels of modest value and a strange rust-free metal plate of marginal artistic interest. We settled the whole matter by falsifying some documents and pretending that those items had been transferred elsewhere. But the complicity of my assistant Rufus cost me a lot. He blackmailed me and I was forced to buy his silence. With my help, that damned ass was able to make a career as quick as undeserved.

"Returning to the remains of two skeletons," he continued, "we accommodated them in Hall F where we had set up a laboratory dedicated entirely to their study and equipped with appropriate tools. Unfortunately, two years ago, the entire section that housed Pavilion F was burnt down by a fire of unclear origin and what remains of it is just a pile of ashes. The only evidence left are the diaries of my son and the drawings therein that prove absolutely nothing."

"Everything was burned?" I stammered.

"Yes. It was a bad fire. The police were certain that it was arson, but the culprit was never identified. I thought everything was lost, but apparently you were able to find the metal plate. I guess you have also recovered the jewels."

"Unfortunately not. Irina told me about it, but in Stahl's workshop, I found only a few of those small spheres and a wooden case."

"Oleg may have taken the rest of it. I thought he took with him nothing but one of the two rings. To be more precise, I thought he did not manage to take more because I kept everything locked in a safe. Did you know that there are two identical rings?"

"Irina told me about it."

"Well, the second ring is still here and Rufus will not separate easily from it. I think there is also one of the earrings left."

I breathed a sigh of relief.

Now his attitude towards me had completely changed and I took advantage of this state of benevolence to venture a question.

"Professor, what did you mean with 'those others' that first you asked me about?"

"Please forgive me. I was unfair to you. I suspected that you had a deal with those gentlemen who came to me with strange questions a few weeks before Pavilion F was burned down. At that time, I thought they were from the police, but later I began to wonder if their visit was just a coincidence or if they were involved in the arson."

"What kind of questions did they ask?"

"They wanted to know if…"

He was interrupted by the bursting into the room of a bony little man, short in stature and with sparse remains of a black and greasy hair, carefully combed in a pathetic attempt to hide its thinning. He was formally dressed.

"Oh, sorry. I thought you were alone."

"Nevertheless, this does not absolve you from the obligation to knock, Rufus. Come in, *then*, since you did it already."

"Let me introduce Dr. Mayer of the University of Vienna."

I stood up and returned his handshake, as slimy as the character suggested.

"But please go ahead," he said, while scanning me with his eyes, small and black as of a reptile.

"I just came here to ask for your help to alleviate the burden of the tedious tasks of which, as the director of this institute, I carry the daily load. But this is perhaps a subject that we may discuss later."

As these words were spoken, he completed the rapid visual scan of the room and, before Oleg's father could prevent him, he jumped like an eagle on its prey on the volume that had been left open on the desk.

"Oh, look!" he exclaimed, getting hold of the diary and beginning to turn its pages under the astonished look of the old man whose face had changed color again.

"Rufus!" he gasped with a strangled voice. ""What are you doing?"

"Oh, I see: a work notebook," he hissed in a faint voice, pretending not to have heard.

"Looks like one of the excavation diaries of your son Oleg. I'm glad that at least some of what he took has come back in custody of this institution," he said with a tone of defiance, staring at the old man who was speechless, as a cobra playing with its prey. I felt a wave of heat spreading on my face and I would have gladly strangled him with my bare hands. He flipped through the diary with an obvious interest and without showing the slightest hurry.

"To what do we owe the honor of your visit, Dr. Mayer?"

I replied that I was passing through Geneva and I came to pay to Oleg's father the greetings from a close friend and colleague of mine who worked in Vienna, but I realized that Rufus was not even listening to me and that he was completely immersed in the inspection the notebook.

After a while he probably concluded that the volume did not contain anything new to him and with a smile accompanied by a smooth and calculated gesture, he restored the volume into its original position on the desk. Finally he took his leave, apologizing for the inadvertent intrusion.

"That bastard!" barked the old man, wounded in his pride as soon as Rufus crawled out of the room.

"And the irony is that it was me who raised up that son of a prostitute."

"It is the very first time I've seen him, but he made a bad impression to me."

"Listen Mayer, I wish to be of help since you seem sincere. I have things to tell you, but this is neither the place nor the right time, with some *animals* that roam around here and maybe would even dare to *eavesdrop* at the door."

He spelt the last sentence, articulating the epithet '*animals*' and '*eavesdrop*' loud and strong. Obviously he had his reasons for doing so.

"Please accompany me out of here."

He did not say a word until we reached the foot of the staircase in the main entrance where he asked me, with a good-natured smile, "How about talking about it tonight, at your convenience. Perhaps in front of a good bottle of wine? Unless you're a teetotaler, I mean. I expect you for dinner at my home. My housekeeper is a great cook, you will appreciate her food. Oh, I forgot… Are you here in Geneva alone, Mayer?"

I replied that I gladly accepted his kind invitation, that I was anything but a teetotaler and that no, I was not alone, but in the company of my friend Fred.

"Very well. So bring along your friend as well. I expect you both tonight at eight. This is the address."

He handed me a small piece of paper and took his leave with a warm handshake.

***

Oleg's father lived in a magnificent top floor apartment in one of the fashionable houses that had been recently built along Quai Gustave-Ador, a name that in reality it would take only a century or so later. Not distant from the present location of the Jet d'Eaux, the Boulevard ran parallel to the lake shore. A long line of tall buildings glittered with the light reflected by the large windows embracing the lake in a breathtaking view.

The sun had just set. An oblique light filtered through the large checkered door windows of the living room casting footprints of purple on the floor, crossed by darker long shadows. The living room opened onto a large terrace where one could enjoy a privileged view of the lake and the dark skyline of the Jura on the West.

Our host welcomed Fred and me with a friendly attitude and, after the ritual introductions, invited us to sit on the comfortable armchairs placed on the terrace where we chatted amiably while enjoying the cool air and the apéritifs. From the kitchen, a promising scent of good French cuisine tickled our nostrils.

As the old professor had promised, the housekeeper was an excellent cook and I still remember with pleasure the delicious taste of a nicely browned meat stew cooked for a long time in a milk sauce and accompanied by an assortment of finely minced vegetables and herbs matching perfectly the taste of sweet and floury chestnuts, the touch of genius of that recipe. A delicacy. The wine was no less: Oleg's father was a connoisseur and let us enjoy a good vintage of Bordeaux. Compared to the negative first impression I had of him at the beginning of our conversation in the morning, now he looked to me as a nice man, a good talker, well cultured, polished, and full of interests.

"I wish to hear from you any hypothesis or conclusion you might have come to," he said, after Fred's description of what he had observed under the microscope during the dissection of one of the spheres.

"We have in front of us a number of pieces of a complex mosaic and they may perhaps be sufficient to grasp the whole pattern," he added.

Fred and I looked at each other, not sure what to say.

"First I would like to hear *your* opinion, professor," I said, a little uncomfortable.

"All right. As an archaeologist I stick to the mere factual evidence. We have found some artifacts in the neighborhood of two skeletons in a good state of preservation and with very similar, although quite unusual, characteristics. It is therefore logical to assume that the two individuals were of the same race or that they were suffering from a similar type of pathology, some sort of disease capable of deeply modifying the morphology of a human being. If we discard the latter case – which is indeed difficult to believe in – we have to ask ourselves which race those two guys belonged to and what they were doing in Herculaneum. It is quite true that the Roman civilization, at that time, had expanded so much as to come in contact with the most exotic peoples. I wonder then if the two individuals were not actually members of an ethnic group with such unusual physical characteristics to induce someone to capture and bring them into the heart of the

Empire as wonders or 'mirabilia' as the Romans would say. The findings in the tunnel, where I presume they were held in custody, indeed support this hypothesis.

"You must also take into account that the Villa of the Papyri was certainly a very special place. I personally believe that the villa was involved in a very ambitious project aiming to store most of the heritage of Greek and Latin culture in a single library. It was definitely a meeting place for scholars. We are still working hard to figure out how many they were and who was the mind, or the minds, that coordinated their activities. All this of course, under the, let's say, 'political' supervision of the Pisone family. It does not seem therefore unlikely that the two 'phenomena' were brought to that place to be studied.

"What puzzles me is the atypical nature of the artifacts: apparently normal jewelry, not particularly valuable, and perfectly in line with the style of the time. However they seem to possess properties that contemporaries of Pisone would not hesitate to define 'magical.' Of these abilities I do not have direct evidence, but I am inclined to believe your experience.

"Is it possible, I wonder, that at that time there could be somewhere a civilization that was so advanced as to be able to forge a plate of an unknown metal alloy and small spheres hiding inside such microscopic and geometrically perfect inlays? And why no trace of such unusual civilization could be found in the historical documents we have discovered so far?

"As an archaeologist, I have long hoped to find a thin thread guiding me to this 'lost civilization'. But after the betrayal of my son – who concealed what he had discovered – and the subsequent events that are well known to you, I have no hope left. Rufus is still convinced that Oleg fled with substantial clues able to guide him to the target and he did so to take all credit for the discovery. As a father, I probably did it all wrong with that poor child. Or maybe I was just unable to fill the emptiness left by the loss of his mom who passed away when Oleg was still a boy."

He said this with such a deep sadness that we felt embarrassed and I avoided his eyes.

"But you did not come here," he continued, "to endure my bemoaning of old widower and father. Tell me rather what you think of this whole thing."

I took courage and began to speak.

"In my opinion, your analysis is very lucid and objective, professor. But no one can guarantee that objects with 'magical' properties, similar to those of the jewelry found in Herculaneum, have not in fact already been found elsewhere. It might well be that no one has ever noticed their potential, or they have been categorized as amulets or ritual objects that belonged to some sorcerer, shaman, or priest and no one has ever really taken seriously the rumors about their magical capabilities. If I decide to believe the story of Irina, I find it difficult to formulate a hypothesis. Sticking close to what I have seen with my own eyes, the only rational explanation that comes to my mind is that of a physical phenomenon, yet unknown to us, that the builders of the spheres have ingeniously exploited to achieve telekinesis. As of my 'mindset' and professional attitude, I am not inclined to explanations that are outside the scope of rationality. In other words, I do not believe in magic."

"On this point I disagree with you," said Fred. "After all, what do we know about how much truth was there in the magic rites of the past? We know that in most cases, the priests of the ancient civilizations were quite smart in their profession. A powerful caste able to influence the rulers and to exercise absolute power over the people. Just think of the Egyptian priests, for example. But I wonder: is it possible that some higher level of reality was hidden beyond the obvious and blatant misinformation? A truth that we may decide to ignore in the name of our rationality, but lives still there, real and untouched?"

"Look, Fred" – I could not help but contradict him – "if something is real and reproducible, then it is a phenomenon that can be studied on a scientific basis, otherwise we are in the field of speculations, a land populated by fabric cheaters."

"Here you are, the scientist. Always with Occam's razor in hand. You damned stubborn scientists had better give more consideration to straight common sense."

"Hey, hey. You two. Don't argue," urged the old man. He looked amused and again filled our glasses.

"It seems to me that your views are both legitimate. I mean that we have got no reliable piece of evidence to decide whether one or neither of you is right. Therefore I will ask you a practical question. What are your plans, what will be your next step?"

"The ring," I answered. "We need to get the ring to be able to feed the power-hungry spheres and be able to communicate with the plate."

So I told him of Anselmo.

"We may try to follow Oleg along his trail if he really escaped using the plate as Irina affirms," I added.

"Do not trust that bitch too much."

As I did earlier, I could not help but notice that the name of Irina had on him a similar effect that a red cape has on a bull.

"She ruined my son. She might well do the same to you, too."

"In any case, with the ring we will be able to verify if there is some truth in what Irina told us. As for following Oleg's footsteps, what do you think?"

"Despite everything… I would give an eye to see my son again. So whatever you two will be able to find out about him, you have my blessing. But keep in mind that this is a decision that you have to take by yourselves. There are risks and ethical issues involved."

"Ethical issues?"

"Sure. You want the ring and earring, right? Well, Rufus keeps them locked in a safe in my old office. He might have changed the key of the room, but it is unlikely that he changed the key of the safe. Too expensive.

Therefore, if you want the ring, you have to go there and get it in one way or another."

"Hence the moral problem."

"Well, if this not a problem for you, then we can move on to the practical part."

"Let's move on it," Fred encouraged him with a broad smile on his face.

"I have no qualms about that weird individual," I echoed.

"Very well then." The old man smiled, satisfied. "Here is how we're going to do."

***

Madame Dauphine's was what we could define, without beating about the bush, a luxury brothel: a two-story house secluded by a high wall and semi-hidden by a well-trimmed fence of thick laurel hedges. It looked unobtrusive and would not have aroused any suspicion if not, perhaps, for the strange habit of keeping all the shutters closed at daytime and for the intense nocturnal activity around the house. In fact, dusk marked the beginning of a veritable parade of carriages concealing elegant gentlemen behind thick dark curtains.

While the house, as seen from the outside, looked modest, the interior was quite the opposite: a profusion of golden decorations, fancy upholstery and seductive draperies, Murano chandeliers in floral pink and pale blue hues, languid sofas, soft patterned cushions, paintings depicting scenes of love, female divinities with generous proportions, and mirrors everywhere.

Oleg's father, who became a widower when he was in his early fifties, had become a regular customer and earned the exclusive favors of the "madame," a handsome woman of high class that, despite her age, still retained an enviable freshness and evident tracks of an earlier beauty that must have been irresistible. The old man now limited his visits to rare occasions when he just paid his homages to her and to the establishment, but his word had retained enough power inside the house to make immediately available to us all the facilities of the well-oiled machine that Madame Dauphine had been managing with intelligence for so many years.

It just happened that our friend Rufus was in his turn a regular customer, though he was deeply despised by all the "ladies." Despised to the point that, every time, Dauphine had to go through a considerable amount of pain to find someone for him, someone who could endure his dirty tastes of a pervert. And the price went up more and more. But Rufus paid well and Dauphine had always managed to resist the impulse that assailed her every time she merely saw him to kick him off or to arrange for him a special treatment by delivering him into the hands of some young and sinewy men with particular tastes that would not ask any better. Anyway, she had sworn that one day or another, she would have him pay dearly. Nobody had forgotten the terrible wounds he had inflicted upon a young beginner when, in the throes of a burst of rage, he took a whip and shattered her with no mercy. Just because the poor woman had dared to spit right into his face what she thought of him as a man and as a client.

"That bastard ought to pay, sooner or later. And he will pay hard," Dauphine used to say. Therefore she enthusiastically accepted the old professor's proposal and organized everything with special care and dedication.

Rufus used to come every Friday on time and on that evening, Dauphine received him in person and, taking advantage of the many years of experience in her profession, she greeted him a warm welcome. She accompanied him upstairs where a peephole disguised in the wallpaper allowed him to peek inside a bedroom where, right at that moment, a young newcomer was expertly undressing.

As Dauphine whispered a few words into his ears, Rufus' wicked little eyes lit up immediately with a lustful greed. Dauphine suggested that, if he wished to, he could spend the night with the woman, a true expert in certain practices that drove people like him crazy. Then she handed him over, quivering with impatience, to the clutches of the woman, one of the most trusted professionals she had ever known in her long career.

Meanwhile, Fred was waiting in an exclusive lounge on the ground floor where he was spending his time in the good company of a mulatto with the eyes of a gazelle and a firm body with breathtaking breasts.

Upstairs, for the professional it was a no-brainer to steal the bunch of keys that Rufus wore tied by a thin silver chain to his waistcoat pocket. Then, through the window of the salle-de-bain, she passed the keys to a colleague who was waiting on the other side. With a sigh, she returned to her thankless job where she resumed the knots of a complex game she would try to keep going for as long as possible.

A discreet, but insistent, knock to the door of the living room was not enough to distract Fred from his pressing occupations of the time, but it was sufficient to prompt the young lady to get free from him and to walk, completely naked, to the door.

"Ah, youngsters!" sighed Dauphine, amused. "You can't be left a moment unattended. On, clothes, quick! You'll end up later. And you, young man, you must hurry up. Here is the key. But... will you be able to walk in that condition?" she asked with a guffaw, soon echoed by that of the girl who, with a professional look, had realized that Fred had some difficulties to tie his pants.

"I recommend you bring back the keys as fast as you can. We will keep the cockroach upstairs all night by hook or by crook. At worst, we will pour a sleeping potion in his champagne. But it is absolutely essential that you will be here before dawn. And... the sooner you come back, the sooner..." – she made an obscene gesture, eloquent as unladylike – "Got it, young man? Not sure you did. You still look a little bit... distracted."

Laughing, the two women left him alone to get dressed.

I was waiting impatiently outside, well hidden inside a coach so that nobody could recognize me.

"Quick, let's go!" I prompted Fred.

He pulled in and I waved to the driver.

The cab moved away quickly in the direction of the old city. Oleg's father was waiting for us at the Pont de la Machine inside his own carriage. We joined him inside and he drove us in the direction of the University. We stopped two blocks short.

"From here on, gentlemen, you have to continue on foot. This is the key that leads to the staircase close to the secondary entrance. From there, you will reach directly the rooms of the teaching staff, as I have explained. This is a copy of the key of the safe. If someone stops you along the street, behave naturally and remember that you are just two tourists. Beware of the patrol. No headshots, gentlemen, and everything will go smoothly. Good luck!"

It was a clear night. Full moon. Not quite the best for such an undertaking. I heard the sound of our footsteps along the deserted street. We met very few people around: an animated bustle of university life during the day, this part of the town was mostly deserted at night. No chance of finding any place open for drink or food. The nightlife of the city was elsewhere.

"Look, Fred," I tried to ease the tension, "maybe I am too tense, but when I left the hotel this morning, I had the distinct feeling of being followed."

"And who would take the trouble to follow you? Some local beauty?"

"Try to be serious, at least once. I think I saw the same guy at least three or four times in the morning and in different places. A guy with a mustache. He might have been following us."

"Maybe he just likes you," he said, broadly smiling.

I told him to buzz off.

Perhaps Fred was right: no point of fearing danger from all directions. Anyway, after a few minutes we arrived at the entrance of a narrow lane that opened on the right side of the University, separated by a block of buildings that housed the offices of the administration. The street was deserted.

Fred was monitoring the road while I easily opened the side door that was normally used by the university staff to get to the offices upstairs, avoiding the main entrance. We stepped inside. The wide windows filtered a pale moonlight that whitened the dust on the sills and cast long shadows on the floor. After a while our eyes adjusted to the dim light. We climbed the stairs to the upper floor where I recognized the large vaults and the long checkerboard corridor I had seen a few days earlier. Oleg's father's room was just in front.

Rufus' studio had to be close by.

In fact, two or three doors ahead we came upon a sign illuminated by the moon. The inscription "DIRECTION" and an arrow pointing along on our right led us to the room. The key was the right one and we entered with no problems. I hurried to the window and closed the heavy drapes to darken the room. Then we lit a candle without fear of being seen from the outside. The room was in perfect order: a large desk in the middle was completely clean of any trace of intellectual activity or administrative work. The walls were covered with shelves full of books in plain sight in their elegant bindings, lined up like tin soldiers. On the wall, behind a tall armchair in dark-skinned upholstery, a row of portraits of austere characters hung over the desk. They were those who, over the years, had served as directors of the department sitting on the same chair. I recognized Oleg's father's severe look and, next along the line, the portrait of a mellifluous Rufus that the artist had well reproduced on the canvas. In the flickering light of the candle, it seemed to me that his evilish eyes were spying on me.

"Now let's find where the case is hidden," I whispered to Fred, "I bet it is behind the most recent portrait, behind his ugly face."

In fact, as it was to be expected, the safe was hidden behind the portrait of the director. A simple model with no numerical combination. It just opened with a key.

With my heart in my throat, I began to tinker with the key that Oleg's father gave us. It was not unreasonable to expect that Rufus had the locks changed. However, Oleg's father was rather optimistic on this point because the cost of such an operation would have showed up in the meager budget of the Department – in which case he would have noticed it – or had been paid personally by the director, a quite remote possibility, knowing Rufus. As a matter of fact, the key eased smoothly in the lock and the safe opened up, revealing its contents: several documents in paper, a few scrolls of papyrus, a locked box containing the cash of the Institute, a small handgun, a silver crucifix, and a number of small wooden caskets. They contained archaeological findings of some value: gold buckles, rings, earrings and bracelets.

In one of the boxes I recognized a massive gold ring with a dark 'pearl' encased on it and veined of blue reflections under the light of the candle.

"Here it is!" I whispered, triumphantly.

I handed the ring to Fred who examined it with his eyepiece and compared it with the copy he had prepared using as a reference the sketches contained in Oleg's diary. All in all, the two rings seemed quite similar as long as one did not take care to observe them too closely. With a nod and a flash of amusement in his eyes, Fred turned his head towards me, a clear sign he was confident that the fake ring was good enough to fool Rufus. In the same box we also found the earring we were looking for. And it was not alone: five small bluish spheres surrounded it.

Fred replaced the gold ring and the earring with the copies he had made. I took from his pocket a handful of small spheres of burnished metal, counted five of them, and replaced as many in the box. Satisfied, we restored with great care all the objects into their original position. Then we closed the safe. After blowing out the candle, I cautiously opened the curtains trying to make no noise. Gradually, the moonlight flooded the room. After a final check I walked to the door, ready to leave.

A faint noise coming from below.

I stopped short.

"Hold on!" I grabbed Fred's forearm.

We stood in silence holding our breath. Now we could clearly hear footsteps echoing on the stairs and voices approaching. Cold sweat dripped all along my spine. I gestured Fred to keep quiet and I held my breath.

We had locked the door of the room and this gave us a few minutes' advantage. I could not imagine any other escape except the window, which was unfortunately closed. Opening it would make noise. Also we didn't know if the ledge was wide enough to stand on. The room at the moment seemed to be the safest hiding place. But we were trapped and the footsteps were approaching.

Two people were walking along the corridor, talking to each other and laughing heartily. Just the opposite to an approach in stealth. I caught fragments of their conversation: probably they were two colleagues heading to the lab, maybe planning to work over night.

The footsteps gradually moved away and the voices faded at the other end of the corridor. I sighed. So did Fred, his face white and ghostly in the diaphanous light of the moon. He closed his eyelids in relief.

"Time to go!" I announced with a thread of voice, flaunting a confidence I didn't have.

We waited a bit longer before venturing – first myself, then Fred – out of the room. Gliding like shadows down the deserted stairs we finally sneaked out in the alley through the secondary entrance.

No one around.

We kept still, holding up against the wall of the building. Then we reached the corner of the main façade and turned to the right. From that moment on, we tried to walk normally, attracting no attention, as if we were two guys coming back from that part of the town where one could still get a decent drink at that time.

I knew I had to keep walking quietly, but my heart was pounding and, despite my efforts to appear casual, my pace tended to accelerate. I kept staring around.

When we stepped right into a patrol I had hard times to master the urge to run. Fortunately, they ignored us and continued on their way.

"It's over! Let's take a breath." Fred smiled, clearly relieved.

We headed to the lake where Oleg's father coach was waiting for us. The coachman had strict instructions to take Fred back as soon as possible to Madame Dauphine's and to wait for him there, even for the rest of the night if necessary.

When I reached the top floor of Oleg's father's building to report the success of the mission, the old professor greeted me warmly and offered me something strong to drink.

Which was just what I needed.

I told him the details of our visit to Rufus' room and, as promised, I gave him the key of a safe in the bank where Fred had deposited the remaining volumes of Oleg's diaries.

The old man gave me a hug when I was setting off. I told him that I would do everything I could to get news of his son. I wished to revive in him the hope that one day he might see him again. But my impression was that he was resigned not to.

I walked slowly along the shore in the direction of the hotel. The lake reflected the pale light of the moon, a silver mirror stained with pointed dark shapes that hung lazily low on the water under a carpet of stars.

***

Given the tension accumulated during the previous hours, I definitely needed a break. Now that the strain was over, I felt tired out, but the night was so beautiful that I decided to take a long walk around the docks before reaching the hotel. I stopped only a couple of times to examine the strange ring that I kept concealed in my pocket.

A large bluish pearl: so it appeared under the moonlight. Too tight for my ring finger, I tried it on my little finger while my thoughts were focusing on my next moves. I intended to try the ring as soon as possible on Oleg's case and to question Anselmo about matters that had been left without a convincing answer since I was a child. But the case had been left in Vienna because I had judged it impractical and not without risk to carry it with us on that long journey.

I had to wait another week or two.

But would it work? And would Anselmo show up as Irina had told me?

I imagined he would not. Irina and Oleg had seen him under two different representations extracted from their memories. How would he look like to me? Not likely as Father Anselmo since I had received a rather secular education and did not have any kind of association with the Jesuits.

As I reflected on these things, I arrived at the entrance of my hotel. I rang the little bell on the side of the door to notify the night porter. I thought I heard some movement inside, but no one opened the door.

I rang again and then again.

I thought that the man must have fallen asleep. Looking through the nearest window, I saw that there was a candle lit inside, but the front desk was deserted.

I kept ringing the bell at the risk of waking up at least half of the customers.

Finally I heard a shuffling of hasty steps and the latch opening. The sleepy face of the hotel keeper appeared in the crack of the door.

"A thousand pardons."

Damn you, I thought.

"Please give me the key to my room. My apologies for the late hour."

I asked if Fred had returned.

No, he had not. The key to his room was still there.

I smiled, thinking that this time my friend was really enjoying himself. After all, he deserved to take it easy.

I climbed the stairs with some difficulty. My eyelids were heavy. Eventually I reached my room and slipped the key into the lock. To my surprise I noticed that the door was open.

I sniffed danger.

I blew out the candle and waited in silence.

In the dark I pushed the door ajar. Very slowly.

It opened without squeaking. I went inside on tiptoe.

The moonlight from the window partially illuminated the room, but I could see only the dark shapes of several indistinct objects. I realized immediately that something was wrong. Black shadows overlapped on the shapeless mess scattered on the floor and after a few steps I tripped over something.

I stood with my heart in my throat.

The room seemed deserted, but muffled sounds were coming from Fred's room which was next to mine. I took courage, shut the door and lit the candle. The dim light of the flame revealed a scene of desolation. The whole room was a mess. The content of my two suitcases were scattered on the floor, drawers emptied, the closet looted, the mattress gutted. Every corner of the room had been meticulously searched.

They were looking for something.

It was not hard to imagine what they were looking for. And I smiled to myself thinking that the object of that vandalism was safe in a metal box inside an armored vault of the bank, protected by a wall of steel, one inch thick.

Meanwhile the noises beyond the wall were going on and gave the distinct impression that there was someone there who was giving the same treatment to Fred's room he had inflicted on mine. I blew out the candle and ventured on tiptoe down the corridor. Fred's bedroom door was closed, but I could clearly hear the noise coming from inside. I heard from a nearby room the protests of a customer who kept pounding his fist on the wall. I decided to go and see.

I plunged back into the darkness of my room and reached the balcony. I climbed over the railing and, a hand first, then a foot, I managed to reach the railings of the next-door balcony. Without caring to look down and with a little momentum, I passed over and landed on Fred's balcony. I flattened against the wall and moved slowly to the window. I peered inside, but the thick curtains prevented me from seeing anything.

Occasionally – under the flickering light coming from the inside – I saw shadows moving back and forth and the looting continued as before. I stood still for a long time, uncertain about what to do. I had no idea how many people were in the room. Two? Maybe. More?

The work of vandalism proceeded briskly, but with little success judging by the curses that accompanied each new failed attempt in the search.

Suddenly the noise stopped. The light went off.

Soon after, I heard the sound of a key that was stuck in the lock. My blood froze because I imagined what would happen next. In fact, as I feared, soon a bustle of a desperate fight arose.

It did not last long. I heard a thud and a muffled cry. Silence.

A flickering light was lit inside.

Without waiting a second longer, I climbed over the balcony and retreated hastily to my room. I lit the candle and looked for my gun in its hideout.

It was empty.

I searched through the overall mess and eventually found it, on the floor, hidden in the middle of a mountain of feathers that came off the entrails of the mattress. Before regaining the balcony, I took a heavy iron poker from the fireplace and held it like a mace. I peered back through Fred's window when a cloud obscured the light of the moon for a while. Through the window panes I saw Fred stunned on the floor, gagged, and two individuals binding him.

I had on my side the advantage of surprise.

Without thinking twice, I threw myself headlong bursting into the room with a crash of broken glass. The two whirled, but the closer of them did not have the time to parry the killing blow that I struck him with the poker. I hit him in the neck and he collapsed on the floor with a gasp of pain. The other one, coldly professional, spun around like a cat and pulled out a pistol from his vest.

But he was not quick enough.

A discharge hit him in the chest before he could take aim. He fired as he fell and the shot missed wide of me.

His body hit the floor, a red stain spreading across his chest.

With a kick I threw away the weapon that was still in his hand and ran towards Fred. I was afraid he could be dead.

Fortunately he did breathe, though with a worrying rattle, but he was alive. I took a breath of relief.

I lifted his head. "Fred, my friend. Say something to me…"

Fred moaned. He opened his eyes with difficulty. Then he lost consciousness again.

I leant him back on the floor while hurried footsteps could be heard on the stairs. The shot must have woken the whole hotel. I examined the guy with the mustache who had been shot. I touched his jugular.

He was stone dead.

The other one lay motionless, but his pulse was good.

Knocks on the door and someone pushing it hastily trying to enter the room.

I moved the corpse clear of the door and found myself in front of a small group of gentlemen in their nightgowns, looking at me frightened and horrified. They were headed by the owner of the hotel.

"Give me a hand, quickly!" I ordered, without explanation. We laid Fred on the floor and I managed to revive him with a towel soaked in cold water. After examining him, I was relieved that he had nothing broken apart from a large hematoma in the parietal zone and obvious bruises to his face and arms. Fred was in no danger.

The other wounded guy instead was still unconscious.

"This guy is seriously injured. We must rush him to the hospital! Call a doctor, right now!" I cried to the hotel guests that surrounded us.

I had hit him very hard. I wondered if I had realized that I was delivering a potentially fatal blow when I attacked him. I worked to save his life and they let me do. Eventually he regained consciousness and we made sure that he did not fall unconscious again.

The carriage bringing a professional doctor took a long time to arrive. Meanwhile I tried to explain what had happened. The doctor examined the body and made sure that someone would alert the police. The injured man was loaded into the carriage, still half stunned. Meanwhile, Fred had fully recovered and was helping me tell everybody around what had happened. I was busy answering questions from the owner of the hotel and some customers who had arrived later than the others. Fred understood that I was anxious to leave.

"Fred, how do you feel?"

"Don't worry about me. Everything is all right. I just feel as if someone had run over me with a carriage. I have a terrible headache, but I can endure it. Rather... how about the police?"

"They may arrive at any moment. They will examine the corpse and for sure will ask a lot of questions."

"That's what I'm afraid of." He looked at me in a way and I understood what he meant. We had to fly, quickly.

"Sure. But... will you be able to?"

"Yes. Full of bruises, but I can do it."

"Then, let's say... meet at the same place where we met last time?"

"Good idea. I go first."

I moved casually. There was a crowd of onlookers around the dead and they were having a hot discussion. No one noticed that I left the room and reached the stairs. Once on the ground floor I lowered myself into the street from a window at the back of the hotel.

I walked away quickly, but with no haste.

Fred instead shut himself in the bathroom and no one found it strange. After some time, they knocked at the door and called for him several times, in fear he had fainted. In the end they broke down the door. They found the dressing room empty and the window wide open. Large enough to let someone out in a hurry.

***

Later on we met at Oleg's father's, as agreed. When I saw Fred again, I hugged him with a great sense of relief.

"Hey, old chap. How are you? You had a busy night, didn't you? First the sweet and then the bitter part, right?"

"You could say that, damn it." He smiled despite the devastating headache.

"I think I know whom we have to thank for this."

"Me too. But let me tell you the nice entertainment we have prepared for that hog. Madame Dauphine made all the arrangements in person. When he will wake up from the effects of the sleeping potion he downed, he will find himself in an isolated house and in good company. He will repent bitterly to having been born. Now listen to the details…"

"Later, Fred. Now we have to hurry up and I fear there is no other option than waking up the old man."

So we did.

Oleg's father listened to us, worried.

A murder, even if justified by self-defense, is always a very serious business and our escape would certainly create problems with the law. We were two foreigners and that was for sure to our disadvantage. We had no witnesses to support our self-defense excuse, and, most importantly, we had failed in our duty to be available for the investigations of the gendarmerie. Enough to finish our days in jail.

After pondering the situation, the old man discarded the possibility of us showing up at the police. Instead we had to flee immediately and leave the country before it was too late.

He pulled the coachman out of bed – a trustworthy man who would keep his mouth shut – and we settled in his carriage just a couple of hours before dawn.

Oleg's father hugged both of us.

I was worried about him. I feared the revenge of Rufus and I was sure the police would find out who had helped us in the escape. I told him. He shrugged.

"At my age, dear Mayer, few people realize they are finally in a position that they can do what they want. And even fewer have the guts to do it for real. It is paradoxical, but true. Many young guys burn their lives for an ideal or for something that at that moment they regard as more important than life itself. We old people, with just a short path left before us, we tend to cling to it with all the forces we have left. Some give up, but hardly anyone decides to sacrifice the few remaining years for a good cause. Do you believe that this is the wisdom of the elders? No, it's just cowardice. The older one grows perhaps the wiser, but certainly no less coward than at the time he was young.

"Anyway, do not worry about me. Travel quickly and be careful. Laurent will lead you to the right place and will introduce the people who will accompany you across the border. Goodbye and good luck, gentlemen."

***

The coach set off. Fred and I took a couple of hours of sleep, curled up on the folding seats and hidden by heavy dark curtains. We were exhausted and woke up only when the carriage came to a stop.

The mountain air was sharp and had the scent of the pastures still wet with the dew. The sun had just popped in, a pink blotch of paint in the blue canvas of a joyous daybreak. From the plateau where we stopped, we could see a large part of Lake Leman to the West and, on the opposite direction, the dazzling white of the snow-capped Alps.

Laurent, the coachman, handed us over to two experienced mountain guides who outfitted us as best as they could with mountain clothes and footwear, a backpack full of supplies, a bottle of water, one of brandy and a blanket for the night. Our guides' wives offered us a hearty breakfast. Awakened by a strong dose of black coffee, we started our trip riding mules along a steep mountain trail.

The journey lasted almost three days and it was hard. Very hard. At night we slept in high mountain shelters or in the open air around a fire, as it was still bitterly cold for the season. After a few hours of sleep we started again at dawn, following threadlike trails along narrow ridges that lined the cliffs. The view was breathtaking.

We continued like that for a time that seemed endless. Deep into the snow, then along the glacier glistening in the sun. At the risk of ending inside a crevasse at any time, we wandered among cascades of blue-violet seracs and threaded for hours along a snowy path. At some point, I realized with joy that we had started our descent.

Not much later we arrived in Italy. Our guides led us further down where we they knew we would be safe. They showed us the way to the Lake Maggiore, then they wished us good luck and turned back, leaving us alone with the mules.

We slowly moved toward the nearest village, a group of houses painted in bright colors mirrored by the clear water of the lake and topped by a bell tower. We stopped at the inn and finally I could lay my body on a real bed.

From there I did not move for the next eighteen hours straight.

When I woke up, it was time for lunch and I had a ravenous appetite. Fred had got tired of waiting for me and had gone off for a ride in the country. The mistress of the inn watched me amused while I was literally devouring one dish after the other in the sunshine of the terrace, my eyes glued to the table set and completely ignoring the fantastic view that I had before my eyes.

"You were hungry, huh?" she said, with a Southern accent.

"It's not just that. It's your cooking. It's... fantastic! I have never tasted anything so good. And this sauce, these spaghetti..."

"It is a recipe of my land. From Sicily. The noodles' sauce is made with eggplant, a breath of fresh basil and lots of ripe tomatoes."

"I am crazy for it." I smiled.

She was looking at me with a smile. "When you laugh, your eyes light up. I like the way you laugh."

"You too. I mean, your eyes speak for themselves. You see, now they are laughing..."

We both laughed.

She offered me a glass of cool white wine and poured a glass for herself. We began to talk and time flew away.

She had become a widow when very young and had decided not to remarry. In her thirties, she was still at the peak of her beauty: black hair, hazel eyes, narrow hips and a firm well-proportioned body. She was happy to meet someone who did not live there and she decided to talk to me, a stranger who happened to be there that day and who would disappear the next day without giving any trouble.

I will not forget her easily. And I will not forget when, as we talked, I approached her and felt the delicate smell of her skin while I gently kissed her neck.

"Not here. They could see us. This is a small village…"

She took my hand and led me upstairs.

A small room full of light with many small flowers on the wallpaper, on the curtains and the upholstery. I had already paid the bill with those flowers and this time they behaved to me in a more educated manner. I don't care if you watch, flowers, I thought.

I closed the door, then hugged and pushed her gently against the floral wall, kissing her on the neck and lips at an increasing rate. I felt her breath become more labored as I began to undress her slowly and kiss her everywhere.

And I will not forget her firm breasts, her long black hair, her beautiful water-and-soap face. I will not forget it, even if it was only for the spell of a sunny afternoon and for a single magical night where time seemed to have slowed down its pace, the glow of the full moon filtering through a small gap between the curtains, painting our bodies with an unreal paleness. A night in which passion seemed to have no end and love came naturally, with the right rhythm and pauses, as an improvised music that comes out, naturally sweet and deep, as if we had rehearsed it for a countless number of times.

Sometimes love is strange. After all, we barely knew each other. Yet, while she slept embraced on my chest and my eyes ran along the wooden rafters of the ceiling, it seemed to me I had known her for a long time.

The next day, Fred and I left the inn heading South. Our carriage skirted the lake, reached the village of Stresa, and then changed course to the East. I slept most of the next day, exhausted from the previous night. It was a long and uncomfortable journey, but we eventually met the imposing beauty of St. Stephen's Cathedral and the city where we were born and raised.

I did not want to go home right away. I had told my wife that I would be on the road for at least one month and I still had a few days left to devote myself to the study of the plate together with Fred.

I slept at Fred's. We woke up the next day, mid-afternoon. We filled his carriage with supplies and headed to the hunting lodge.

***

In front of me stood a building I was vaguely familiar with. The image was still uncertain and the contours were blurred, but slowly it stabilized and became sharper. I recognized the door of my old Lyceum in Grintzwald. I reached out cautiously and knocked at it.

I waited. No answer.

I knocked louder, my knuckles aching.

It all seemed real.

Footsteps inside, approaching.

The door opened and I found myself in front of my old professor of mathematics.

"Ah, dear boy. Here you are."

I recognized his sly smile under a thin mustache cut short, a slim gray line that curved upwards or downwards depending on his mood. A man I had learned to appreciate during the three years of his mentoring.

He was a good teacher. He challenged us with difficult problems and fascinated us with some bright new trick to solve them. I remember that his lectures were crystal clear and he could hold the audience firmly in his hands until the end of the lesson, just like a professional actor. He was able to light in our young minds sharp images full of details that seemed to bloom like flowers and take a life of their own. This way, I learned from him the rudiments of calculus with minimal effort and with great interest.

"I guess you'll have a lot of questions for me," he said with his usual good-natured smile.

Until then I had remained silent, my mouth wide open. After so many years, I was seeing again those places full of memories of the time when I was a teenager. Everything was exactly the same as I remembered.

All except one important detail: there was no one around.

A great silence, as if the school was closed.

I missed the busy hum of my companions, their sudden bursts of laughter, the fights, the runs down the corridor, the background noise made of whispers, of jokes, of stifled giggles, of coughs when one of the professors passed nearby.

"Excuse me, I got distracted. I am still looking around. It's all so... real!"

"You mean it is exactly as you remember it?"

"Yes, though I should not be surprised at it."

"Right. You've always been a smart guy. But look carefully around: don't you think that there is something that should not be there?"

I looked around, uncertain. Then my eye fell on a detail that seemed out of place.

"That door over there, perhaps? I do not remember it. The front door of the library was smaller. Yes, now I'm sure of it. It was white, I mean, painted white. And then it was much smaller. I do not remember a door so huge and massive."

"You are right. Even the library is slightly different *inside*. Please have a look."

Slightly different, he said.

He was surely joking. Our school library was a tiny thing with a maximum of two or three hundred books in all. On the contrary, what stood before me seemed like the interior of a cathedral, as I realized as soon as I walked through the door. But on a second look, it became quite clear that it had actually nothing to do with a cathedral. Rather, it was modeled on the architecture that resembled a seashell, with a large empty space at the center, illuminated from above by a skylight and surrounded by a large spiral terrace narrowing in width as it climbed higher up.

The walls along the spiral ramp were covered with shelves full of books. And in the central hall I could see books scattered everywhere. Open on the tables, matted on the floor, or piled here and there, in small towers. Somebody must have been working feverishly, looting the shelves on the walls and turning everything upside down.

"I guess our friend Oleg has been here, am I right Professor?"

"Yes. He must have been in a hurry, as you can see. He did not bother in the least to put the books back in their place."

"It seems to me he was looking for something. And I can probably guess what it was. But first, tell me, are you… also Father Anselmo, aren't you?"

"Yes, for Oleg I was Anselmo."

"And for me?"

"I think in your case the character of your professor of mathematics, who was your idol at the high school, will suit you best."

"But can you also manifest yourself as Anselmo, if you wish to?"

"Sure. Why not? After all, I know that character by heart."

The image had a slight tremor and seemed to dissolve while is changed shape rapidly. Then it stabilized. Instead of the plump face of my old professor, now I had in front of me the bony face of the Jesuit brother.

"Are you satisfied now? Here is good Father Anselmo."

He looked at me with an air of amusement. He must have caught me with an idiotic expression on my face, probably open-mouthed. I forced myself into a normal look and tried to challenge him with an intelligent observation.

"I suppose that Oleg was looking for a clue about those two strange individuals of Herculaneum."

He looked stern. Any trace of fun had disappeared.

"Maybe."

"And what could good Father Anselmo tell me about it?"

"Not much more than he said to Oleg."

"And that is?"

"Just as I said to him, this library is full of information of all kinds. It contains most of the knowledge that mankind has accumulated so far. It is like having gathered in one place all of the major collections of books of the world. However, despite this vast abundance, you will find nothing other than perfect copies of books or documents that are in fact stored elsewhere. It is therefore a waste of time trying to find here solutions to issues that have never been solved or at least to which humanity has not yet given an answer in writing. Also, I am afraid, you will not find an answer to the question you asked before."

"You mean about the two gentlemen in Herculaneum?"

"Yes, for example. And on many other things."

"You mean all these books," I traced a complete arc in midair with my index finger, "they do not contain anything new, anything that is not already known?"

"No, I didn't say that. I just meant that there is information that you cannot access. For example, try to see what is written in that book over there."

"Which one? This one?"

He nodded. I picked up the book he had pointed at and opened it. It had every appearance of being a manual of medicine with beautiful hand-drawn pictures, illustrated with inks of various colors and printed in crisp characters. I looked at it, puzzled.

"Everything looks normal, right? Now, try the next one."

I took the book he was now indicating. Outside it looked quite similar to the previous one: same leather binding, same size, more or less the same weight. I started to turn over its pages but the first one was blank just as all the others, till the last one.

"But it's empty!" I exclaimed.

"Not really. It's you who cannot read it. In a sense, you are not authorized to read it. For this reason, all the pages look blank to you. But that book is full of interesting things, believe me."

"And who decides what I can and what I cannot read?"

"That I cannot tell you."

"Then, let me try to guess. Let's start with this question: Oleg was the last one to come here, wasn't he?"

"Yes. The last one before you."

I examined the books on the tables, then those that had been thrown on the floor without any regard. There was a whole shelf that had been virtually emptied and most of its contents lay scattered on the floor along the ramp or had been thrown off the spiral terrace and now cluttered the central floor of the library.

"This destruction looks like the work of someone who was looking for something in those books and, not finding it, at some point has gotten really mad at it. Given that most of the books thrown here and there have blank pages – blank just for me, of course – while many of those on the tables are readable, I would say that no more privileges were granted to Oleg than to me. Am I wrong?"

"Smart deduction. So?"

"So, if we go back in time and we ask ourselves who were the last users of this library before Oleg, we come again to the two strange guys in Herculaneum." Assuming that what Irina told me was true.

"Continue."

"In this case, I am willing to bet that some of the data contained in this library were somehow locked by the two guys."

I picked up one of the volumes with blank pages.

"I wonder where the key might be. It could be hidden in this room. For instance a personal object like a ring or an earring, or even something immaterial. Basically everything in here is a piece of mere fiction."

Anselmo looked at me amused, with a defiant smile on thin lips.

I looked him straight in the eye. Perhaps I had understood.

"After all, if is true that you are nothing but a visual representation of a *machine* or an intelligence of some kind or something else that is hidden in the plate, then it is not unlikely that once you took orders from those two guys. So, what if, right now, I give you orders? For example: Father Anselmo, please unlock this book because I want to read it."

Anselmo smiled and disappeared.

The whole huge library flickered and disappeared as well.

I suddenly found myself in a smaller room with no windows and a low ceiling. A series of objects with perfect geometrical shapes were arranged on several shelves. Each shelf contained a number of copies, all identical, of the same solid. I recognized the sphere, the cylinder and the five regular polyhedra: tetrahedron, cube, octahedron, dodecahedron and icosahedron.

I took a copy of a tetrahedron and I rolled it over my hands. It looked to be made of crystal, smooth and perfect, with neither a flaw nor a scratch. It was an extraordinarily tough and resistant material, but at the same time very light. Too light to be ordinary glass or crystal.

At the center of the narrow room I saw a long line of stony pedestals, each no more than three feet tall. I counted sixteen of them, all lined up. They seemed made to lean on something. I tried with the small pyramid that I kept in my hand and placed it on the nearest pedestal. The size matched perfectly. I took another solid from a shelf, an octahedron, this time, and arranged it on the next pedestal. Choosing at random different types of solid, I repeated the operation until a sequence of sixteen objects was completed.

At that point, Anselmo reappeared.

"My compliments. You are definitely smarter than your predecessor. You got it almost immediately. Too bad that the sequence is not the right one."

"Right. And what is worse is that there are, let me see… just about forty billion possible combinations. To pick the right one is not a children game."

"Of course. Unless one does remember the right sequence."

"This is the key, right?"

"Yes. But I believe you have to give up. However…"

"However?"

"I may help you in a different way, if you wish. For example, I could answer a few more questions if they are formulated in the proper way. What would you like to know?"

"What happened to the two guys in Herculaneum?"

"Here is just an example of a kind of question I cannot answer."

"How about this, then. Where did Oleg end up at?"

"This is a question to be expected. Let me show you."

Suddenly, right in front of us, a globe of intense blue with white streaks appeared floating in mid-air. I could easily recognize the profiles of Africa and South America both illuminated with bright sunlight in a clear sky with few clouds. The Northwest of Europe was instead partially hidden by a thick gray blanket of clouds spiraling in a cyclonic system with the center more or less above the Shetland Islands. Stunned, I made a tour all around the globe to observe the other hemisphere still in darkness. I reached out to touch the globe with caution, ready to withdraw my hand. Anselmo let me do it. I was expecting to feel the resistance of a solid object, instead I discovered that I could go through it with my whole arm.

Anselmo was watching me, amused.

"Do you see that red triangle down there?"

"Close to Madagascar?"

"More or less. For the record, it is closer to the Mauritius island."

"Great place. I've sailed over there in the Indian Ocean," I said without thinking.

"I know."

And how couldn't he, being able as he was to draw freely from my memories?

"That is the target that Oleg had chosen. It corresponds to a point in the sea, not far from the reef. You can reach the island just swimming, unless you stumble into a bad encounter before reaching the barrier."

"Sharks?"

"Yes, for example. But usually they do not attack humans. Unless you have bleeding wounds or another prey has been killed nearby and the smell of blood makes them all crazy."

"But, why Oleg did not choose a safer place on the mainland?"

"Because it is dangerous. Even if you choose carefully, an empty lot of land where you see nothing around today, it's hard to predict what you will find there tomorrow, or in a hundred years. They might have built a house on it or a tree could have grown just there. Who knows? Offshore instead, the only solid object you can happen to bump into is a boat or a ship passing by in that precise point in the middle of the sea and at that very moment. As you can imagine, the probability of this happening is extremely small. But if it does, then…"

"Boom!" He spread his arms upward, mimicking the shock wave of an explosion.

"Yes, I know that. Irina told me. Why did you say in a hundred years? What did you mean?"

"I should explain that. I told you *where* Oleg chose to go, but I did not tell you *when* he chose to arrive. You see, even a journey of a few meters, for example from a wooden case to another, takes some time: it cannot be instantaneous. But I am able to stretch this time at will, and in this way, you can choose the time of your arrival."

"You mean that in this way one can travel through time?"

"Yes, if you want to put it in these terms. But only in one direction. A trip to the past is not possible. We all follow the arrow of time and there is no way to go back. And this, I think, you should probably know pretty well."

"The second law of thermodynamics, eh?"

"Yes, I think you know it by that name."

"All right. On this point you don't need to convince me, Father Anselmo. I never thought that travel to the past would actually be possible. It would generate well-known paradoxes. Such as the guy who goes back in time to kill, before it's too late, his own murderer. As for traveling to the future, I do not know what to say. It does not seem to create any logical paradox. But, from here to believe that it is a doable thing…"

"In fact, it is not easy to understand. But trust me."

"I was taught at school that time is absolute. It always runs along the same direction, no matter who watches its flow."

"I'm afraid that it is not quite so simple. But it is too early for that. And, believe me, I talked even too much. As a matter of fact, your friend Oleg is really far away, both in time and in space."

"And what happened to him?"

"To Oleg?" Anselmo laughed heartily. I regretted to having made such a stupid remark. It was obvious that he could not know.

"And can I follow him there?" I asked immediately in return.

"Oh yes. If you want, I can help you to do that."

"But the wooden case would remain here and the plate with it. In this time, I mean."

"Of course."

"So it would be a one-way trip?"

He did not answer. He studied me in silence, then walked away, slowly, toward the entrance of the library. He turned his head to greet me with an enigmatic smile and finally disappeared beyond the high portal, leaving me alone.

I awoke from the state of trance.

Slowly, Fred's face came into focus. He was watching me, worried.

"Hey, friend. Are you there?"

"Yes I am."

"Welcome back among us. Come on, tell me what happened. And then move aside because I want to try this nonsense myself."

I told him about Anselmo and all the rest.

"How long did it last?" I asked.

"A couple of minutes, I think. You've been quite fast."

"What? Anselmo and I talked for at least half an hour. Are you sure?"

"I saw you when you tripped away: numb like a stockfish and wide-eyed. I'm sure it did not last more than a few minutes. It is absolutely impossible that you've been away for half an hour."

"Strange." I was not convinced.

"What are we going to do? Do you want to try?"

I handed him the earring and asked him to lay his hand on the plate and touch it with the bluish pearl encased on the ring. As expected, the first time the attempt failed. He could only see some colored spots and little more. However, during his second attempt, suddenly Fred opened his eyes and stood there, his stare lost in another world like an opium smoker.

Fred remained in a trance for two or three minutes, then he regained consciousness.

He told me that he met his fencing master and they talked a long time in the gym where they trained together. Fred had even shown him a shot of which he was particularly proud and that he had learned many years after leaving the school.

He also had the feeling of having been away for a longer time.

"You were right. One does not realize it, but the dialogue with our friend Anselmo may have actually occurred at high speed, at a much higher rate than that of a normal conversation. It must be so. That's probably why the state of trance lasted so little."

"You mean that when in interaction with this *machine*, one believes to be talking with Anselmo at normal speed, but in fact the subjective time is dilated."

"Could be. However, it is a fantastic experience. It all looks so real. Hey, you know what I asked your friend?"

"No, tell me."

"I asked him if he could show me where those two gentlemen of Herculaneum had decided to go. I mean the place and the time they had chosen as a destination, starting from the tunnel under the villa."

"And of course Anselmo replied that he could not tell you."

"No, dear. You are wrong. He told me. And I also know why."

"And that is?"

"I would bet that... those two guys died before they could escape from the tunnel. Perhaps the glowing cloud coming down from the Vesuvius hit and killed them instantly. In any case, they probably had no time to activate the transfer even if the destination was already decided. And they did not give Anselmo any specific order to prevent others from accessing that data, differently from what they normally did."

"Interesting! Go on please."

"Anselmo showed me the coordinates they had set for their departure from Herculaneum. They wanted to go or, more likely, to return to Rome. Given the short distance, the transfer would have been practically instantaneous."

"To Rome? Of course! The capital of the Empire with hundreds of thousands of inhabitants. A good place to hide for two ugly faces like them. And Anselmo?"

"He did not give a wince. But I doubt that we will get any more from him."

"And in your opinion, why Oleg left?"

"Who would not be interested to know how the world will look like in a few centuries?"

"I would. But there are still things that I do not understand. For example, why he left in such a hurry and did not bring Irina with him? And what happened to the paintings?"

"I have no idea. It's hard to speculate. I think you'd better ask her. You may go tomorrow, early in the morning, to pay her a visit at the prison."

I nodded.

"You do like Irina, eh? Don't even think to try to fool me."

I replied with a shrug. "It's time for you to sleep, my friend. We are both tired and you already begin to tell random numbers," I said, yawning.

I was in fact really tired. I threw myself on the bed, hoping he would give up. But he didn't and continued to tease me until we both fell asleep.

***

The next day I saw Irina.

She was radiant. I could tell she was glad to see me because her eyes were shining with joy. She had combed carefully, collecting her hair behind her delicate neck. She was just beautiful. On her face there was no trace of the paleness and of the deep dark circles I had noticed when I saw her for the first time. She no longer gave an impression of extreme thinness that had worried me at the time. She was still young and, after a long time, she was now back in blossom. In all its glory.

"I was so worried about you, Mayer. You spent such a long time abroad, you and that friend of yours."

"I am happy to see you, Irina. You… you look good. They haven't treated you too badly here, did they?"

"No, no. I was treated quite well. And I owe that to you. I feel much better now. But, do not keep me in suspense. How did it go? Please, tell me everything of it."

I told her everything, or almost. The meeting with Oleg's father, the night raid in Rufus' room, the ambush at Fred's, the flight from Geneva. I just neglected to tell her some details related to the final part of the journey.

"That's horrible! So you have killed a man?" asked Irina impulsively grabbing my arm and squeezing it hard when I told her about the shooting in Fred's room.

"What else could I do? He would have killed Fred. And without a second thought."

"Oh, my God. He could have killed you as well… It must be terrible to kill someone."

"I kept having nightmares for several nights. I woke up suddenly in a sweat when I revisited the scene in my dream. It is not easy to forget having killed, even if you were forced by the circumstances and you had to do it to save your life."

"Was it your first time?"

"No, unfortunately." I lowered my eyes.

"No? You mean during the war?"

"A duel."

"Ah, for a woman, I guess." She stared at me, cross with a look of disappointment on her face. I remained silent, eyes glued to the floor.

"I was very young," I finally said with a faint voice, "and also very stupid and presumptuous. I do not like to talk about it."

Her eyes softened.

"Never mind. However, looking at you, one would not guess. You do not look like a callous killer. And now that we know each other better, I can tell you what you look like."

"And what would that be?"

"You look rather like... a sacristan. Sort of."

A silvery laugh: she had already forgiven me.

"Ah well. As you wish, but a sinner sacristan, I am afraid."

"Could be..." she said, laughing, a somewhat mischievous tone in her voice.

"But, tell me about Anselmo. I bet you've already tried with the case, right? And did you see him? It was him, Anselmo, I mean, or somebody else?"

Then I told her about my professor of Mathematics from my time at the Lyceum, and I told her about Anselmo and everything else.

"And now, we just have to get you out of here," I said, at the end of the story.

She frowned and looked at me in silence with an open expression of skepticism.

"Anselmo will help us," I added, "and maybe we can find Oleg. But, first we have to get you out of here, one way or another."

"Shhhhh! Softly. The guards can hear us."

"I do not know exactly how. We still have to work it out. Myself and Fred. But don't worry: we will succeed."

"Are you sure you want to leave, Mayer? It is a journey of no return."

"The way you ask me sounds like it is *you* who have now changed your mind."

"No, I have not changed my mind. But are you aware of the consequences? You will no longer see your wife, your beloved ones, all your friends, the world as it is now, the world you lived in."

"I know. I have thought about it at length. It's a big risk. The world that we will find will be certainly different. It may be better than the one we have lived in, but it might as well not please us at all. And I will miss my wife and people I know and love."

"And that is not enough?"

"That's all. As I said, Irina, I've thought about it for a long time. Ulrike will suffer, but I think that if I leave her now, and forever, she might at least have the chance to rebuild her life with someone who might give her more than I did. There is not much left between the two of us. I should have had the courage to leave her earlier and that would have been more honest on my part. But, perhaps, if we had children… I do not know, maybe everything would have been different."

Irina was studying me, and something in her eyes had again changed.

"You could leave her in a less definitive way. But… would you go into this trip anyway? I mean, without me?"

"Yes, I think so," I lied.

"I hoped you would say that. Even for me it is the same. And that relieves me from feeling guilty. So what really drives you to leave?"

"Do you mean that you would leave even if you were sure not to find Oleg?"

"I think so. In this long time, locked in here, I thought of so many things and I have often wondered how it will be in tomorrow's world and what kind of people will live there. It is the dream of every one of us to be able to lengthen our life and see what will happen, what will be the fate of mankind. The evolution of the human race is such a fascinating story that it would be a real shame not to know where it will go from here."

"Right. I never liked the stories in serial form. It's a vicious editorial ploy. I find it cruel. As a child, I was dying to know how some story I cared for would end. So, sometimes I tried to imagine how the next episode would develop. And often I did not like it, so then, I invented another thread of the story and then yet another…"

"Yes. I did that too. As a girl I always had a galloping imagination, limitless and effortless."

"But in any case, we only can guess part of what may lie ahead. The wooden case will remain here and we do not know if we will be ever able to retrieve it. Probably we will remain stuck in the era in which we will happen to fall, whether we like it or not."

"We will love it. I am sure of it."

"Uhm. If so, then we just have a technical problem to solve."

Irina followed my gaze and turned her head to that part of the garden where the armed guard was taking care of us with great discretion. She smiled.

"Yes. We do have a problem, but now I believe that we will succeed."

"I need time to prepare everything. I must try to get more information from Anselmo. And maybe you can help me: Oleg might have told you something useful. When you were in Paris, for example, do you think that Oleg had already clear in mind what he wanted to do?"

"I don't think he did. We were both striving to achieve a break-through, to be successful. At first it was disappointing, but then, thanks God, things quickly took a turn for the better."

So, Irina began to tell.

We made our debut before an audience of scoundrels who drank and smoked and laughed and whistled every time I entered the scene. It was a stinking room in the Marais. It smelled of beer and smoke and of people who rarely took care to wash. With all those eyes glued on my body, I felt so humiliated that I hardly could go on with our show. Oleg too was disgusted and I don't think he would have agreed to perform a second time in that place. But fortunately that very night we were noticed by a small theater impresario who engaged us for the whole season.

So we moved to a small theater nearby, a hundred seats or so.

Soon it filled up. People stood on a long line at the box office after being told that some real magic took place in the theater, not just the usual tricks of magicians. And the rumors soon spread outside the neighborhood. Within a season, Oleg had already gained a good popularity and the reputation of a true magician.

New opportunities came when theatrical impresarios started competing again each other to win exclusive rights to the show. The number with the two cases was our workhorse. Each spectator received a numbered coupon and, during the show, a blindfolded child extracted at random one volunteer from the audience.

The spectator climbed on the stage and we asked him to inspect the case thoroughly. If there was anyone else in the audience who wished to have a look we encouraged him to do so. And it was fortunate for us when some important person, a notable or an officer well known to the public, committed himself to make sure that both cases were empty and they did not hide one of the usual tricks like a fake bottom. Then the volunteer was closed into one case which was then sealed with the metal plate. A bit of staging, with Oleg muttering a few words of a magical ritual, and.. voilà! The case was reopened.

And of course it was empty.

An ovation of incredulity from the audience.

At this point Oleg showed his talent with the cards until, after a while, from the second case – a normal wooden crate similar to the first one and placed at the opposite end of the stage – some noise could be heard from within. Oleg pretended to be surprised, opened the lid and... voilà: the unfortunate spectator slowly rose from the case and stood uncomfortably numb on the stage, semi-drowned by the roaring of the public. The theatre was in a frenzy.

The person on duty checked again both the first and the second case, then he turned to the puzzled public and spread his arms helplessly, bewildered and dejected at the same time.

The public stood up in ovation.

From one success to the next, we performed in front of an increasingly large audience. Within two years, we climbed all the rungs of popularity to the summit of the Opera House. One of the businessmen offered us a lovely apartment on the Île de Saint Louis and we happily abandoned the two lousy rooms in the Marais and moved there with no regrets. Everything was going very well at that time. We were popular, well paid and satisfied with ourselves.

But one day something happened and, since then, Oleg was never the same again.

One evening, after the show, two men asked to see him in his dressing room. It had happened many times before. Usually they were impresarios who wanted to discuss some business with him or just enthusiastic spectators begging for an autograph. So I did not worry too much and I introduced them to Oleg leaving them alone to talk. When they left I realized immediately that something has happened."

"What's going on with you? Bad news?"

"No. I do not think so. But it's strange…"

"What is strange?"

"Those two guys. I do not understand. They were claiming to be our fans. But they posed some curious questions. Not directly, of course, but cleverly disguised in the middle of a lot of gossip and congratulations on the show and other more mundane questions and so on and so forth."

"What did they ask?"

"First of all, one of them was too much interested in my ring and he asked me if he could examine it."

"And you?"

"What else could I do? I held my hand right close to his glasses. He must have been short-sighted, I guessed. He examined the ring for a bit and then he declared that it was a remarkable stone. Probably a mineral containing some kind of rare earth. So he said."

"And that's all?"

"No. Then they started asking about the case. I tried to wave them goodbye, but they insisted on giving a look inside. Anyway, the case was there and I could not hide it. What is strange is that the first thing they began to inspect closely was precisely the plate."

"You mean even before checking the inside of the case?"

"Yes. This is what puzzles me. I would have expected that the first thing they would have checked was the bottom of the box to see if it had a hidden trapdoor. On the contrary they took their time to observe the plate and its mosaic of beads. Does it not sound strange to you?"

"Perhaps you are exaggerating, Oleg. The lid of the box, with that oddly shaped plate, draws the eye perhaps more than the rest."

"Maybe you are right. Yet I do not feel comfortable."

"For two curious onlookers who went to pry under the lid of your case?"

"No, there's more."

"Then, tell me."

"Anselmo told me that someone tried to enter the case."

"Tried to... enter?"

"Get into the case. I mean that someone from outside tried to take control of it. Maybe he wished to send us a Christmas gift or to come in person for a visit."

"Are you kidding? And who might that be?"

"I do not know. Anselmo realized that someone was trying to take control of the system without taking the trouble to ask his permission."

"And when did that happen?"

"Some days ago. Anselmo is sure that there have been at least three attempts so far. Luckily he knows his job of guardian. Most probably his masters of Herculaneum had decided they did not want intrusions and had left him a set of tools designed for this purpose. That's what he told me. What kind of tools I haven't the faintest idea."

"That's frightening! And Anselmo cannot guess who this guy is who wants to come in?"

"No. It seems that he does not communicate with Anselmo and does everything to conceal his identity and location."

"And Anselmo, what did he say about that?"

"He has some suspicion, but he does not say much. However, he is concerned. He says that sooner or later the intruder may succeed. Anselmo has prepared a series of tricks and traps to protect the system against these attacks, but it seems that the guy is insidious and the siege could also end up badly…"

"That's terrible! You mean we could have something monstrous entering our house from the box?"

"I did not want to tell you, but I'm afraid so."

"Then, damn, we have to store this case in a safe place as soon as possible!"

"That's what I intend to do."

So we locked the case down in the basement behind an iron door and Oleg unlocked it only when he had to carry it to the theater for the show, or to communicate with Anselmo. And every time he approached the door cautiously and, before entering, he peered through the grate as if afraid that a wild beast was lurking inside, hidden in the gloom.

Since then, Oleg began to behave more and more strangely. I think he had decided to keep me unaware of what was happening. He was convinced that I would have panicked and be of no help. He said that everything was fine and that Anselmo controlled the situation, but I could see very well that he was worried.

A few days later, he told me that he had moved the case to a safer place and it seemed more relieved and more self-confident. But it did not last long and soon he fell back in a state of acute depression. I did not know what to do to help him because, despite my insistence, he continued to evade my questions about Anselmo and the case.

This went on for a while, until he received the visit of a dealer of antiques, a gentleman I had never seen before. Tall, thin, probably in his fifties, with a gray mustache cut short, smartly dressed, and always carrying an elegant stick with a silver knob. They met often in the following months and each time the dealer, very polite and kind, showed up with a package for Oleg and a bouquet of flowers for me. From the unmistakable shape, one could easily tell that the package contained a picture.

Oleg seemed more relaxed now. He told me that Anselmo had not recorded new attempts to force his surveillance system. Our shows were going well and now we were two celebrities in Paris. I did not pay much attention to the frequent meetings of Oleg with the antiques dealer. After each visit, the wall of the study was enriched by a new canvas and I had no reason to be suspicious.

Actually I had other concerns, because Oleg had begun to go out alone in the evening, after the performance. I was jealous, I admit, and I could not stand that he could leave me at home alone. Furthermore, he began to squander considerable sums of money to purchase artistic objects, ancient books and scrolls that he bought regularly from all kinds of art markets in Paris or that he ordered from far away, especially from Egypt and Mexico.

For the first two years, we lived mostly in Paris. They were two memorable years. Then we began to make tours abroad, in various capitals of Europe, and we were welcomed by an enthusiastic audience everywhere. But one day, while we were on tour in Antwerp, the news reached us that the antiques dealer had been arrested and that the police had raided our home in Paris.

Oleg tried to minimize the importance of these facts. He said it was nothing but a misunderstanding and that perhaps the antiques dealer had unwittingly purchased some object of art that was later found to have been stolen. Everything was going to be clarified and we had nothing to fear. Meanwhile we had better be cautious and, instead of returning to Paris, we should anticipate our next tour. So we left Antwerp.

Back in Vienna, we discovered that our reputation had preceded us and the same evening of our debut in the capital, we received the official invitation to perform at the Royal Court.

It was a triumph.

The Imperial Family appreciated the show enormously and, in addition to the honors, we received a generous reward. It goes without saying that our popularity in Vienna grew vertiginously and everyone was talking about us.

"I heard about you, too. From my wife."

"Yes, sure. We were very well known and appreciated at that time. But Oleg seemed indifferent and he got increasingly aloof and absent. He started neglecting me and could always find a good excuse to keep me away from Anselmo. Instead, at this time, Oleg and Anselmo spoke more and more often, that's my guess. I'm not entirely sure why the case was no longer kept in the usual place and Oleg had decided to hide it somewhere else.

One day he told me he was going to make an important experiment and he needed my help. I would have done anything to get him back to himself and so I agreed willingly.

This time he had decided to try the transfer of his body across a large distance and without the help of the small guiding spheres that usually were hidden in the second case. It was dangerous, and Anselmo, to play safe, had suggested him to choose as a target any place with deep water.

So the choice fell on the Millstättersee Lake in Carinthia. It was not only a leap of one hundred and sixty miles, but also Oleg opted to test a time gap of almost one month. The appointment was on the shore of the lake at dawn on the twenty-eighth day after his departure.

"And what did you do?"

"I spent twenty-eight days in pain and went to the appointment convinced that I would never see him again.

Instead, Oleg arrived on time.

The surface of the lake had been completely flat until then, except for small ripples caused by a light breeze. Suddenly it got furrowed by deep ruts and became restless. A surge of water and a loud thunder propelled a myriad of water drops to the cloudless sky, screaming and dancing in a giant spray. Then the perturbation quickly faded away and the waters adjusted themselves and became quiet again.

Slowly, from the surface of the lake a dark shape emerged.

Oleg was back.

After an absence of twenty-eight days, he surged from the waters of Lake Millstättersee exactly where and when he had predicted. It was the culmination of many grueling tests and a kind of conclusive experiment or rather, as the subsequent events would have shown, a sort of dress rehearsal.

When he pulled out from the icy water, exhausted and shivering, I hugged him tight in my arms and in that moment I hoped that everything was finally over and he would return to be the same Oleg I knew before. But as soon as he started talking, I immediately realized that this was not going to be the case.

He was excited by the success of the experiment. He explained to me that those twenty-eight days had passed for him in a single instant. A moment before, he remembered to have curled upon the case and a moment later he felt propelled out, upwards, toward a hazy blue sky and then he was falling into the icy water, like a stone. He was happy as a child, though shivering from the cold.

Comfortably warm inside our carriage during the return trip, we long dreamt of the voyages that we could take using the case and the exotic and faraway places that we could easily reach. Oleg also mentioned the possibility of venturing into the future to an age yet to come, with the help of Anselmo. I thought he had in mind to share this new adventure with me, but I was wrong.

In the following weeks, things turned worse. Oleg had begun to attend the golden world of art dealers and took on debts beyond our means. I was really worried about him. He was often brooding as haunted by a fixed idea.

One day when he was in the mood to, he told me:

"I cannot understand how people can resign themselves so easily to the idea of dying, when I am ready to bet that in a few centuries humanity will be able to defeat most of the causes of death other than accidental and we will be able to delay, if not eliminate altogether, the aging process."

According to Oleg, senescence had to be considered on the same footing as the growth process: a programmed phenomenon triggered with continuity by the previous steps. Childhood, adolescence, maturity and then a scheduled decline toward the final outcome were nothing else but the subsequent steps of a same program.

"I'm sure," he said, "that one day mankind will be able to take over and replace nature in the control of this mechanism, correcting or perhaps eliminating it entirely."

He was no longer desperate at the idea of being born too early, in an epoch not yet mature for all this, because now he did have a hope. A hope that had become certainty that very day on the shore of Lake Millstättersee. He now had the proof that he could make it. He had stumbled, quite by accident, into something mysterious, utterly incomprehensible, but now he owned a winning ticket for the lottery that gave him the opportunity – so far denied to all men before him – to escape his fate. The fear of missing this opportunity did not let him sleep at night.

"It is quite understandable that he was haunted," I said. "No one, to my knowledge, has ever come even close to have in his hands an opportunity of this kind."

"Yes, but I think his depression was not due only to this, but rather to something that threatened him directly. Something that literally terrified him. And this also explains his determination to keep me away at all costs from this danger."

"And you have no idea about what he was afraid of?"

"No, I haven't the faintest idea. Only some hints. At that time I was sure that the cause was to be sought in the case, and I wanted to confirm my suspicions, questioning Anselmo. But, as I told you, Oleg allowed me to get close to the case only when it was absolutely necessary, that is, during the show."

"It's strange. Maybe someone threatened him?"

"Maybe. Yet, the paintings acquired by the antiquarian of Paris and all other objects of art must be somewhere."

"Anselmo might know."

"Yes, maybe. But Oleg may have instructed or compelled him to not tell anyone. "

"Most probably. Please continue. What happened, then?"

One thing, apparently inexplicable, made the situation even worse. We had been absent from Vienna for a few days and, on our return, we were struck by a bitter surprise. Our house had been visited and turned upside down by burglars. Actually, almost nothing was missing and this was rather odd given the large number of valuables that were there. It seemed that our visitors were after something. As soon as he realized the situation, Oleg panicked and rushed away. He returned later, still upset but more relaxed. The case was still where he had hidden it, in a place known to him alone.

After taking care of the sort of a battlefield that our home had become, we realized that the magician's hat and the ivory wand had disappeared. A rather disturbing circumstance.

On the following day Oleg disappeared without notice, without a farewell message. He took with him two oil paintings of Flemish school that he had bought in Antwerp for an exorbitant sum. I tried unsuccessfully to track him down, mobilizing friends and acquaintances, talking with art dealers with whom he had been in contact, and I questioned the staff of the theater. We sought him everywhere in Vienna sifting through local taverns and brothels that he had begun to attend recently.

No trace. I feared the worst.

To complicate the situation, the police were investigating the burglary at our house and they sent off immediately an alert to search for Oleg. They questioned me at length, showing little interest in the burglary and hammering me instead with questions about the paintings and objects of art that Oleg had recently purchased or on those we had brought with us from Antwerp. They showed me some shady characters I'd never seen before and asked if I had seen any of them with Oleg.

I was outraged and perplexed because I expected that their duty was to identify those who had broken into our house and not investigate us. But the facts that we know at present, and of which I was unaware at the time, show that they were doing their job.

In fact, after a few days, an officer of the gendarmerie came and told me that they had tracked down the place where Oleg had taken refuge after his flight and had recovered some of his personal belongings. Still no news about him, but they were confident that he would be caught soon. He said just like that: "caught." I could not believe my ears!

Unceremoniously, he told me that Oleg was charged as receiver of stolen works and of having commissioned some thefts of paintings that had taken place recently. The accomplices, common criminals, had been arrested and had confessed. I should consider myself in custody, as suspected of complicity in Oleg's illegal activities.

My heart sank.

When I regained consciousness, I was lying on the sofa and my household around me were trying to assist me as best they could. I saw tears in their eyes. I was incredulous, completely dazed. I made no resistance and followed the police officer. Escorted by guards, he led me to a cab that was waiting outside. Only later, during the long journey, I came out slowly from the state of near-unconsciousness I had fallen into. Gradually, I began to put together the various pieces of the whole mosaic and reconnect some episodes dating back to the time of our stay in Paris, facts I had not given much weight to.

The coach left the outskirts of Vienna and continued along a dusty road across the country and a few villages.

After a couple of hours of travel along narrow and winding mountain roads we entered a small town surrounded by a dense forest of fir trees. It was not distant from a small lake.

Once in the main square of the village, we stopped in front of the inn close to the church tower. We were received by the head of the local gendarmerie and by a second lieutenant who made himself immediately available to his superior.

The owner of the inn, a fat, pig-like faced man with greasy hair, led us upstairs where the bed rooms were located.

"Here, this is the room," he said, bowing slightly and letting us get into a dingy room furnished with excessive parsimony: a single bed, a bedside table, a wicker chair. From the window nothing of interest could be seen, except the top of the trees of the forest that wrapped and protected the village from the north wind. The best rooms, with a view of the lake, were on the other side of the hotel.

"We moved his stuff to the closet next door. Follow me, please."

He opened the door to a small storage room and dragged out a wooden trunk.

"Here. We put everything inside the trunk."

With a sinking heart I recognized the case. No doubt about it: it was ours!

The host opened the lid, bowed and picked up some clothing that I recognized immediately. The police officer gave me a quizzical look.

"Yes, it is Oleg's. This jacket is his. I'm sure."

"And the traveling trunk?"

"Yes, that also belongs to Oleg."

"Well, at least he could not take it away, that son of a bitch," said the landlord with little grace.

"Moderate your terms in front of a lady!" ordered the officer.

"Excuse me, *ma'am*. But I just cannot understand how that s... I mean how he managed to slip away, damn him, without paying for his stay. We found the door locked from the inside and the key in the lock. And. How the hell did he get out? From the window? I do not think so. The window was closed and in any case he would have broken his neck."

"As soon as we get hold of him, he will tell us everything, no doubt," the policeman assured him with a menacing tone.

I knew immediately what had happened: Oleg had used the case to quit our time and I would never see him again. I felt my legs give way and I collapsed in tears on the floor. They thought I was desperate about what could happen to Oleg after his capture, so the policeman hastened to reassure me.

"Don't be afraid, madam. We not are going to hurt him. We all hope that he will be captured without resistance. You said he has no weapons, didn't you?"

"Yes..." I sobbed "Usually he does not carry weapons with him."

"Good. Calm down, now. You will see that he will be fine with little ado. A few years in prison at most."

The host appreciated the cynicism of the joke and roared with laughter.

"But is it true that he is a… magician?" asked the innkeeper, with a broad grin and stroking his chin.

I said nothing and avoided his eyes.

***

Fred had taken the whole matter to the heart. After resigning from the laboratory where he was working as a gem carver and thanks to the intercession of my uncle, he got an employment as a clerk in the administration of the prison. By coincidence, or perhaps it was not just a coincidence, an equal-grade employee was moved to another location, leaving a vacancy at the prison where Irina was in custody. With the qualifications he had obtained from our college, a private school with a high reputation for strict discipline, Fred got the job immediately.

He reported to the director of the prison with an appointment letter in his hand and a voluminous luggage containing his belongings which included a wooden traveler trunk reinforced all around by a sturdy metal frame. He took possession of his office located on the same floor as the direction and worked there for about two months, gaining the trust of the director and of other employees of the administration.

Meanwhile I was busy with other preparations. I signed some legal papers that would secure Ulrike financially after my demise. She could count on a generous annual income as I transferred to her practically all the properties that I had inherited from my parents.

I sold the farm and the land to collect the money I needed for the trip.

But which currency of today, I was wondering, would be still in use after a few centuries?

None, I thought.

Only gold, perhaps, could be trusted to maintain its value, but I discarded this solution because gold was heavy and therefore not suited for the kind of journey ahead. Instead, I decided to follow Fred's advice: "Listen to me, a diamond is always a diamond. It will always have considerable value, it is easy to carry and easy to sell, especially if not too large."

So I converted most of my money into diamonds, a handful of glittering stones that I could carry comfortably in my pockets. Fred told me that I got a good deal.

In addition to these activities, I spent a lot of time with Anselmo. Following his instructions, I built a sort of life jacket that I derived from an old waistcoat by applying a number of extra pockets stuffed with pieces of cork and sewn all around. It could be fixed to the body with leather straps. It was cumbersome and primitive, but allowed one to float even in a state of complete unconsciousness thanks to a collar that supported the head out of the water in the upright position.

With this ridiculous equipment in stand-by, I asked Anselmo to send me to Lake Millstättersee. I wanted to repeat Oleg's test, but I decided to shorten the time.

Fred came to take me out of the lake only three days later.

Everything went perfectly well and from my point of view the journey seemed a matter of seconds. A moment before I was folded inside the crate, with my temples throbbing strong, and a moment later I was falling into the icy waters of the lake where I kept floating thanks to my lifesaver. Fred pulled me out half frozen.

The next day I handed the wooden trunk and the lifesaver to Fred who carried them to the prison.

Two months passed and finally the opportunity we were looking for was at hand. The director had left the night before and it was rumored that he would stay away for a few days. That morning I showed up, as usual, at my appointment with Irina.

We had been talking for about ten minutes in the usual garden inside the courtyard reserved for the direction when a guard came over and motioned us to follow him. We set off, escorted by a second guard who closed the small procession. We crossed long empty corridors then we climbed the stairs two floors up where the offices of the administration where located. Shortly after, we stopped in front of the door of an office not far from the director's.

The prison guard knocked, waited respectfully, and then escorted us inside the room while the other jailer stood guard outside the door. Fred was sitting behind a desk surrounded on three sides by shelves full of papers and files. I avoided eye contact with him because I was afraid of the risk that we might burst into laughter.

He stood up and held out his hand.

"Sit down please, Herr Mayer. The director told me about you."

"Give a chair to the prisoner," he ordered the guard.

"So, Herr Mayer, you have asked to see the manager. Unfortunately he is absent at the moment. If it is a matter of simple business I can handle your request myself, otherwise you will have to wait for his return."

"You see, it is a problem of the prisoner. She complains about a serious matter that has happened again and again and now it is time to do something about it. But maybe it is better that she herself exposes the facts."

"Please explain," encouraged Fred, with a winning smile to Irina.

"Well, I…" stammered Irina. "It is something… unpleasant…" She turned her head toward the guard who was standing upright at the side of the desk.

Fred looked in his turn in the same direction, then he asked gravely, "What, exactly, unpleasant?"

"Here, I do not know if…" Irina continued. "You see it is… a person, another prisoner… she is harassing me."

"Harassing? What do you mean?" Fred snapped.

"It is embarrassing to say. I am ashamed… but believe me, it's not my fault."

Irina bowed her head and began to sob, apparently desperate. I was fascinated how she was playing the part to perfection.

"It's a shame!" I intervened vehemently. "Incidents such as these should never happen again. To serve a sentence in prison does not mean to give up one's dignity, to put oneself at the mercy of..."

"Calm down, Herr Mayer, please. First, please explain to me what happened and then I will see what can be done."

"It is sexual harassment... That's what it is. A serious matter that has repeated too many times now. It is natural that Irina is embarrassed to talk about it in front of three men..."

I glanced significantly toward the guard. His little eyes were peering Irina, excited.

"I understand, of course," Fred said, standing up.

"Guard, leave the room! And stay at ready outside the door!" he ordered with a perfect aplomb.

The guard snapped to attention and executed what looked like a sensible order under the circumstances. As soon as he had shut the door, Fred turned to us with a broad smile.

"At work! We have no time to lose. And you Irina..." He bowed to kiss her hand. "You have been superb, a wonderful actress."

"Pleased to meet you," Irina replied,"I'm glad that my stage experience served to a purpose."

Fred retrieved the wooden case from a pile of garbage that covered it almost completely in a corner of the room, opened the lid, bent over, and pulled out the rudimentary life jacket he had built.

"Please help Irina put it on. Pass me the ring... quickly. And you Irina, keep talking. From outside they must continue to hear your voice."

I activated the plate, touching it with the ring, and passed the earring to Fred. He rest his hand on the plate, focused for a moment, and then stood still, frozen, eyes wide open for about half a minute.

"All done," he said, taking back control of himself and shaking his head as if he had suddenly awakened from a nap.

"Anselmo is ready. Let's ship the luggage first. Hey, you two! Strip off some of the stuff you wear, otherwise you will drown."

Paying attention not to make noise, he began to pull out from a closet the few things we had decided to take with us.

Irina looked at me puzzled. She did not know what to do.

She kept talking in a colorless voice, reciting her phony story about the alleged sexual harassment perpetrated by her cellmate.

Fred took our luggage which had been carefully packed and tightly fastened to a separate life jacket and shoved it inside the case.

I began to take off my jacket and waistcoat.

Irina ran into a corner and, turning her back to us, she took off her jacket first, then the prisoner's uniform. Fred made himself busy with the case while I took off my pants.

Eventually, Fred closed the lid.

"Ladies and gentlemen, your luggage has just been shipped off. Now it's your turn."

Irina was now wearing only a light camisole and a pair of knickers that reached to her knees.

I was left shirtless with a pair of equally long knickers.

She blushed to the tip of her hair.

When we turned around and looked at each other, Irina could not hold back a chuckle. I smiled too, but I couldn't help but staring at her. She looked much better than I had imagined having seen her dressed in no other way than in those horrible grey clothes that imprisoned her slim figure. The eye lingered just long enough on the thin fabric that barely concealed two well separated breasts that did not fear the force of gravity.

"Come on, hurry up. And you Irina, put this on. It will help you stay afloat."

Fred helped her to wear the life vest and asked me to tighten the pair of straps that laced on the back.

"Let me help you."

I could not help but let my eyes slip on those parts of her figure that I had not yet dared to look at. Fred, on the contrary, was behaving as a better gentleman and assisted Irina in taking position inside the box.

"You should try to curl up at the bottom. There you are, that's better. Fold in your legs more."

The floating harness that we had imposed on her for precaution made her trunk stiff and it was not easy for her to find the right position at the bottom of the case.

"Here we are. Now I can close the lid. Irina, you are ready?"

"Yes, but I'm so frightened…"

"I understand you. I would be the same in your place. But everything will be fine, don't worry. I wish you a happy life in the world yet to come. You deserve it. Farewell, Irina."

"Farewell, Fred. I will never forget what you have done for me and the risks you have taken."

Fred kissed her hand. Irina then curled back inside the case.

"I'm ready, Mayer. But hurry up, do not leave me alone in the midst of the sea… That sea that lies beyond… It scares me."

"Don't be afraid Irina. Just the time to say goodbye to a friend and I will join you. Good luck."

Fred closed the lid.

I touched the plate with the ring and waited a few seconds.

Fred lifted the lid: Irina had passed.

"Now it's up to you, Herr Mayer," said Fred with a big bow, pointing to the case.

"Be serious, Fred, at least once. It is the last time we see each other…"

"Yes, I know... damn. I wish I could change my mind and come with you two, but I cannot. We have already discussed that."

"My dearest friend, I'm sorry to leave you here. You are like a brother to me."

"The same for me."

We hugged.

"Hope everything goes smoothly and you will be happy," added Fred, moved.

"I'll think of both of you. And I hope you will still remember me even when I will not... But, enough of this sentimentality! Rather, remember what I told you about the case."

"And, I almost forgot to mention," he added, laughing. "I hope you and Irina..."

He brought his index fingers together.

"Me and Irina what?"

"Come on. I saw how you were looking at her before..."

"Shut up, Fred, or I'll give you a blow."

"That's exactly what you have to do, remember? Come on, quickly. Let's do it."

We raised up our voices and feigned a fight. Fred took advantage of the noise to carefully lock the door with the massive deadbolt. Then, we pushed the desk against the door and began to stack other heavy pieces of furniture on it. The two guards realized that a fight had started inside and tried to open the door to rescue Fred. But the door held.

"Come on, soon. You have to. Hit me! Now!"

"Farewell my good friend." I hit him in the neck with a cut by hand. He collapsed to the ground without a sound. I immediately checked his pulse. It was good, thank God.

The screams and the blows on the door brought me back to reality. The guards outside were hammering the door with their rifle butts shouting and cursing like madmen. The door was about to give. Now I had little time left.

I slipped quickly into the case and closed the lid. The plate from the inside was hot. I touched it with the ring just in the very moment when the door broke down in a final crash and the two guards rushed into the room.

Darkness.

A sensation of free fall.

Falling down… deeper and deeper.

A strong sense of dizziness and a terrible noise in my ears.

I had already experienced all that, but this time it was different. It was lasting much longer. When Anselmo had sent me to the lake, the whole trip had been for me just a matter of a few seconds.

Not this time.

I was fully conscious and my brain was working well, but my head was about to explode.

"My God. I must be about to die. And Irina?"

A sudden push, very strong, propelled me upwards.

A thumping noise shattered my ears.

"I can't breathe…"

A sudden ray of light. Dazzling.

Blue sky above.
Warm, moist air on my face.
Freefall again.
Silence.
A final stroke of time.
A loud splash in the water.

To get back my youth I would do anything in the world, except take exercise, get up early, or be respectable.
- Oscar Wilde, *The Picture of Dorian Gray*, 1891

"I am sure they invented the whole of that ridiculous story" said Rajiv, coughing.

He tried to wave off a cloud of bluish smoke spreading out in his direction and pervading the small room with a sweet smell. He passed a handkerchief over his neck. Sweat ran in rivulets down his back, soaking his shirt of a faded yellow. He returned to stare quizzically at his interlocutor who didn't say a word and kept himself busy with his briar pipe.

"This scrap of a conditioner…" growled Rajiv, oppressed by the stifling heat of the room.

"Everything is going down the drain here. Every day's worse than the day before…"

"Keep quiet, Rajiv. If you keep struggling like that, you will suffer the heat even more," declared the other with a calm voice. Standing by the window, he had remained silent, his gaze fixed on a point far away on the horizon, beyond the palm trees, along an indefinite line where the blue of the sky melted into the metallic sheen of the ocean.

Tall, dry, salt-and-pepper haired, the skin covered with freckles, he looked like the portrait of his British ancestors in the good old days when India was a colony of the Empire.

"You have to admit, however, that it is strange indeed: why make the effort to invent such a crazy story?"

"How should I know? Perhaps they are both insane," replied Rajiv, fishing a piece of paper from the desktop and using it as a fan.

"They are definitely *not* crazy. Indeed, given the progress they have made, I would say they are quite brilliant."

Rajiv raised his eyes to the sky.

"Which progress? They are just two crooks. I don't buy it. "

"Maybe. But in that case you have to admit that they have chosen to act in a play that sounds definitely unconvincing. And there are many things that do not fit."

"Like what?"

"Look, Rajiv. We have been watching them day and night. And for a long time. Although trained perfectly, human beings always end up making some small mistake, betray a minor detail or fall into some contradiction. Instead nothing at all has happened with them! They have not done or said anything that has betrayed them. If they are impostors, they are damn good."

"And what else could they be?" Rajiv retorted stubbornly, spreading his arms in a gesture of despair. "The heat must have cooked your brain if you believe their story. Herr Mayer and Frau Irina coming to us from a distant past: two fossils from the times of the Kaiser being found afloat on the ocean centuries later. And all thanks to a kind of… a time machine. Give me a shred of evidence, Vincent, and I will believe you."

"Okay. So let's start from the beginning. They were found adrift, burned by the sun, half dead of thirst. And how were they dressed, remember?"

"With the knickers of our nineteenth century ancestors. And this would be a proof of evidence? Just go to a theatre, on the backstage and you can get whatever you want. Grandma's knickers, for instance. Or you may try at the sex shop. There are perverts who…"

"That's enough, Rajiv. But what is the purpose of this masquerade? Everyone else we have caught so far, you know, had infiltrated secretly or was acting undercover. To what end, I wonder, did they decided to play the castaways?"

"Maybe they wanted us to find them."

"Perfect. But why this farce of pretending that they came from the past?"

"Don't ask me. *You* are the devil's advocate."

"All right. Then let's follow the opposite hypothesis that they are two impostors. In this case, we must assume that they knew they would be constantly observed because they never made a *single* mistake. We never caught them turning on a switch with the natural gesture of someone who already knows what it is for. At first they looked completely disoriented even with simple low-tech stuff as if they had never seen anything like that before, as if they had grown in the trees. And the truth tests, how could they possibly pass them all?"

"How many did they go through?"

"A dozen. First, three or four during REM sleep, then those under interrogation and last the online mapping of Malakhov's potentials. They also passed the level 12 test. No failures."

"What is the probability for a liar to be able to fool level 12?"

"Virtually zero. Something like one in ten million."

"May be that those guys who sent them here took care to give them a special psychological training so to be able to fool our truth machines."

"It seems unlikely to me, given their low-tech level," said Vincent, exhaling a cloud of smoke exactly aimed at Rajiv.

"And speaking of…?" asked Rajiv, with a broad smile and a significant gesture of his hand.

"They are like brother and sister… There is no sex between them. Even though they have been living under the same roof for quite a while now. They are both perfectly normal and heterosexual. Though, I do have the impression that there is an attraction between them. Probably at a latent state."

"Or maybe they are so clever to do it in the darkness, when we do not look at them."

"Forget about it. The surveillance system provides full coverage around the clock. Our computers never sleep and peep into the darkness as well as in daylight."

"Yes, I know."

"Also, another strange thing. They spent weeks navigating through all the material we have provided them.

They first devoured the few books they found in their rooms and immediately asked for others. History books and an encyclopedia. Later we explained them that it is more practical to use the database and we taught them how to use a computer. Since then, they have done nothing but spending their time glued to the screen. From the records of the files they have opened, it seems they have systematically studied all that happened after the second half of the nineteenth century.

"That's exactly what they may have done to make us believe their ridiculous story, you will say. But how much patience does it take to fake *for weeks* genuine interest, surprise, bewilderment, sadness, joy and sorrow for the fate of humanity, for facts that everyone knows? It needs a strong will and a perfect training. Too perfect to be real."

"So, in your opinion, they were expressing genuine emotions."

"How about you, if someone would hand you a book where you can read everything that will happen in the next couple of centuries?"

"Well, I would certainly read it all in one breath."

"And then, what else would you do in their shoes?"

"I would try to find out what happened to the people I know. I mean... I can imagine the end of it, unfortunately. But maybe I'd like to know how they lived, what happened to them..."

"And that's precisely what they did: Irina and... Dr. Mayer, or whatever the guy's name."

"Heinrich. That's what she calls him."

"In short, those two folks, after about four weeks of relentless study, began to make a series of cross-searches on a number of databases. They ended up fishing out the scanned copies of the old archives of the Vienna Rathaus. Following their digital footprints through our computers, I reconstructed much of their alleged relationships and friendships. See it for yourself."

He handed to Rajiv a voluminous file with names and dates.

"I even found their birth certificates. She was born in Vienna on August 31, 1811, while our friend Heinrich was born on April 18, nine years before."

"I see you still enjoy yourself in fooling around..."

"No. Please check. It's all in that file. Obviously if they have invented the whole story, they may have done the searches intentionally, to make it plausible."

"And... did you find their death certificates?"

"Of course not. We found those of their relatives and friends. But not theirs."

"Why not?"

"I actually made a search on my own. I did find the birth certificate of a woman, named Irina, who had actually been sentenced to jail. I found a record about her in the archives of the judiciary and of the prison administration which, thankfully, were scanned about a century and a half later. I had to get help from a German woman, an expert of the old language. She has been so smart to be able to decipher patiently the calligraphy flourishes of the time which, I assure you, are not within our reach. From the archives, it finally came out that Irina had escaped from prison never to be seen again."

"Of course. You can bet on it. And her friend Heinrich?"

"I have not found much about him. But I discovered a deed signed by his own hand in which all of his assets were transferred to his wife Ulrike. With a subsequent act, the court of Vienna decreed the dissolution of the marriage for abandonment of the marital home and unavailability of the spouse."

"Everything fits together with Heinrich's diary."

"There is also a 99.5% match between the diary's handwriting and the signature of the deed, according to our bright brains in Cleveland."

"This is ridiculous: of course they must fit together. The diary, as you call it, was written just to trick us. And, as for imitating anybody's handwriting, it may not be a problem."

"Or vice versa, they are telling us the truth. But can you believe that?"

Vincent did not answer. Instead he began fiddling with his pipe which, in the meanwhile, had gone off again. A proven tactic, which allowed him to gain time.

"In my opinion," he replied after a long pause, firing a volley of smoke in the direction of Rajiv, "not in the least do they suspect that the diary is checked every day and every new page is on my desk not later than twenty-four hours after it was written."

"Or maybe they know and let it be."

"Maybe. But the motivation, I ask again, what is it? I cannot guess."

"Let's put them to a test."

"How?"

"Let them flee. Let's see what they will do."

"I think this is an excellent idea, Rajiv. No alternative. We can't keep them here forever."

"Leave it to me. You will see that, once away from here, we will catch them with their hands in the bag."

***

A gentle breeze blowing from the ocean caressed Irina's face. Leaning motionless against the railings of the wide wooden terrace, she kept staring at the yellow disk of an oversized moon that was lazily floating on the horizon. She narrowed her eyes for a moment and savored the air filled with the scent of tropical flowers. She became aware of the breeze under her shirt: thousands of invisible fingertips dancing gently on her nipples. She blushed, in the shelter of darkness, and let her thoughts wander back in time.

It looked like yesterday, but centuries had passed since she had seen him for the first time from behind the bars of the parlor room and had heard his voice, the same voice that now she could recognize among thousands. What was going on with her? Where had all her love for Oleg gone? It was useless to try to fool herself and she knew it very well. There was something about that man she could not...

She stiffened and tried at all costs to dispel that idea, to clear up her mind. But she found it increasingly difficult to carry on with this exercise of will. How could she have forgotten so quickly a love she had nurtured and fought to keep alive during those long days within the walls of that squalid prison? She couldn't come up with an answer. Yet she felt that there was something special in that man's voice, something special she could read in the depths of his eyes and her emotions were growing so intense as she had never experienced before. Even with Oleg.

A muffled sound behind her. She recognized his tread followed soon by the unmistakable timbre of his voice, now so close to her on the balcony. She narrowed her eyes.

"It's a wonderful night. I may have seen a moon like that, but only a few centuries ago."

Goose-pimples ran all along her skin, but she kept her eyes fixed at the moon.

He came closer and closer and, slowly, gently kissed her neck.

She closed her eyes, her body stretched into a slim arch, like a bow.

When he reached her earlobe, she drew back slightly and turned her head, meeting his eyes. Two tiny yellow moons mirrored into them.

"Bad idea," she said, in a whisper.

"Why?" he asked, annoyed.

"Because it is a bad idea. We shouldn't..."

"We are far away from our past, Irina. In a totally different world, and I…"

"I know. But, the time has not come yet."

A long pause. The moon had stopped her motion and was staring at them, puzzled.

"Are you still in love with him?"

"Don't know. I suppose I should be. But, now… I am so confused…"

"I am also very confused myself, Irina. From the very first day I met you."

"Really?"

"Something has been growing in my mind since I saw you first… behind the prison's bars… Don't know how it could happen, but since then I've not been able to think of anything else. Tell me, what do you want me to do?"

"You have to be patient with me…" She stretched towards him and slightly pressed her lips on his.

He tried to kiss her. But she slipped away.

"Please, stay!" He failed to stop her from freeing herself from his arms.

She moved aside a few steps along the balcony, her eyes now locked again on the liquid path of light that seemed to connect the beach to the distant moon, low on the horizon.

He reached her again and encircled her waist with his arms, from behind. Warm lips crawled all along her neck and the tip of his tongue slowly penetrated Irina's ear.

She let him.

They remained like that, in each other's arms, for a time that seemed forever.

Like two teen-agers, he thought.

His fingers now moved smoothly on her skin under the shirt. But they did not reach very far, as she pulled herself free again and ran away from the terrace, leading toward the interior of the house.

"Well... it's just a question of time" he said, confident of himself, to the moon.
And the moon, bobbing up and down on the dark waters, nodded to him in sign of her approval.

***

The opportunity they had been waiting for came unexpectedly during a walk over a part of the base they had not explored yet. For the last two months, they had been able to move freely inside Perimeter B, reserved for the guests. They explored it with one of those strange three-wheeled electric vehicles that everyone used to move around inside the base.

An officer had shown them how to drive one. It was simple. They had just to sit behind the steering wheel and look through the windshield. Immediately some colored symbols appeared in transparency: an arrow along the direction of travel, an arrow pointing to the opposite direction, and a red disc. It was sufficient to stare into one of the two arrows to move the vehicle along the corresponding direction. Appropriately dosing the intensity of the stare on either icon one could increase or diminish the speed or reverse the direction. The red disk was used only in the case of an emergency stop.

That was all.

The amazing thing was that the machine guessed, so to speak, the intentions of the driver as if reading his mind. In fact, a distracted look on the wrong icon had no effect. For example, a glance that was falling unwittingly on the forward arrow was simply ignored if one would not really wish to increase the speed. One could steer left and right using the steering wheel or just casting a stare at another pair of arrows that pointed right or left.

At the beginning, Irina found more natural to use the steering wheel, but once she got used to it, she could go exactly where she wanted with a few glances here and there, sitting comfortably in the driving seat with legs crossed and hands free. There was an emergency pedal to stop the vehicle in the unlikely case of a failure of the guidance system, but nobody ever had to use it.

Irina enjoyed this new game and rarely left the driving to Heinrich, who gave up any competition for the driver's seat and just let himself be carried around like a suitcase. The vehicle's maximum speed was relatively low and Heinrich estimated that in case of danger he could just jump off and roll on the ground without any major injury. This thought gave him solace, given the fact that Irina was always driving at full speed.

Along the river, close to one of the less frequented piers that had become over the years a kind of graveyard for old boats in disuse, Irina discovered a small wooden sailboat, semi-hidden under a clump of reeds and presumably long abandoned there. It was exactly what they had hoped for, because all the other boats of the base could be used only by the authorized personnel. Tapered shapes of tinted glass and metal featuring elegant designs were slipping fast on the waters leaving long trails of white foam, propelled by quiet and powerful engines. Getting hold of one of those dream-boats was unfortunately hopeless as the machine could, in a way that was totally beyond their comprehension, identify the person who was authorized to use it. The boat recognized its master and simply remained inactive for anyone else. A system that discouraged any kind of theft and that worked perfectly.

With the abandoned sailboat they could instead hope to slip, undetected, upstream along the river taking advantage of the breeze that rose from the ocean at night blowing toward the inland. They had first to repair some minor flaws and patch up the sail, a patient work of needle and thread that Irina had learned to do quite well during her long months in prison.

After two weeks of furtive visits to the boat, everything was ready for the flight. No one seemed to be aware of their preparations.

That night, the moon had reduced to a thin crescent. Heinrich waited for the arrival of the breeze from the sea, then loaded the bare essentials on the boat and lowered it into the shallow waters. He started to walk the boat to the opposite bank, away from the bright lights of the base, hidden in the darkness of the lush vegetation that grew along the river.

The base was well protected along the whole perimeter. Outside, the desert took its revenge on the green lawns generously irrigated inside the fence. On the side facing the river there were two guard posts, one upstream and the second downstream of the base. They were considered sufficient to guarantee a proper level of security.

Heinrich lowered himself into the water up to his waist. Pushing hard with his feet on the sandy bottom, he managed to slowly advance the boat against the weak current of the river, always keeping at shelter under the thick foliage of the vegetation. Irina lay on the bottom of the boat, holding her breath. She was frightened. What would become of them if they were caught?

The lights became more intense as they approached the guard station. Already they could hear the voices of the sentries chatting and their bursts of laughter. They were smoking, relaxed. The last attempt to raid the base dated to many years ago and as a result the discipline had considerably relaxed.

Heinrich was sweating from the effort and tension while the boat was advancing amid the foliage with an exasperating slowness. Eventually, they passed the guard station and the lights behind them began to fade. Heinrich continued to push the boat until they were completely out of range and finally he decided to hoist the sail.

The cool breeze from the sea, funneled along the river, took them and let them fly away from danger. Irina straightened up from the bottom of the boat and looked at him with a sigh of relief as soon as the lights of the guard station disappeared behind a bend. Freedom was just in front of them in the shape of a strip of dark water, barely lit by the crescent moon.

Heinrich directed the boat to the middle of the river and coasted there with the wind that engulfed the sail. With a firm hand on the tiller, he put his other hand over Irina's shoulders and pulled her toward him. He could feel her trembling. He stroked her back until he felt her tension getting loose.

Irina hugged him tight with her face pressed against his chest. Her eyes were moist and she did not want to let Heinrich know it. So she kept still in that position even when his lips started slipping along her neck. A sense of safety was spreading like a warm wave throughout her body. Then, on a sudden impulse, she straightened up her head and their lips met. They kissed for a long time, passionately, while the boat, more or less left to itself, proceeded unevenly, barely keeping the middle of the river.

Downstream the river, the watchman on duty inquired of the monitor, then chose a pair of images recorded by the infrared camera and appended them into the message he had just finished typing on the keyboard: "They transited about ten minutes ago. We've got them on the monitor.

The satellite is locked. Everything is going according to the plan."

He sent the file with a high priority code.

A couple of minutes later, he received back on the monitor a short message of congratulations from Rajiv.

***

At sunrise, they had already sailed a long stretch of the river without unpleasant encounters. Except for a wide barge loaded with containers heading in the opposite direction and a small motor boat that had overtaken them. The appearance of the boat behind them was scaring, but when Heinrich heard the cracking sound of a diesel engine, he calmed down. They probably were fishermen returning from the sea. The military patrol boats, with their electric turbines, were much quieter and faster.

The vessel, covered with antennas, aluminum frames and networks everywhere, easily passed them, but no one on board took the trouble to greet them. The cockpit was completely obscured by a polarizing filter and none of the crew could be seen at work outside.

After a few minutes, it disappeared around a bend of the river and Heinrich breathed a sigh of relief. Soon, he thought, the breeze would drop and they would have to find shelter somewhere and hide the boat.

He felt exhausted, but just a look at the delicate features of the creature that was now sleeping quietly in his arms was enough to give him the strength to go on. He deeply inhaled the scent of the flowering shrubs on the riverbanks and felt filled with their fragrance. To him they smelled of freedom, a feeling that became gradually more intense and aroused his imagination at the thought of what the next few days would give them and the emotions he will be able to share with Irina.

Past the bend, the river widened and soon revealed a small village that climbed up the side of a hill, bare and rocky, covered by tiny whitewashed houses, a small harbor teeming with boats, white minarets soaring against a background of electric blue. In the distance, he could see the sinuous forms of the sand dunes, now painted in yellow and rose in the early morning light.

Heinrich squinted trying to distinguish the activities inside the port. He reduced the sail and pondered what to do. Entering the harbor directly would be suicidal: just the right way to finish in the mouth to the lion, so to speak. How about docking outside instead, amid the dozens of boats moored along the river bank and entering the village on foot, concealed inside the crowd? It sounded like a good idea, since a long row of people flocked to the main gate through the ancient city walls of stone that surrounded the village. Women dressed in brightly colored robes and men with long caftans were leading the animals to the market in a long procession. It looked like an important event, perhaps a village festival, from the way they were all dressed up for the occasion. Nothing better than hiding in a crowd, thought Heinrich. He veered sharply to the shore and passed the sail to the other side of the boat, a maneuver that woke Irina up.

"Where are we?" she moaned shielding her eyes from the light and looking around, confused.

"We have just arrived."

"Arrived where?"

"I haven't the faintest idea. But we'd better leave the boat and walk."

Irina looked puzzled, but she said nothing. The boat maneuvered skillfully and stopped a few feet from the shore. Heinrich furled the sail and pulled the boat aground. Irina picked up the few things they had carried with them and lined them up on the shore. There were dark-skinned fishermen, who raised their heads from their networks under repair and stared at them with a look not at all benevolent. Then someone pointed toward Irina, said something in their language and they all roared with laughter. Fortunately, they soon turned back to their nets, continuing to exchange jokes, but essentially ignoring the two. Good sign, thought Heinrich, who had feared a hostile attitude, given the fact that it was dead easy to realize that Irina was a foreigner.

The path leading to the village was not far away and soon they found themselves surrounded by a multicolored crowd who spoke a guttural dialect, fairly incomprehensible, and for sure from an Arabic root. They probably were used to tolerating white people and no one bothered about them. Only women cast occasional glances at Irina.

Now it was quite warm and the smells of animal dung and of the sweaty crowd were strong. Fortunately, the trail soon spilled into a paved road and the air became a little more breathable. Along a row of mats, on one side of the street, were exposed colored fabrics, richly embroidered caftans with gold threads and pottery, copper cookware, kitchen utensils, tools, and all sorts of spices and merchandise. Not far away began the real market, the suk: an explosion of colors and pungent smells. Irina's stomach was churning.

Strolling aimlessly among the stalls of the market and making their way with difficulty through the crowd, they were led by a scent of roasted meat that was becoming more intense as they were getting closer. In fact, soon after they saw a small crowd crammed around a kebab which rotated slowly on a vertical spit, spreading an intense spicy scent in the air. The seller was slicing down the roasted meat with a long sharp knife and was stuffing it into freshly baked golden buns: an irresistible temptation for an empty stomach. Irina felt she was going to faint.

"I have a huge appetite, so to speak."

"Me too, but we do not have money."

"I cannot help this perfume. How about if I ask him politely?"

"Come on, Irina. We have to find a place to hide in a hurry. By this time, they must have noticed our escape and started the search."

"Yes, I know. But… I cannot resist…"

"Then, we must try to get some of the local currency. And the only way we have are…"

"The diamonds."

"Yes. We must try to sell one or two of the smaller ones. It's a miracle that they have not seized them at the base."

"Well, your hideout was ingenious."

"Sure. But it sounds strange to me that despite all their technology they have not discovered it. As a matter of fact, we still have the diamonds in our hands and we may just want to sell only a minimal amount and take care not to be cheated. We should not call too much attention to ourselves, otherwise we will have soon to face a gang of thugs who will try to rob them all."

Heinrich gently pulled Irina away from the roasted meat she was staring at, enchanted. But scents of exotic food were rising all around them from every stand and mingled into one single irresistible lure. They left the square, entering an alley that climbed up the hill. The houses, whitewashed, were mostly of one floor, with a large terrace instead of the roof. Sheets and caftans fluttered in the wind to dry. Here, too, there were mats stretched everywhere along the way with merchandise of all kinds on display.

They explored some of alleys that radiated from the main square haphazardly, until they stepped into a larger street, paved and lined with shop-windows protected by metal bars with earrings, bracelets and gold chains on display everywhere. They guessed they had entered the district of the goldsmith craftsmen. Despite her stomach in turmoil, Irina stopped here and there in front of the shop windows, while Heinrich was trying to peek inside in search of an honest face to whom he might propose the sale of the small diamond he kept clutched between, his fingers. The choice seemed difficult because Heinrich was suspicious by nature. It would have taken forever, if not for Irina who unintentionally broke the deadlock.

One of the goldsmiths noticed a beautiful blonde foreign woman in front of his shop window who was admiring a pair of earrings of elegant shape and he immediately rushed outside. He could speak a passable English, though with a strong Arabic accent. With affable and courteous manners, he introduced himself as the owner. Irina asked him to show her a pair of earrings embedded with precious stones shed had noticed in the shop window and asked for their price. Then he called Heinrich, who was keeping himself in the background, and introduced him to the goldsmith. The latter sniffed a good deal when he first saw the small diamond.

After reviewing it carefully, the jeweler scratched his head and asked where it came from. Heinrich replied that it was a family jewel that had belonged to his grandmother. The goldsmith laughed and explained that natural diamonds had not been mined for at least two centuries because of the exorbitant costs as compared to synthetic ones. The authentic stones had become a rarity reserved for art collectors. Since buying and selling genuine gems had been banned, a flourishing black market was born. In short, his honesty before the law could allow him to close one eye only in the case of a very beneficial exchange.

Heinrich had no idea of the commercial value of real stones and so asked the goldsmith to make an offer, which turned out to be approximately three times the price of synthetic stones as Irina had been told. Heinrich was unaware that on the black market a real diamond was worth at least ten times as much, but he shrugged and, at the end of a short negotiation, stipulated an agreement with the goldsmith at a price slightly higher than the first offer. After the deal, the merchant inquired if they had more stones of the same kind and if they were inclined to sell them. At that point, Heinrich became certain that he had been duped. Nevertheless, he pretended to be satisfied and, flashing a winning smile, he lied saying that that it was the only diamond he had.

"Are you foreigners? Where are you from?" pressed the goldsmith, not too convinced and determined not to pass up the prey.

"We are just tourists. We are looking for a quiet place to rest. "

"A quiet place. Let me think… Ah, of course. My sister could accommodate you for a modest fee. She is a very private person and not at all inclined to meddle with other people's business."

"Does she live close by?"

"At a stone's throw from the village. It is a house on the river, without too much fuss, without too many curious people around."

"It sounds good. Can we have a look at it?"

"Gladly. Ahmed will accompany you."

He dialed a number on his mobile phone and waited for a good minute.

"Damn. Here everything is going down the drain. Our satellites are now old carcasses and these phones are getting worse. Let me try again."

After a couple of failed attempts, he managed to establish a communication and Ahmed, a young and sturdy man, appeared after about ten minutes driving an old car with crusts of rust over the whole bodywork and a smashed and roaring catalytic. Irina took her seat in the back and Heinrich sat next to the driver who addressed them with only a few words of broken English.

Just outside the winding alleys of the country, the car went along a road that ran parallel to the river and in the opposite direction of the base. After about two miles, they arrived to an isolated house, surrounded by tall palm trees and a high wall. Heinrich was expecting something less luxurious. Instead the house denoted a standard of living far more wealthy than the houses they had seen in the village.

The goldsmith's sister, a woman of refined manners in her fifties, was wrapped in an elegant tunic. She received them graciously and offered drinks in the shade of a porch overlooking the garden. She did not pose too many questions and led them upstairs to see the room. It was simple, sunny and with a view on the river. They agreed to a price that seemed reasonable to Heinrich. She asked them how long they intended to stay and if they wished to have some food. Irina, at these words, barely refrained to hug her, grateful.

Their host let them in the porch and immediately offered a basket with fresh fruits, while a more substantial meal was being prepared in the kitchen. Given the abundance of servants and the quality of the furniture, it seemed odd to Heinrich that the woman had a real need to rent rooms to foreigners passing by. Also, it seemed that they were the only customers. A maneuver of her brother, he guessed. Maybe someone would come tonight to see if the small diamond was in good company. Better keep his eyes open. He passed the word to Irina who barely listened to him, totally focused as she was on a delicious couscous of mutton in a spicy sauce, garnished with pineapple slices.

After a hearty lunch, the hostess led them in their room and took her leave. The decor was simple, but the room – freshly whitewashed – gave the impression of being clean. Not least it had a bathroom of its own.

Heinrich went to the window that overlooked a shady part of the garden and allowed a broad view of the river, while Irina was looking puzzled at the great double mattress on a large bed covered with a nice blanket ornate with floral motifs and with many colorful cushions. They had lived for months in the promiscuity of a small wooden building equipped with every comfort that had been their golden cage in the military base. Yet, until then, they had slept in separate rooms. Heinrich seemed to guess her thoughts and struggled to hold back a wry smile.

"Which side do you prefer?" he asked with nonchalance, pointing to the bed.

"It doesn't really matter because you'll have to sleep on the floor."

"I see. And are you really amused by such a mischievous request?"

"I see no other alternative. Hmm… maybe it could be me sleeping on the mat, but it would not be very kind of you…"

"Don't you trust me?"

"Not a bit."

"Well. Then I choose."

Heinrich lay down on the left side of the bed, his hands folded behind his head.

"It is quite comfortable," he continued with a broad smile on his lips. "I suggest you take a little siesta. Outside it's unbearably hot. You'll feel better, after. Come on, Irina. You know I'm a gentleman…"

Irina, deeply convinced of the contrary, raised her eyebrows and looked at him for a while, in silence. Then she sat down on the opposite side of the bed and finally curled up on her side.

A thin breeze from the river pleasantly caressed her bare shoulders.

She closed her eyes and waited.

They slowly opened in narrow slits when the caress of the wind turned into the unmistakable touch of warm lips sliding gently down her spine.

Slowly. Very slowly.

Irina closed her eyes again and sighed.

Paris, four centuries or so after the Universal Exhibition of 1889

Oleg's glance embraced the ancient part of the town. Crossed by an almost dry Seine River and surrounded by a forest of glass and steel towers,*"the Old Paris"* was now confined into a kind of Central Park. Right at the center, the Eiffel Tower still stood where it had been for centuries, kept alive by constant restoration work, rusty metal beams being replaced gradually over the years. Despite all that, *"la ville lumière"* still retained her unique charm. An irresistible attraction for the brightest architects over the centuries, the city had become accustomed to their extravagance, as when the crystal pyramid of architect Pei made its first appearance right in the center of the austere courtyard of the Louvre. That event, and the sensation it aroused at the time, was now the key to understanding the Paris of today: an example of successful co-existence between the ancient and the ultra-modern.

"I'm getting old," thought Oleg. "Soon, I will have to decide for the big leap."

His gaze shifted from the line of the horizon to the garden, thirteen floors below, where a five-year-old child was kicking a soccer ball hard.

"Nothing of this makes sense at all," he heard himself say aloud.

"What is absurd, dear?" echoed a bored voice from the bedroom.

"Nothing. Don't worry."

"Anyway, you would not be able to understand a great deal of it." He grinned, casting a glance beyond the door and meeting a pair of panties abandoned on the carpet near the bed.

"You have so much time ahead of you," he thought.

She lingered on the bed, sporting a pair of practically perfect buttocks, legs raised in the air, swinging back and forth. A stunning blonde, thumbing lazily through an electronic journal.

"No, you will never have the chance to know what it means to grow old, because it is simply not a problem for you and for all those who were born like you. Your cells do not age like mine and you will remain as you are now for at least a century and a half. "

Oleg felt himself as the victim of a cruel joke of fate. Despite all the risks he had run, he had only managed to come one step closer to his goal, but he had fallen short of it. He was trapped into an epoch where science was not yet able to save him.

"I jumped into a time when aging is nothing more than a forgotten disease and no longer scares anyone, but for me it is too late," he thought sadly.

"Oleg, please be gentle. Come here. I'm getting bored…"

***

Dawn was already gilding the spires of the minarets and tinging in pink the walls of the whitewashed houses on the hillside. The dark shadows of the dunes were slowly retreating into the background, while the sand of the desert was gradually getting redder.

Irina was quietly asleep after a night that had left little room for rest. Heinrich was lying close to her, comfortably numb in deep sleep when, all of a sudden, something awoke him. He stood up and quickly stepped to the window in tiptoes. Furtive shadows were moving down there, in the courtyard. Blind in the darkness, he groped for something to get dressed. First, his hand fell onto a silk slip. Next, on panties of modern cut that Irina had learned to use during their stay at the camp. He gave up the search for his briefs and instead found his pants, put them on quickly and left the room without a sound. He slowly descended the stairs to the ground floor. From the large windows that overlooked the river, he could see the dance of distant lights from the helicopters that were probing the shore.

"They are chasing us," he thought.

A muffled sound of voices from the garden brought him back to reality. They sounded like a bunch of men arguing with each other. The discussion was animated.

Carefully, he opened the door to the garden and found himself in front of a half-dozen people sitting on the stairs of the patio. Among them, he recognized the merchant of precious stones. A cigarette on his lips glowing red at regular intervals, he was listening in silence at the discussion between a bearded and rather massive guy sitting next to him and an individual who – by the sound of the voice – sounded younger. Heinrich could see him only from behind. They were discussing animatedly: bursts of words followed by long pauses, in a harsh language that he could hardly understand. The discussion was suddenly cut short by Heinrich's appearance and everyone turned in his direction.

The merchant threw away his cigarette butt and waved him over.

"They are searching the river," he said with a sweep of his hand, "using an entire flock of helicopters. They must be after something of importance."

Heinrich tried desperately to figure out a plausible explanation, but preferred to keep silent.

"Is it you guys they are looking for, right?"

Heinrich nodded.

"We escaped last night from the base."

"Well done. You did the right thing. But why did you have to run away? Are you not one of them?"

"No, we are not. They rescued us from the sea. A shipwreck... not sure of it."

"I see. You don't know, right?" he asked in a mocking tone.

"...we have lost our memory."

"Both of you?" the merchant chuckled, skeptical. "Come on. Now listen carefully to me: who you are and where you do come from is just your business. If you do not want to be captured, we may be inclined to give you a hand. But under two conditions. First, it will cost you a little fortune. Second, if you are two people that they hope to infiltrate as informants..." He gestured his hand with a dry running cut across his throat. The meaning was unmistakable and Heinrich knew he was not joking.

"We are not. But I have no way to prove it and you have to trust me. I can reward you for that."

"I guess you probably realize," added the merchant with a condescending tone, "that we are not bandits. All you have to offer, we could take it anyway. And at any time. You may easily encounter people with far less scruples. Also, you better be aware that your woman can be sold at a good price. Plenty of us would be inclined to vent in a pleasant way their hatred against your people."

The tone of his voice had hardened. Heinrich had no doubt that he was in their hands.

"While I may decide to be of help, most of my people think of it differently. To them, you're just spies. I really hope you are not. Where are you heading to?"

"Austria. We want to go to Vienna."

"To Austria? It's far away. On the other side of the wall. Where are your papers?"

"We carried no papers with us when they rescued us. They have not been able to identify us."

"From your accent I would not be surprised if you were really an Austrian. Do you speak German?"

"Sure."

"Uhm. You don't remember who you are and where you do come from, but you want to go to Austria. Right? May I ask you why?"

"Listen. I understand your doubts and concerns, but I have no way to prove what I say. I know I was born in Austria. Don't ask me how. I just know. And the only way to try to get back my identity is to return to my country."

"You take me for a fool? The guys at the base must have done cross searches and your names have certainly spilled out from their computers. Your story does not hold."

"Believe it or not, no one has been able to identify us. They have studied us for months, digitized all our biometric information, watched us constantly, spied our intimacy, interrogated us under the influence of drugs, but they didn't get away from a spider hole."

"Then, why have you not just asked the base commander to let you go back to Austria to regain your lost identity?"

"I don't like those guys. They treated us as guinea pigs. At the first opportunity, we escaped from the base."

"Uhm… or maybe they have facilitated your escape and now they are tracking you. Before moving into the open we will make a full scan of your bodies to be sure that you have no electronic bugs implanted somewhere."

"In this case they would already found us quite a while ago."

"Right. Unless they are waiting to find you at the right time. Anyway, we do know how to deal with them. We can get you to the other side of the wall, but it will be a long and hard journey. You will travel blindfolded for most of the time and if you behave well, we won't harm you. What are you planning to do, with no papers, once you have reached the free zone?"

He spat on the ground as a personal appreciation of the popular term 'free zone' to indicate that part of the world occupied by the infidels and their allies.

"I have no idea. Can you procure false papers for us?"

"It's difficult. But not impossible. Surely it will cost you a small fortune. How are you going to pay?"

"I have some other natural diamonds with me, similar to the ones we have sold. Apparently they are quite rare nowadays."

"How many carats?"

"They are more or less all of the same size, same cut and brilliance you have seen."

Heinrich caught a glimpse of greed in the merchant's eyes.

"Why not just tell me where they come from?"

"I've already told you. They are family jewels."

"I may give you credit for that. The cut of the stone is very special. I was puzzled when I saw it for the first time. I consulted the database at De Beers. That original type of cut was introduced by a diamond carver in Vienna more or less during the first half of the nineteenth century and used for a couple of centuries later, as a legacy of the disciples of his school."

"Fred would be glad to hear this," thought Heinrich and added, "I guess they have a considerable value and maybe what you gave me in exchange for the first stone is just a downpayment?"

"I don't think you are in the best position for a good deal. You will give me five more stones now and ten more after you've reached the free zone."

He spat on the floor again.

"Go and grab the diamonds. I want to examine them. Wake up your woman. We are leaving in less than an hour. We must be on our way before the sun is high."

"I have to trust you."

"You have no choice, my friend. But as of now, you have my word."

He spoke the last sentence in German, with a bit rough grammar and a heavy Arabic accent, but he could make himself well understood.

"Remember to keep your woman away from my men and keep her well covered up. Nobody should see an inch of her white skin, otherwise I do not guarantee for her. Is that clear enough?"

"You speak German?"

"I speak five western languages discreetly. Do you think we live on the trees just because we are on this side of the wall? We are the heirs of an ancient civilization. A cigarette?"

Heinrich accepted the offer and when the flame of the lighter revealed for an instant the face of the merchant he tried to decipher his expression.

"Shall I trust him?" Heinrich asked to himself as he climbed the stairs heading to the room. "On the other hand, we have not much choice," he thought.

When he reappeared on the patio, the five precious stones wrapped in a cloth, the merchant was still holding the cigarette between his yellowed nails, ready to throw it away after one last draw. They stepped inside while the other men were busy with the preparations for the imminent departure.

The merchant pulled his instruments out of a drawer and examined the stones in silence, one after the other, while scribbling on a notebook. Half an hour later he declared himself satisfied.

"It's time to go. Your woman is ready?"

Irina had approached in silence, wrapped in a robe that covered her from head to toe, leaving only her face uncovered.

"Very well," approved the merchant. "It is not necessary that you cover your face, but I believe it is far better to keep your hair well hidden."

Irina raised her eyebrows and could not suppress a look of defiance. The merchant shook his head.

"Believe me. It's for your own good. Our women learn very soon to keep their eyes down. A proud look like yours, would be interpreted as a provocation, a challenge…"

"I thought that times had changed," Irina hissed through her clenched teeth.

The merchant smiled. "You are right. Maybe I'm exaggerating. Here in the village it would not be a problem. But once in the desert, the old gestures, the ancient habits will prevail. Man's relationship with the desert has not changed. It is a deep bond that goes to the roots of our nature. The survival instinct and the harsh discipline gained over the years will drive our camels through the perils of a hell of sand and fire. But these same instincts…"

"I do understand," Irina cut short. "I will follow your advice."

The merchant introduced them into a small study that looked like a dentist's office. Machines with long telescopic arms and monitor plates hanging over the walls, chrome and steel pipes all around. He sat down at the main console and switched on a scanner that began to buzz lazily.

He asked Irina to lie down on a small bed. A detector head mounted on a boom began a scan of her body from head to toe.

"Good. You clean. Now let's try it with you, gentleman."

He repeated the same operation on Heinrich and seemed satisfied with the result.

"We can set off. It seems that you are not wearing transmitters or locators. At least not of the most common type. Unfortunately, not a day passes without those damn guys inventing new devilry that we cannot identify with this old equipment. I hope you have not been chosen to test some new type of bug."

Outside, two rovers were being loaded with supplies and luggage. Irina and Heinrich took place on the back seat of the car while the merchant sat in front, next to the driver. The others took place on a second car and eased slowly on a dirt road, uphill, heading away from the village in the direction of the desert.

***

The sun was still low on the horizon when the two cars stopped next to a clearing on one side of the road. There, they waited until two individuals leading a small herd of camels were seen approaching from a distance. Not far away, a caravan route penetrated into a complex mosaic of lighter and darker shadows surrounded by a sea of dunes that extended as far as the eye could see. Irina stared around, worried.

Under the orders of the merchant, the supplies and the equipment were immediately unloaded from the rover and divided among the mounts.

"Am I supposed to ride *that*?" asked Irina pointing her finger at a camel squatted idly on the ground. The animal looked at her, indifferent. It sported the typical contemptuous attitude that places the camel higher in rank and status among all the beasts of burden.

"Once you get used to his rhythm, this way of traveling is not so uncomfortable," said the merchant. "But

I am not at all sure that this equally applies to your friend," he added with a vicious smile. Prophetic words that should have seriously worried Heinrich, had he known what was going to happen to him before long.

The two rovers set their way back while the small caravan pulled away slowly, on a single line, heading to the dunes. Heinrich, in his awkward position on the camel, soon began to curse the day his mother made him a male, rather than a female.

Lazily ascending above the horizon, the sun was performing a breathtaking show. All around them, colors were slowly turning from yellow to reddish under a sky of lapis lazuli. Irina watched, fascinated, the elegant silhouettes of the dunes and the restless shadows getting shorter and dimmer. Taken by such a beauty, Heinrich became oblivious to his plight. But it did not last long.

Three hours later the heat had become unbearable. Though bandaged with a heavy harness that protected her from the sun and from the extreme temperatures, Irina realized that she was not going to make it. Heinrich was dripping with sweat. He felt hurt everywhere. The professional camel drivers instead moved slowly, with measured gestures, wasting neither energy nor a single drop of sweat. Totally careless of the pains of its driver, the camel seemed perfectly at ease, even amused.

The merchant approached Heinrich and announced that in about half an hour they would reach an oasis where they would stop and wait for the night.

"In half an hour I'll be cooked to perfection," Heinrich thought as he pushed his camel to flank Irina's.

"How are you?" he shouted.

"I'm melting down. The heat is killing me. How long shall we have to endure this torture?"

"For another half hour. So the boss said."

"Then?"

"We will stop at an oasis where you will be able to strip off and swim in front of everybody, including the camels."

"You are kidding. But I dream of getting rid of this stuff they gave me. It smells of damn camel."

"Maybe you should ask the camels what they think of our smell... Do you think they appreciate yours?"

"Have no idea about camels. How about you?" Irina smiled, winking at him.

The minutes passed slowly and Irina felt exhausted, her last bit of strength fading. She began to stagger, unable to breathe that fire any more.

After climbing the next dune, the mirage of a lush palm grove suddenly opened up before her eyes. Irina thought it was a hallucination. The camels started to lengthen their stride, attracted by the irresistible lure of the water that now could be seen distinctly, glittering right at the center of the oasis. But the refreshing bath that Irina craved remained a mirage: with a parched throat, she could but keep watching enviously the camels drinking from the muddy pool while the water for the tea was being boiled and the air became full of scented spices mixed with a pleasant smell of dry wood and smoke.

In the shade of the palm trees, the temperature was bearable. After a hearty meal of roasted mutton, they all set down to rest.

After sunset, the camel drivers resumed their activities. Irina and Heinrich were awakened from a sound sleep with the grim perspective to be exposed again to 'the torture of the camel,' as Heinrich had decided to call it. The caravan went back on the move and the journey lasted all night, interrupted only by short pauses. Heinrich tried to get oriented watching the stars and concluded that the caravan was moving roughly to the northwest.

During the night, they left the expanse of sand dunes and turned onto a dirt path that climbed over a chain of hills that rose above the desert. It was near dawn when they reached the watershed of a ridge and Heinrich could see what awaited them on the other side: a stone desert marked by mountains that seemed a giant's skeleton buried in the sand. The merchant reached him beside his mount and pointed to a distant line: dashed dark spots, here and there, were running through the entire plain in front of them.

"That's the wall. Down there. You see it?"

Heinrich shook his head.

"See those dark spots? Try with the binoculars."

Heinrich took the binoculars and focused on the closer dark spot.

"It looks like the fuselage of a small plane. Totally burned."

He focused and magnified the image of another dark spot not far from the first. They were all, more or less, clustered along a wide band one mile across: mostly blackened carcasses of animals and scrap of vehicles of any type.

"Old wrecks. People no longer dare to pass the wall this way. But, at the beginning, when the wall system first came into operation, many people were killed because they believed they could approach in stealth and then cross the area as fast as possible."

"Instead?"

"Instead, the satellite detects moving objects on the ground with a resolution of a few centimeters. When the beam that comes from space is locked onto the target and turned on, suddenly everything starts to burn within an area of one hundred meters or so around the target.

"And how about if one moves very slowly?"

"It doesn't help either. Digital photos of the same area are taken at regular intervals and compared automatically by a computer. All objects that have changed position, albeit slightly, by comparison with the previous frames are incinerated by the beam."

"That's why they call it the wall?"

"Yes. It is a modern version of the Great Wall. On this side, a large population continues to live using outdated technologies and making use of what little oil remains. Pollution, overpopulation, poverty are more or less everywhere. On the other side of the wall, instead the western civilization defends itself from the assault of a lesser humanity. But I am sure that, as in the case of ancient China, this wall will eventually backfire on the civilization that built it."

"Once they lost all interest in the oil," he continued, "this part of the world has been left to fend for itself. Not enough resources for everybody: the western standards of living are not easily sustainable on a planetary scale. Therefore, today's immigration is tightly controlled at all possible access points and the task of keeping an eye on the thousands of kilometers of border between the two halves of the world is carried out by the wall system."

"But walls can be bypassed. For example, by digging a tunnel," said Heinrich.

"True. In fact, over the years people have been seeping under the wall at various points of the globe. But eventually they have all been discovered and the tunnels blown up. It is a war that the western intelligence has been fighting for years."

"That's why you suspect they want to use us to locate a new access point?"

The merchant nodded while he stared at a luminous point moving in the sky.

"And now I'm sure of it. Do you see that bird flying over there?"

"Yes. But what's wrong with it?"

"Look."

With a whistle, he called one of the camel drivers and gave him sharp orders. A few minutes later, the man reappeared with a falcon trained for hunting, perched on his arm protected by a sheath of leather.

Freed from the black cap on its head, the bird of prey unfolded the large wings and set out for the hunt. The hawk continued to spin in long and large rounds over their heads, high up in a cloudless sky. But it completely ignored the other bird that was hovering more or less perpendicular to the caravan.

"It has been following us since yesterday. I noticed it when it flew over the oasis. There are basically no birds here."

"You mean…"

"The hawk does not recognize it as a prey. For him it is just a cold object, inanimate. Probably it received the signal from a bug and remained on the reconnaissance, receiving the signal at low power and retransmitting it to the satellite. Let's see if I'm right…"

He pulled out a gun and quickly locked the intruder into the telescopic sight.

Two shots rang out in the dry air and the black dot crumbled into smaller fragments that fell to the ground a couple of miles away. They reached the area of impact on foot and the merchant as well as the camel driver began to search the ground. They did not take long to find the first scrap.

"Here is the proof!" exclaimed the merchant, showing to Heinrich a fragment of plastic and some circuits that had been part of the anatomy of the bird.

"Those bastards! By now they must have realized that they lost the signal and will send other surveillance systems."

"You mean that Irina and I may still have in our bodies some hidden electronic device that your scanner failed to detect?"

"Exactly. And it will not be easy to find it as it is probably not much larger than the diameter of a hair. We'll have to keep our eyes wide open until we can hide underground. We will travel during the cooler hours, but only as long as there is light. At night we would not be able to see what turns over our heads. I had planned to travel at night to spare you the torture of the daytime heat, but I have no choice: you'll have to travel during the day. Blindfolded. It will be uncomfortable for you until we reach the next wadi where we will find shelter in the shade."

He spurred his camel away from Heinrich. A series of whistles and guttural sounds notified his people of the schedule change and of the new orders.

***

"We lost the signal from Horus," complained Rajiv, unhappy.

"So soon?" The answer was preceded by a broadside of smoke, shot with precision into his direction.

"Did you expect that?"

"Of course. That stupid toy-bird would not fool even a blind man. They have shot it down, I am sure."

"And what are we going to do about that?"

"Do you have their last recorded position?"

"Sure. They are about thirty miles from the wall, but now they will watch out."

"Send the insects then: spray the camels with a little bit of electronic flea. They won't notice the difference."

"Okay. We will deploy them immediately."

"No. Better wait for the night."

"But we will lose them…"

"For the moment, they are clearly visible from the satellite, but they will not go very far during daylight and will be forced to stop somewhere.

"Do you think they are close to the entrance of the passage?"

"I doubt that. For the moment they have taken very few precautions. I expect them to make a surprise move during one of these nights. Already other people have disappeared there. If we lose the signal, there will be nothing we can do."

"I would be surprised if they had found the buzzer," chuckled Rajiv with a glint of mischief in his eyes.

"We'll see. With the obsolete scanners they have got, they will surely be unable to find it. But I fear that they will keep their eyes wide open now. I told you that the idea of using Horus was dangerous. Come on, get busy with your bugs!"

The order, highlighted by two consecutive rings of smoke, had the desired effect of getting Rajiv rushing out of the room waving his arms as if to ward off a swarm of wasps.

***

Oleg returned to the window and sat back to watch the boy who was playing with a ball, down below, in the garden. He moved agilely, with fluid movements, already taller than the average of his peers. The long, slender hands skillfully mastered the ball that kept bouncing again and again on the wall in front of him with a staccato rhythm.

"He is so much like me when I was a boy," thought Oleg, "and he is growing up quickly. But it will take some time…"

He glanced toward the bedroom. From inside, a voice even more persuasive than before reached him, repeating the earlier invitation.

Oleg looked up in the sky with an air of resignation. He felt nothing for her. Beyond the physical attraction, that pretty doll had never meant anything to him, if not the means to carry out his desperate plan.

"I ended up in the wrong time," he repeated to himself. "I should have continued along. Perhaps another hundred years ahead in the future would have been enough. Now I've made myself a prisoner of this time and I'll finish my days here!"

He cursed himself once more for not having a second chance left.

"I wasted a unique opportunity. I should have hidden the wooden box in a safe place so I could recover it and continue my journey. I was a fool to panic when the police were about to arrest me. But what else could I do? Had I been arrested, I would still be rotting in jail… and the box, where would it have ended? Maybe taken by that animal, the owner of that squalid inn… and turned into firewood. Damn him. I should have hidden it in a place where no one would have dared to desecrate it for hundreds of years, perhaps a tomb or a famous monument… Is there anything else capable of surviving the changes of the centuries and the horrors of wars? I should have thought about it in advance: identify a safe place, hide the box and then start my journey from there."

He cursed himself once more.

"I stepped into this future just to discover that the secrets of life and death had been revealed some time ago and that mankind is now able to put its hands into the genetic program that regulates the organization of the cells. It is the very program that deals with us ever since we are conceived, that makes us grow in the womb and then out of it, that determines when it is time for childhood to end and finally decides when the adult must begin to run the downward spiral that will lead to replacement by younger individuals. This mechanism has worked automatically for million years, until man unveiled its secret working principles and managed to rewrite most of the program."

It was just what he had always hoped for. Mankind had finally found the key to avoid the most common, but invariably lethal, disease: aging. A "genetically programmed disease" to which thousands of generations had surrendered, helplessly. Mankind had finally rebelled against a fate that seemed immutable, had succeeded to escape the natural course of things and freed itself – at least in part – from its mortal condition. Sure, immortality was still a long way to go, but the average lifespan had been extended by at least a factor four or five compared to the times when Oleg was born.

And one could remain young for more than a century!

But this wonder would simply not work for him.

It was like a vaccine delivered to a child. They got immunized against aging, too. Unfortunately for him, genetic reprogramming could not be done with adults of Oleg's age. When he had first realized it, Oleg had gone through a period of deep depression.

"It's helpless," he thought. "I get into this time, so different from mine, to see accomplished before my eyes what I have always been dreaming of, and I soon realize that I am excluded from all of this. It is a cruel hoax."

He considered the past, the history of mankind and all those individuals who had striven to live, of the many who had struggled to survive and had been forgotten. He thought of the dust, the only remains of the once powerful men that had raised huge monuments to their memory so that the imprint of their existence would not be deleted from the sands of time. He wondered how far into the future their imagination had been able to go. He wondered if they could have ever believed as possible what he had seen with his own eyes.

Sometimes later, he shook himself from those grim thoughts and peered down at his clone who was still playing with the ball thirteen floors below. A perfect copy of himself, he had been genetically reprogrammed to live for a long time, young and in perfect health. The uterus that had generated him had been a mere necessity, a vital cog, but nothing more.

"My God," he thought,"if only that woman knew that he is not our son, but only mine: the exact copy of myself!"

And with a sigh, he turned from the window and walked into the bedroom.

"At last, dear… you made up your mind! I was getting bored to death!"

***

Irina was exhausted. Four days in the desert had driven her into a state of extreme physical weakness. The rocking gait of the camel, the unbearable heat that had been enveloping her for hours, the acrid smell of a sweaty body that had not a single chance to be washed for days, the blindfold that kept her isolated from the surrounding reality and from the comfort of the gaze of her companion, all of this had caused her to fall into a state of complete apathy and resignation. She was no more ashamed even to rid the bladder in public by crouching as Berber women used to do. In any case, no one paid attention to her. Men urinated as needed, without the least concern.

Heinrich was no less tired. His bottom was covered with sores. He felt so exhausted that he did not feel pain anymore. The only solace came at nightfall when, finally free from the bandages over their eyes, they jumped like hungry wolves onto a dinner of dried meat and dates. Then they retired to their tent. Before falling asleep, they barely had the residual strength to sprinkle scented ointments on each other trying to soothe the pain where the flesh had formed blisters or sores. Tired as they were, they managed to make love only once. And it was not much of it.

The merchant assured them that their torture would end soon. In fact, on the fifth day, they reached a rift in the mountain area where the caravan pulled into a narrow passage between two almost vertical walls of bare rock. The sudden drop in temperature woke them from slumber and the unexpected sensation of coolness restored in Irina the hope that their sufferings were about to end. In fact, after a long tortuous path between the walls of a narrow canyon, the caravan came to a point where the rock opened abruptly into a big space. Irina and Heinrich were freed of their bandages and, half-blinded by the intense light, they looked astonished at the wonderful sight of a natural cave carved out in the limestone rock, over the centuries, by an underground river.

Pristine water emerged at the center of an emerald pond. Light filtered through the cracks on the ceiling and illuminated the calcareous concretions surrounding the pool with the colors of the rainbow. Irina, as if in a trance, stared at the reflections of the light that danced on the walls of the cave and could not refrain herself from thinking she could wait no longer to jump into the water. The merchant seemed to read her mind and, with an inviting gesture of his hand, made it clear that they were allowed to plunge.

Heinrich did not need to hear it twice. He broke free of his fatigue caftan, dirty and unpleasantly stuck on his skin, and threw himself naked into the pool of water with a shout of joy. It was soon followed by the merchant and by the other caravan members. Irina, embarrassed, stood on the edge of the natural pool, uncertain.

"Come on, Irina. It's wonderful!" shouted Heinrich, excited as a kid.

Irina hesitated a moment and then jumped into the water.

A bad move.

Her long robes got soaked with water and wrapped around her body preventing any significant movement. Irina realized with horror that she could not stay afloat and shouted for help. Heinrich immediately swam closer and grabbed her by the waist.

"Hey, you. Don't want to get drowned with these clothes, right? Come on, get undressed a bit!"

But Irina, surrounded by what looked like an infernal circle of naked men, judged it more prudent to get rid only of the outermost layer of her clothing. She remained well covered, but now she could swim alone. The wonderful feeling of contact with the fresh water made her cry of joy and she couldn't help hugging Heinrich and brush against his lips.

When – after a long and refreshing bath – Heinrich helped her out of the water, Irina felt upon herself the eyes of the men who clung to the visible curves of her slender body, made even more sensual by her wet clothes. She ran away and took shelter behind a large rock where she changed her clothes into dry ones.

After the bath, dinner was prepared around the fire in an atmosphere of general good humor. Camels were unloaded of the heavy compressed-air cylinders and diving equipment. Two camel drivers brought the animals out of the cave and traced in reverse the long narrow passage between the rocks, back to the entrance of the canyon. There, they resumed the original direction of travel as if the caravan had simply stopped by to take a rest. Inside the cave the merchant was imparting to Irina and Heinrich the basics of scuba diving.

***

"There is something that does not fit," muttered Rajiv observing the images on the monitor,"look here! The signal from the flea we placed on the camels was strong enough until the caravan stopped at this very point."

He pointed his finger to the monitor where a map in color showed the path of the caravan during the last days.

"The signal began to fade after they resumed their travel, here. They stopped near this ridge and left after two hours. We continue to follow their path from the satellite, but at this rate, the signal will be soon too weak."

"It looks as if they have dumped our two heroes," replied the other voice.

"You mean they have abandoned them in the desert?"

No reply. Loading the pipe required concentration and allowed time to think.

"Can you show me the satellite images of the point where they stopped?"

"Yes. But we can't see much. They seem to be stuck in a deep depression that runs parallel to this ridge and stopped at a point where the visibility from above is almost zero. Since they left, the signal began to fade."

"We can't lose them now. Send someone to check."

"But it is risky. They may see us," said Rajiv.

"I know. But the caravan has already left. Flying at low altitude from the south, your men can be there in a couple of hours. If they have abandoned them, they are still alive."

"Okay. I will send the helicopters."

"Send also a diving team and continue to monitor the caravan from above."

"Divers? In the desert?"

"That one is a limestone area and there might be water running under the surface. They may have abandoned them inside an old well where they stopped by to refill the camels. Indeed... we need a map of the prospecting hydrological subsoil of that area, as soon as possible."

"Why?"

"It is still too early to tell. Just order them to send the maps in the meanwhile."

"Okay, boss." Rajiv snorted. He looked grim. He didn't like at all being treated like a child and hated even more that his boss did not allow him to share his brilliant ideas. However, he had to admit that on more than one occasion that arrogant son of a bitch had been right.

***

Off the ground by less than one millimeter, the train was traveling smoothly and perfectly safe at about five hundred kilometers per hour on a magnetic cushion that a few centuries earlier had replaced the old rails.

Oleg was working quietly inside an elegant soundproof carriage ignoring the landscape that changed continuously. Low hills fluttered up and down like waves in a stormy sea. A group of houses, some cattle grazing, a line of trees along the river, the bell tower of a church, strips of cultivated land: images torn apart and flashed to the eye as colored brush strokes. He adjusted the transparency of the window glass so that the bright sunlight would not disturb his reading.

He pulled the newspaper from the bag, turned it on and let the headings of the main articles roll on the screen, as flexible as a sheet of paper. He loaded the first page of the *Frankfurter Allegemeine* and looked admiringly at the gothic characters of the heading, the sharpness of the characters and the high-resolution photos. He still could not get used to the miracle that had transformed the printed paper into an electronic spreadsheet, thin and flexible.

The subtle fragrance of the paper came to his nostrils, a scent of old times. Not only images and sounds, but also satisfaction for the other senses. He slid the finger over the screen and started fiddling with the controls that regulated the roughness of the sheet at the touch. The surface became first silky smooth and then wrinkled like an old parchment. Finally he opted for something in between, but slightly tuned the parameters of the paper, adding a little nuance of sandalwood scent. Were it not for the presence of an elderly gentleman sitting next to him and who watched his maneuvers with obvious disapproval, Oleg would have pulled out his tongue to see if the paper – as he had selected – really tasted of dark chocolate with a slight tinge of orange peel. He refrained from doing so and concentrated instead on reading the news.

Nothing new: an earthquake in Japan, some folk murdered in Los Angeles, an attempt to trespass the wall in Afghanistan. This time they tried with a bus covered with highly reflective material and built in a way similar to a dewar. However, the ingenuity of the designer had not been sufficient and his invention ended up in a tangle of smoldering wreckage and seven charred bodies.

Oleg shivered.

To distract himself, he decided to download a large-circulation monthly magazine known more for its articles of tabloid gossips than for sport news. He flipped the pages, bored, focusing only on the images. Jumping from one page to another, he paused to read the news of the last race of the World Cup. The article reported the account of the sinking of a sail boat in the Indian Ocean. The reporter recalled the curious analogy with the rescue of two castaways which had occurred almost a year ago, more or less in the same area. The two had completely lost their memories. Kept afloat by a rudimentary lifesaver, they had been found adrift by a patrol boat of the US Navy and then transferred by plane to the hospital of a military base located on the southern coast of the Arabian Peninsula. Intrigued, Oleg followed the link to the original article and dumped it on his spreadsheet.

His eye was caught by the photo of the two castaways and guided by the forms of the woman, wrapped into wet clothes. It reminded him of something familiar.

Oleg startled and immediately enlarged the photo.

"I can't believe it!" he muttered aloud. The gentleman next to him cast a malevolent glance in his direction.

There could be no doubts: he would have recognized that face among a thousand!

That was Irina!

Incredulous, he continued to examine the photo at various magnifications, up to the point where the image resolution did not allow him to go farther. The more he looked at it, the more Oleg became convinced that it could not be a mere resemblance.

"It cannot be true!"

Suddenly, he was struck by the idea that Irina had found the wooden crate and she had used it to follow his footsteps. He felt a chill running down his spine. He turned his head to the grim passenger and returned him an intense and menacing stare with such determination that the other lowered his eyes.

Oleg rushed to the date of the article and ran through the math.

"She arrived almost eight months ago. Where is she now? And who is that dude with knickers next to her in the picture?"

He launched a computer search of all the sources of the article, but the track dried up soon. He could find no more news of the two castaways after the time they had been embarked on a military ship.

"I will find them!" said Oleg, furiously typing a series of numbers on the electronic sheet now turned into a telephone at the push of a button.

"Albert? Still alive? Listen, old rogue, I have a job for you. Utmost urgency. Money is not an issue. You have to find two people. Right now. That's what it is…"

***

The merchant allowed them to take a rest until the following day. Once they had restored their strength,

Heinrich and Irina went through a severe underwater training. They made them submerge several times until they learned to perfection how to empty their masks during the dive by using the air regulator. Irina gradually managed to dominate panic and to suppress the natural urge to drop everything and emerge in search of some fresh air. The merchant explained that complete control was necessary because they would cross long stretches underwater with nothing but rock above their heads.

Heinrich too had to struggle against the sense of claustrophobia that took him whenever he considered the perspective of dying like a rat inside a hole dug in the rock and full of water. But, after a number of immersions, he became an expert in handling the equipment and reacted calmly and quickly to emergency situations. The two instructors were doing their job well. Sometimes they even amused themselves leaving their students suddenly airless after cutting off the pipe from the regulator or causing water to enter into their diving masks.

At the end of an exhausting day, they declared that the training was over and made preparations for the true dive into the depths of the waters of the cenote. Heavy crates were unloaded from the camels and a couple of men started the assembly of a small torpedo driven by a jet engine which could be ridden by two divers. In the course of the day three torpedoes were lowered in the water and tested in immersion, one after the other, in the deepest part of the cenote.

Irina and Heinrich learned to ride the metallic animal holding the yellow handles fixed to the rear of the vehicle and sitting behind an instructor at the controls.

A hearty dinner with roasted meat and couscous was served around a bonfire on the shore and everybody ate in a good mood. When the sentries mounted the first quarter, everyone was already asleep. Inside the cave the temperature was pleasantly cool and there was not too much moisture, contrary to what Heinrich would have expected. But Irina had a different opinion and curled up shivering inside her blanket. Soon she fell into a deep sleep, leaving him awake and wondering what risks they would face on the following day.

Their rest, however, was short because before dawn the cave began to come alive with voices and the noise of the activities around the compressed-air cylinders and submersibles. The merchant ordered three men to stand guard at the cave and to wait for their return. Armed with light equipment, they began to test the communication system with the divers. They received the signal in a built-in headset wetsuit, a special model designed to keep the body warm during long dives. A microphone kept them in contact with the base and the other divers.

The merchant took his place on the first torpedo behind the head instructor. Irina followed him on the second one, driven by the other instructor, while Heinrich and the third driver closed the line.

The merchant was the first to submerge. He reached the depth of fifteen feet and then moved horizontally, guided by powerful lights that barely pierced the water. It was dark down there and the light reflected the ghostly white of the sand at the bottom. Spaced approximately thirty meters apart, the three torpedoes moved silently, driven by the engines near at idle. Irina was struggling to breathe at a regular rhythm and felt her heart pounding loudly in her throat. The dark shape of the rider in front worried her and she hugged the handles even more tightly, her hands protected by a pair of fluorescent orange gloves. Small schools of pale fishes darted aside quickly from the beam of light that intruded in the darkness of the still waters.

The column slowed down and pulled by a narrow margin inside a gallery that descended smoothly. Heinrich pressed a button of the instrument on his wrist and the dial lit up with the digital readout of the depth.

Twenty meters.

The walls of the gallery were rough, covered with calcareous concretions, and showed no signs of human activity. The pilots were careful to keep their vehicles well in the center of the narrow gut not wider than five meters in diameter. The gallery began to spread in large curves while the color of the rocks grew darker. They continued for about half an hour when suddenly the gallery walls faded into the darkness beyond the reach of the headlights.

The leading craft began to climb up, slow enough so that Irina could compensate the pressure as she had been taught. At last they broke through the surface.

Following the example of the pilots, Irina and Heinrich closed the switch of the respirator and took off the mask with great relief. The air had the characteristic odor of the caves, an undefined smell of musk, damp and sealed environment. But for Irina that air was a blessing and she breathed eagerly while rubbing off the imprint left on her face by the diving mask. The headlights now were illuminating the gray vault of a huge dark cave with stalactites hanging here and there.

The pilots slid the three crafts to a dry shore covered with gravel, while the merchant began to inspect the cave with a powerful flashlight, looking for something. Heinrich and Irina sat down, exhausted, on a beach of small dark pebbles, ignored by the drivers who had meanwhile reached the merchant and were helping him in the search. One of them shouted something and the others moved in his direction, a clear sign that they had found what they were looking for.

***

A black limousine was waiting for him outside the station. Oleg slipped quickly into the car to escape the oppressive heat that radiated from the blacktop exposed to a fiery sun. The driver closed the door behind him, made a half turn around the car and returned to his position, not less than three meters ahead, at the wheel of the long vehicle. Oleg, comfortably sitting in the rear, poured himself a martini on the rocks and stretched his legs to relax, enjoying the cool from the air conditioner while the car slipped silently through the London traffic. He felt tired and soon started sliding towards that state of drowsiness that precedes sleep. With semi-closed eyes, he watched the driver at the wheel on the right-hand side of the car, a tradition that nobody had been able to eradicate from what once had been the UK.

"They will never change not even in a million years," thought Oleg, smiling.

He rehearsed what he would say at the imminent meeting and figured out a pair of possible alternative strategies in the case where the negotiations would not go as smooth as he hoped.

He would meet the man face-to-face for the first time: a man who had become a legend of planetary dimensions. He was known to be shrewd and merciless. And what else he could be, given the fact that he was still alive at his remarkable age, a long trail behind him paved of murdered victims? He was a very dangerous man, but Oleg was confident that they could come to an agreement because they shared a common goal.

An ambitious one.

Meanwhile, the car emerged with difficulty from the suburbs of London and was now running along the green Essex countryside. And the green landscape brought back to him the memories of the pastures around the village where he was born and the world where he came from. A world so different from the present one: a cage with no possible escape for him.

Everything had changed – he thought – from the very moment science had freed humanity from the gloom destiny of a whole species condemned to live a too short life. Until then, mankind had settled for a progressive improvement of health, for the elimination of the most dangerous diseases and a gradual increase in life expectancy. During the first two millennia of the Christian era, lifespans had practically doubled, but people had continued to age as before. A few centuries later, the scientific and technological progress had gained a total control of the genetic process and reprogrammed the life cycle changing the human condition forever.

At first, when the new technologies were still in the testing phase, only a privileged limited number of people had been able to afford them, at great cost. The mirage of a life where individuals reach full maturity and remain in that state for an average time of a couple of centuries – in practice without getting old – was a commodity that could be sold very well. As expected, there had been wild speculations and a secretive black market flourished where one could gather confidential information on the most recent research outcomes and eventually gain an expensive access to the new therapies.

Nothing new.

Something similar had happened many centuries before with the black market of organs for transplantation. But in the end, such a huge discovery could not be kept for long out of reach of the many. So, when the technology became mature and the new elixir of life available on a large scale, the new techniques of genetic remodeling began to be practiced routinely in hospitals. Very similar to the old vaccines delivered to children.

At first people were enthusiastic, but soon important social repercussions and side-effects followed. Paradoxically the most serious problems were not, as everyone expected, birth rate increase and overpopulation.

"When you become able to reprogram life" – Oleg thought – "you can do whatever you want, for the better or for the worse. It is a natural consequence of any new knowledge: you can use it either to destroy or to build. It is relatively easier, for instance, to use nuclear power to make a bomb than to harness it in a power plant. In a similar way, with genetic control one can create new monsters, develop deadly weapons of mass destruction, or alternatively one can finally solve the problem of feeding the whole world by growing an army of useful micro-organisms – as, for instance, genetically engineered bacteria that continuously replicate themselves and work night and day in silence to produce food – or create entire new species of animals and plants designed for nourishment.

"What was unexpected is that the worst problems would come not so much from an increase of the global population, but rather from the impact of specific individuals, or groups of individuals, on the society. In the absence of a natural limiting factor, they remained active for too long and quite often this turned into a serious problem."

Oleg was well acquainted with the academic environment and he smiled at the thought of what his father might have become had he access to an extra century of life after reaching the apex of his brilliant career. Probably, he thought, no one would have been able to dig a hole even in his own garden without his permission. And this for archeology. So much worse was to be expected in the world of business and finance! An aquarium with a few long-lived predators, getting increasingly stronger and determined to tear each other apart after eliminating all the small fishes. It was exactly what had happened: life had become difficult and social tensions had skyrocketed.

Oleg woke abruptly from his thoughts alarmed by a sharp crackling sound when a boy armed with a slingshot hit hard on one of the side windows of the car. The stone left just a scratch on the bullet-proof glass, but the car swerved dangerously to one side of the road while the driver, taken aback, gave out a profusion of expletives.

"Excuse me, sir. But that little bastard… we almost fell off the road… if up to me, I'd give him a lesson that he would remember for a while."

Oleg made a grand gesture, raising his hand in midair and letting it fall down, as if to say "What can we do about it?"

"The streets are full of these little thugs. They are the consequence of the carelessness of their parents. A hundred years old, they continue to marry, to divorce, then to mate again and make other children. They do not take care of them and let them grow on the street, like wild animals."

It was true.

And the laws that were introduced could be easily circumvented. For example, at a certain age, law enforced an individual to withdraw from his main activity. The maximum age depended on the kind of work, but in general, people retired with more than half of their life ahead and in good shape. For people with their feet on the ground, an extra half-life could be an opportunity to achieve a higher social status and there were many who started looking for another employment immediately. This was allowed by law as long as the new activity was completely disconnected from the previous one. And here, as expected, everything that could be envisaged to circumvent the law was soon invented.

In public institutions, a consolidated habit flourished of hiring as 'consultants,' well-experienced people that had to clear the field for reasons of age. In private enterprises, the title of honorary office became quite common in favor of the 'old lions' who actually held the real power of the company, delegating executive duties of pure appearance to a group of young managers. In politics, after reaching the age limit, one was required to leave the stage and could not be re-elected. But power does not give up so easily, and old people continued to be influential behind the scenes and to strengthen the lobbies and the groups of power.

"The world changes" – Oleg thought – "but mankind remains the same as always."

He remembered as a boy to have seen people who had to work from sunrise to sunset to barely feed a family. Lifespans were short at that time and the elder people were a respected minority for their experience or maybe just because of a millenary tradition. The world that one was given to know, at that time, did not extend much beyond the city or the county where one was born with a few rare and lucky exceptions. Later, everything began to change more and more quickly, under the pressure of an unprecedented technological development and – despite the wars – in the homes of the many, one could now breathe a level of prosperity that was once the privilege of the few.

The information revolution, which took off in the late twentieth century, had woven a highly interconnected world and the individual horizon – which was once the village, the county or the city – was soon extended to the entire planet. But, at the end of the first century of the third millennium, the crisis of the energy sources had divided the world in two. Now there was a 'wall' that separated a relatively large portion of humanity, out of the reach of the modern technologies and with an economy that still depended largely on oil and natural gas, from the other side of the world that was instead running at high speed and did not tolerate to be endangered or slowed down.

Silence had regained its place inside the car that was now moving faster. They soon left the highway and turned onto a narrow dirt road, in the middle of the fields, leaving behind a trail of white dust. The villa was built on an isolated hill where it dominated the entire valley. It was surrounded by tall trees stemming from an imposing high wall.

At the end of the driveway, a wrought-iron gate opened automatically as they approached. Oleg noticed a camera surveillance system and several guys with a disreputable look.

"Here we are. In the lion's lair," he thought.

Two bodyguards made sure that he was not armed and escorted him into a spacious living room tastefully furnished in the late eighteenth century style. Oleg immediately noticed a profusion of oil paintings on three walls that almost reached up to a coffered ceiling. The fourth wall was almost entirely occupied by a huge sandstone fireplace, topped by a coat of arms with the cross of the Knights of Malta.

Sitting in an armchair by the fireplace, a hard-featured man motioned him to come closer, stretching out his hand with a winning smile.

"Forgive me if I do not stand up to greet you. Age plays its tricks and today my back does not allow me to do more."

Oleg returned the handshake and sat on the couch.

While talking, he could not help but study the man who stood in front of him. The deep wrinkles on his forehead and at the sides of his lips, the hunched back and a certain slowness of movement were those of an old man, while his general appearance, black hair and stainless skin were in some ways closer to a forty-year-old man. But the general impression was of someone who was very tired or perhaps ill. People said he was almost two hundred years old. For individuals of that age, the genetic therapy that had kept them young for so long eventually gave way to the burden of the years. While most of the tissues and organs could indeed be regenerated, the nervous system suffered a long-term slow degradation and science was not yet in a position to provide a remedy to it. The individual sitting in front of Oleg was definitely an old man, apparently harmless. But his eyes darted a fierce look that was frightening.

"Let's see, dear Oleg. Where are you with your experiments?"

"At a crucial point. There is no doubt that we have made enormous progresses. As you may know, we started from the results of dedicated research carried out by the army some time ago, just before the Ethical Committee blocked everything. Or, to be more accurate, before they prevented all information from becoming public knowledge. Some confidential sources tell me that even today there are some experts in the field that are induced, more or less voluntarily, to collaborate in some project of which we know almost nothing."

The old man nodded.

"The goal of their research is always the same. Their dream is to build a new type of fighter, a perfect war machine. Their goal is to completely eliminate the personality of the individual and control his brain by loading dedicated programs. Now, as you know, the human brain has a distributed structure and some areas of the cerebral cortex have highly specialized functions. It took centuries to build a model of its operation. But now we have a fairly good one. In addition, we have made great advances with the external interfaces. You can buy today, at bargain prices, memory banks and arithmetic-logic units that you can hold in your pocket and run wireless connections to the neural network. They enhance our ability to store data and carry out arithmetic calculations.

"All of this became relatively easy after the creation of the first chip that connected an opto-electronic circuit to a network of neurons. The next step was to identify and patiently reconstruct the fragments of a memory, of an image, of a tactile sensation, of an odor…

"If the brain were organized like a computer, it would be sufficient to copy the relevant memory regions and you would get an exact duplicate. But the key to the long failures in this area is that we have been negligent in treating the brain as if it were an electronic computer. Instead, the way to 'draw' information from it is totally different. It was necessary to emulate its working mechanism, improve it and make it faster.

"How many times are we trying hard to remember someone's name and, after a few minutes of fruitless efforts – when we are ready to give up – the answer comes unexpectedly?"

"It is true," interrupted the old man. "Sometimes you seem to have the answer on the tip of your tongue but... but, please, continue," he said with a smile.

"Using this principle, specialized hardware has been designed that manages the assembly of memories starting from the various regions in which they are distributed and with the forced cooperation of the brain itself. But there is a drawback."

"Which one?"

"The machine 'dries up' the brain of its memories and in doing so this inevitably changes the delicate spider's web structure on which they are woven. In other words, the complete reading of a brain damages its memories irreversibly. And what remains is an individual that is left with the intellectual capability of a three-year-old child. This is the main obstacle that has blocked our research for a long time."

"It does not seem much of a problem. There is always someone who has to be sacrificed for the advancement of science," remarked the old man cynically.

"Unfortunately," Oleg replied, "the information taken from an individual cannot be easily implanted into another one for an analogous reason. You cannot download the information into another head without reconfiguring, in a sense, the whole structure of the target brain. This implies that the personality and the memories of the host are washed out."

"Again, it does not seem to me a real problem. You can make a copy of the host brain and possibly implant it into another guest."

"Technically it is possible. Or rather... almost possible. But from the ethical point of view, we do have a problem there."

"Leave aside this crap. Rather, what do you mean by almost possible? Can you do it or not? And are we sure of the result? I do not have much time to waste."

"That's precisely what we're trying to understand. As of now we have only partial results that look encouraging."

"Partial?"

"Yes. It works well with children, but with adults there is a problem."

"What kind of problem?"

"It seems that the structure of the neural network of an adult is more difficult to replicate into the new host. It gets increasingly harder with the age of the donor, that is, with the amount of accumulated memories. The process freezes up... and often we lose both the guest and the donor."

"They both get stupid?"

"More or less. Depends on the case."

"That does not sound very encouraging."

"Yes, I understand that it may seem so, but the results we have achieved are still a huge leap with respect to the past. We have shown that we can actually transfer the mind of a young individual, his personality, his ego, into another body. Some centuries ago, someone imagined all of this in a tale of pure fantasy."

"Yes, I remember well the story of an old man who took possession of the body of a young fool. Well, this is exactly the only option I have left. I do not care a fig about ethics. Can you solve the problem? What do you need?"

"This is the last chance for me, too. At birth I was not subjected to gene therapy and now I can no longer do so. So I have little time left. I'm already getting old. We are on the same boat."

"True. We are on the same boat. As you may know, I can help you in many ways. You have only to ask."

"We need new experiments. We suspect that the process gets blocked because we do not give enough time to the host brain to develop new connections and to reconfigure itself. Simplifying a lot, the idea is this: the information transfer into the host can proceed fast until it needs to reconfigure the existing network and when you wish to pour in more than is already there, then we must proceed in another way. More slowly."

"How much slower?"

"We do not know yet. Certainly months, maybe years."

"But is it going to work?"

"I hope so."

"Well. Go ahead, then. I've heard about your laboratory and I know that all this costs a little fortune."

"It is not a question of money. It's a matter of… volunteers."

"Volunteers? Aye, I see. Human material for the experiments. Guinea pigs, in fact."

"They are still human beings and we do not have the right to…"

"Right? Don't make me laugh. Humanity is full of derelicts. Sacrificing some of them for such a noble cause is a unique chance of redemption for them, to give a meaning to their miserable existence. If this is what you need, do not worry. I'll take care of it. Volunteers will be fully consenting, I can guarantee. So you can account them on my conscience, not on yours."

He laughed in a vulgar way while staring at Oleg with a look of disapproval and disgust for his guest's weakness of character.

"I guess it's not a problem for you, old rascal," Oleg thought. "I wonder how many people you have convinced to shove a bullet in their skull, with the promise that you'd spare a painful death to their loved ones. Horror is your territory, not mine. But I have no choice but to serve individuals like you. Unless… I can find that damn wooden crate and get out of this time. Curse on me. Perhaps it would be sufficient to move forward in time by a hundred years and I would be okay."

The old man seemed to guess Oleg's thoughts and looked at him with an inquisitive look.

"It is just what we need right now to proceed further," Oleg hastened to add.

"In addition to that, I intend to contribute significantly to the costs. My lawyer will pay you a visit to define the details. Thank you for coming here."

Oleg realized that the interview was over.

"Before you go, take a look at the walls and tell me if there is anything that looks familiar to you."

The old man's voice was once again affable and Oleg felt the tension easing down. He started to inspect the paintings one by one, until his eyes fell on a painting he knew very well. A painting by Breugel the Elder.

"So the mysterious buyer was you!" he exclaimed.

The old man smiled.

"Do you expect me to attend in person at a public auction?"

Oleg remembered what had happened at Sotheby's. Dizzying offers grew higher and higher until a lawyer representing an anonymous buyer fired a figure that silenced everybody else. They kept talking about it in the newspapers for two weeks trying in vain to uncover the identity of the mysterious tycoon. The readers got extremely interested at hearing the story of the painting stolen centuries before in Vienna. It was found out that the painting that had been on display for years at the Kunsthistorisches Museum was actually a copy, while any trace of the original was lost until the painting had reappeared in London. An unknown guy of Russian origin claimed to have found it while rummaging in the attic of an old building he had recently purchased. As the legal owner, he decided to sell it to some wealthy art collector and the painting ended up at Sotheby's.

Oleg could not take his eyes off the picture that he knew in detail probably better than anyone else. For a moment, he felt again his heart pounding at the sight of that masterpiece as it had happened to him when – in another time and in another place – someone had unrolled the canvas before his eyes at the flickering light of a candelabrum, the edges of the canvas still fresh from the offense of a blade that, guided by expert hands and without doing any damage to the masterpiece, had gently separated the painting from its frame.

He had a clear recollection of the nights when he used to descend into the basement where he had locked it. He remembered standing for a long time in front of it in admiration, and the care with which he had sealed it in an airtight container before carrying it, tightened to his chest, in that crazy adventure that had separated him forever from the world where he had lived until then. He could not believe that he had become so rich thanks to the money of that disreputable individual, thanks to money tinged with blood.

"So I owe you my fortune," said Oleg, trying to find the right tone of voice.

"In a sense. At that time I did not know anything about you. It is the circle of life that closes up. But I'm glad to have given, even if unconsciously, an initial contribution to your research. But all credits are for you, dear Oleg. Good luck."

A shiver ran down Oleg's spine as he heard that 'dear Oleg.' He hastened to shake hands with him and then left the room escorted by the two bodyguards.

The black limousine was waiting outside with the engine running.

***

The helicopters arrived from the South and came to a rest at the entrance of the wadi a mile or so from the cave. A group of well-armed soldiers moved swiftly ahead guided by the satellite. In less than an hour they found the entrance of the canyon. The tracks left by the camels were still fresh and indicated that the caravan was heading North, but it was also evident that there had been considerable traffic of beasts of burden with multiple entrances and exits to and from the canyon. With extreme caution the men ventured into the narrow passage between the steep rock walls. They were forced to proceed in a single line, in silence, weapons at ready to respond to an ambush. Their passage, however, was detected by a couple of motion sensors that had been cleverly concealed along the way so that the men guarding the *cenote* could not be caught unprepared.

Meanwhile, the merchant had ordered one of his men to retrace his steps and to monitor the two foreigners. Irina and Heinrich were sitting on the beach of small pebbles inside the giant cave and they watched a group of pale fishes with large dark eyes that had come close to the shore, attracted by the headlights of the submersibles.

When she saw him coming, Irina frowned. A big man, with a nasty scar on his chin, small darting eyes, dark and thin lips. A murderer's face. He had treated her with extreme rudeness throughout the training. She sensed in him a passionate hatred for western women and a savage inclination, barely controlled, to hurt her. The way he was now staring at her again expressed his aversion, but at the same time an unbridled desire to take her by force.

Irina shivered at the sight of his rotten and yellowed teeth in a broad grin of satisfaction when he realized that the two had not moved from where he had left them.

Suddenly, the radio began to crackle and they heard the excited voices of the men guarding the *cenote* amid the noise of gunfire and whistles of tracer bullets. The man jumped and screamed on the radio in a guttural Arabic. Totally incomprehensible. Heinrich knew that something big was happening at the *cenote*. The man immediately called his boss on the radio and made him aware of the situation, yelling and screaming, completely outside of himself.

"Damned spies!" he hissed through clenched teeth in the direction of the two.

He launched himself against Heinrich with all his weight striking him hard with heavy fists. Engaged in a desperate fight, they rolled over the gravel, clinging hard to one another.

Irina picked up a stone to hit the man in the head, but she was too late. With consummate technique, the man had blocked Heinrich's jugular and made him lose consciousness. With his hands now free, he spun around, slapped Irina on her face and pushed her down. A moment later he was over her, a cruel smile on his face.

"Now you will have to deal with me, filthy bitch!"

Irina tried to hit him in the lower parts, but the man avoided the blow and, crushing her with all his weight, began to fumble to pry open her wetsuit. Irina wriggled and struggled desperately. She bit hard his hand, sinking her teeth deep into the flesh until they stopped at the bone. The man screamed in pain and hit her face even harder. Then he grabbed her by the throat while continuing to undress her.

The stripped-off wetsuit now showed her naked white skin and the sight of her breasts made him even more excited. Irina tried to deep her nails into his left eye, but the man grabbed her hand and twisted her arm so much that he almost broke it.

Now the tight lock at her neck had become unbearable.

She needed air.

She tensed her slender body in a futile attempt to breathe. The man was working below her waist to free her – just as needed – from the wetsuit. Irina struggled in a last desperate attempt, while he was trying to pry open her legs by brute force.

Suddenly, a rush of warm blood completely blinded Irina.

The man froze in a strangled gasp. The body slowly stiffened.

With a kick, the merchant rolled the body to the side. He was holding a long, bloodstained dagger in his left hand and a gun in the other. He had acted without hesitation and, grabbed the man by the head, had slit his throat from side to side.

At the sight of the dead comrade, one of the men grabbed the long diver's knife he carried fastened to the calf and lunged at the merchant. With a good deal of cold blood, the latter swerved to the side and shot him twice at short range. Then he turned the barrel against the last man who hastened to raise his hands.

"I do not think we will have problems, the two of us, Yussuf. Is that right?"

"No, boss," promptly replied the other, shaking his head and keeping his gaze fixed onto the bodies of the two companions.

***

"They got them like a bunch of amateurs!"

The reproach reached Rajiv like a whip and without being accompanied by the usual broadsides of sweet smoke.

His boss was furious. The pipe had gone out in distress.

"We lost three men in there! And what have we got? Nothing. Not even the shadow of those two."

Rajiv did not know what to say and judged wise to keep quiet. As a matter of fact, the operation had been a complete failure. The men who defended the *cenote* had ambushed the team that penetrated into the canyon and two soldiers were killed during the first minutes of fire. Then the team was reorganized and they decided to blow tear gas against the occupants of the *cenote*. But in the later shooting, they had lost another soldier.

It was a disaster. They had failed to capture even one of them alive. Before succumbing, the defenders had sunk the submersibles and now a team of divers was scouring the bottom of the *cenote*.

"They found a passage at the bottom !" cried Rajiv. In his headset, he received the divers who were inspecting the tunnel entrance underwater.

"Pull them out immediately!" the chief ordered. "It could be a trap. We already lost too many of them."

Rajiv transmitted the order by radio and soon the divers emerged, one after the other, from the waters of the *cenote*.

"Show me on the big screen the hydrogeological projections and the images of the radar depth scan."

The pipe was back on and the tone of the voice calmer.

The boss was back. Thinking.

On the screen appeared the high-definition images from the satellite and, overlapped on them, the maps from the synthetic aperture radar. It was a technique used routinely to search for water on the outer planets, satellites and asteroids in the solar system which had been used, centuries ago, in the exploration of Mars. The radar could scan in depth and the images of aquifers were now visible, in false colors – from deep blue to red while the geological background from the geological survey was painted instead in shades of yellow, ocher, hazel, and turning to deep brown where the desert gave way to the mountains.

"There. Look there," said the boss, indicating a blue vein on the screen with a laser pointer.

"Yes, I see. The cenote is connected to a deep aquifer."

"It's there! Look, Rajiv: do you see that branch going toward the North-West? The passage must be there! It is where they manage to cross the wall! Why didn't we think of it before?"

"Aye, why?" asked Rajiv in his turn.

It all seemed so obvious. The passage wound and wound again at increasing depth before joining a branch of an underground river that flowed for miles into the free zone beyond the wall.

"I'm sure they are there!" The triumphant statement emerged from a thick curl of smoke. "And soon or later they will have to come out somewhere. Let's see how many possible exits there are. Enlarge the dial on the upper left side."

Image zooming revealed the complexity of the maze, like the coils of a long snake that wound and unwound lazily.

"Uhm. It will not be easy to predict where they will get out from there. But maybe…"

The boss focused his sight to inspect the entire area within a radius of about fifty kilometers in search of a road, a small airport, a group of houses.

"Nothing. Perhaps more to the North," ventured Rajiv.

"Unlikely. I do not think they have the means to surf down there for such a long a stretch. Enlarge this area please."

The boss meticulously studied the ground until it sought out a dirt road coming from the North and ending suddenly in the vicinity of a relief. Below, in depth, the river bent in a large loop.

"What's there? Why this road ends up into nothing?"

Rajiv started a search. The computer did not take long to return an interesting answer. "There's an old mine down there. The road starts from it and continues northward, then folds to the North East and joins the road leading to Baralla."

"Perfect. It might be the right place. Someone will pick them up. How long will it take?"

"I do not know what their plan is. The compressed-air tanks will take them little farther and to recharge them…"

"Rajiv, do not forget that it is not the first time they use the passage. It may be equipped with refilling stations. Maybe it will take them a few days to pull out."

"Sure. Why it wasn't me to say that?" thought Rajiv.

"We have to get things right this time. Search the whole area with the satellite, around the clock and at the highest resolution. If a snake moves by two inches, I want to see it there, on the screen. Send a reconnaissance team during the night to the mine. And take care. They are likely to have surveillance equipment. Send first a team equipped for cleaning up the area. Had we done the same at the wadi, perhaps we wouldn't have lost three men."

"Okay, boss. No one will set foot inside the mine before we make sure we have cleared off the bugs."

But the boss was not listening anymore. His pipe was pulling furiously now, a sign of intense speculation.

Rajiv looked worried.

"It looks like the boss is preparing a few more surprises for us," he thought.

***

Irina felt sick. She was in tears, clasped in Heinrich's arms, her hands still shaking, her face scratched and bruised. She had vomited a couple of times.

The merchant and the instructor moved the two bodies, hiding them from Irina's eyes and walked away. They reached the hideout where they found the compressor and a survival kit. After a while, the merchant retraced his steps carrying a woolen blanket and offered it to Heinrich without saying a word. With his face swollen and one eye knocked out, Heinrich smiled with gratitude and wrapped Irina with the blanket. He held her in his arms, until, little by little, she stopped sobbing and finally she fell asleep.

The other man had turned the compressor on and started to refill the bottles. Heinrich settled something soft under Irina's head and let her rest. He walked away a few steps and sat down, exhausted, with his head in his hands. He could feel his blood pulsing, strong and warm, where he had been hit and felt a stabbing pain on his right shoulder. The merchant sat beside him and handed him a bottle containing a clear liquid.

"A couple of sips of this stuff should help."

Heinrich followed his advice and drank a sip. The drink, with a pungent smell of brandy, made him cough and brought tears to his eyes, but within seconds a warm feeling spread throughout his body.

"My men at the *cenote* are all dead," the merchant said with a grim voice. His stare wandered into the darkness. "And the passage is now compromised. We cannot go back. I activated the explosives into the tunnel and if those hogs dare to chase us I will blast them asunder."

Heinrich did not know what to say.

"It is obvious that they were following us. When I destroyed their bird-spy, I should have imagined that they would trace us by other means and that the trick of the caravan would not be enough to fool them. All those dead people… it was entirely my fault," he said in a faint voice.

There was a long silence. Then the merchant turned to Heinrich and, looking him straight in his eyes, said, "I do not think you two are responsible for this, although it is clear that it is thanks to you that they located us. I believe that you have been used. But, as you have seen, most of my men think otherwise."

"If they did hide a bug on us, it is unlikely that they can receive the signal from this depth," said Heinrich.

"That's what I guess too."

"But they can easily locate us when we get outside."

"Probably. Perhaps it would be wiser for me to kill both of you and leave your corpses right here."

Heinrich said nothing, not believing that he would. In fact, he was mistaken, because the merchant was seriously considering this possibility. He could no longer go back and knew very well that he would be severely criticized for the failure of the whole operation which was under his responsibility. They had lost a valuable channel to infiltrate people beyond the wall and there would be many who would ask his head for this. After all, killing those two and stealing the diamonds might have been more practical than to bring them along, at the risk of being caught.

And yet... there was something that prevented him from doing so. Perhaps the clear eyes of the white woman? He did not know how to explain it, but he knew he would not be able to hurt a hair on her head. If those two were still carrying concealed bugs in their bodies, he had to invent something to avoid being spotted once they reached the surface.

"Maybe they will wait for us at the old mine. They are not stupid and they will inspect the maps of the subsurface. The mine is the only logical possibility within fifty kilometers."

The merchant had a cunning flash in his eyes.

"Yeah. The maps of the underground river. But, I do not think they know just as well the galleries of the mine. The dry ones, I mean."

He walked away from Heinrich and approached one of the headlights illuminating the cave. From a waterproof bag he pulled out a map, spread it on a rock, and began to study it very carefully.

***

The car stopped in front of a long fence. A young black man who wore the security uniform came out of the guardhouse and peered through the tinted glass of the car. He recognized Oleg who sat behind the driver and saluted him respectfully.

The gate slid silently to the side, the car entered a large parking area and stopped in front of a two-story building entirely covered with green-blue mirrored panels that reflected a bright sky dotted here and there with puffs of white.

Oleg went up to the top floor and entered his office, welcomed by the smile of a young secretary. He sat down at the desk, turned on the computer and looked around. The small company that he owned numbered no more than twenty-five employees. Of these, twelve were young researchers, led by four senior scientists with considerable experience.

A few years earlier, Oleg had taken over the company that at the time was in rough waters, betting on the talent and expertise of the team of researchers in the field of neuro-sciences and opto-electronics. Time gave him reason. Revitalizing the research with an injection of fresh capital, the company had soon registered a couple of patents and within three years, Oleg could report a budget surplus. Now the company was in bloom.

The workshops were located two levels underground. The East Wing, in the lower level, was dedicated to his personal projects and access was restricted to only three or four people.

"Neurotech. Access level four."

As soon as the computer gave him access, the logo of the company appeared on the screen. Oleg quickly scanned the list of files that informed him of the progress of the various lines of research. He opened the one labelled with the name of "Project Evesham." He did not expect to find anything significantly new. He had given mandatory provisions not to store in the computer any details of the project: it would be too risky. The file consisted of a single sentence labelled with the date of the previous day:

"New volunteer being checked. Experiment in preparation."

Oleg called the manager of the project by phone and announced that he would come down to see him in half an hour.

"Better check it out in person," he thought. He began to read a number of e-mail messages and his attention was immediately caught by a short message entitled: "News from your faithful Albert."

The message was terse.

There is some interesting news about the research I have been assigned to. It is best to talk about it on a secure line.

Oleg consulted his computer and connected with his man on a secure line.

"Dear Albert. How are you? Tell me everything. You can speak freely: the line is clean."

"I found that those two escaped from the base where they had been kept under observation after they had been fished up from the sea. There's a hell of a lot of people now who are working hard to find them. They must really be two special guys, because searches are being made sparing no means."

"You do not have to spare yourself either, dear Albert. Were you able to anoint someone to get first-hand information?"

"Not yet. Nobody so far has given any detail. They are all scared: it is classified material. I fear that the bill will be quite high."

"Don't worry about that. What did you find out so far?"

"Sounds like the two are trying to pass the wall with the help of people skilled in these things. In my opinion, the operatives at the base are trying to locate one of the tunnels by tracking the fugitives. They have been searching this area for years."

"Do you think they are on alert?"

"Likely."

"You may be able to get the codes and frequencies, won't you?"

"Very difficult. This is stuff for court martial. I can try, but it will cost us a fortune."

"You have *carte blanche*. But be careful. If your informant has second thoughts and makes a complaint to the military authorities, you will find yourself in big trouble and I will not be able to do anything for you."

"I know. It is part of the risks of my profession. However, it seems that a big operation is under way in the desert. They also committed divers."

"Divers? In the desert?"

"Perhaps there is an underground passage. There is limestone there and water is likely to flow below."

"Try to understand where they might pop out and get a team at ready. You know what to do."

"All right, boss. But it will not be easy to get there first. It seems to me that our competitors are well organized and it will be difficult to beat them."

"It is true, but we have channels that they do not have. I'll put you in touch with someone who knows the traffic through the wall in that area. He can put you on the right track and maybe you can catch them before the others do."

"Okay. Good idea."

"See you soon, dear Albert. Good luck."

Oleg hung up the phone and kept thinking for a few minutes. He made a long phone call to England and then, satisfied, left the office and took the lift to reach the laboratory, three floors below.

***

Irina was recovering slowly. They had to work hard to persuade her to swallow down a hot drink. The merchant invited them all to regain their strength with a hearty meal before tackling the difficult part of the trip.

"It's damn cold down there and you risk hypothermia. You have to take a good supply of energy." But Irina was not listening. She felt dizzy and her stomach was closed. She refused to touch any form of solid food and they could barely persuade her to drink a cup of tea.

They decided to bring with them an extra torpedo, as a spare unit, and hooked it firmly under the belly of one of the other two. With such a burden, the underwater craft became slower and less maneuverable, but – after trying it out under water – the merchant said he was confident they could make it and decided that Irina was his passenger, being the lightest of the four.

Heinrich took place behind Yussuf, while Irina, wearing an electrically heated waterproof jacket, sat behind the merchant. It was the only one they had. The others would feel the bite of the cold despite their wetsuits being quite thick.

They dove one after the other and reached the bottom in a few minutes. A natural tunnel linked the cave to the underground river that flowed deeper below. As they descended, the water temperature decreased and the river current caught them increasing their speed. The two pilots had to constantly maneuver to avoid being pushed against the rocks and to keep their course at the center of the gallery.

Suddenly, the turbulence subsided and the rocks, illuminated by the headlights, became more distant. They were now at the center of a large underground river where they would coast for several miles, carried along by the current.

After about fifty minutes of immersion, the first compressed-air cylinder was almost exhausted and the system of self-breathing switched automatically to the second. The merchant had calculated that it should take no more than twenty minutes before getting to the second refilling station. Therefore they had a good margin of about forty minutes of air, but could not afford to make mistakes.

When the front vehicle began to rise, the merchant pointed a flashlight on the rock above their heads. After a few minutes he finally spotted what he was looking for: a phosphorescent strip painted on the ceiling, followed by a second and then a third one. Past the last strip, the merchant made the engine of his vehicle roar up and pushed it firmly upward to escape from the grip of the current of the river.

They ascended slowly and finally emerged in a cave smaller than the previous one.

The air was breathable and the gas station contained a generator, a compressor for air-bottles, food and blankets. They were all shivering and exhausted. They stripped off their wetsuits and rubbed their skin with an ointment that warmed the body. Wrapped in heavy blankets, they prepared a hot meal and this time Irina did not have to be persuaded to eat as she now felt ravenous. During the journey, the jacket had protected her from freezing, but now she felt tired and hungry.

After the meal, everyone lay down on the ground and soon fell asleep. The merchant did not fear any attack from Yussuf who had been his servant and companion for many years. Nevertheless, before going to sleep, he judged wise to load the gun and hide it under the covers.

The next morning, after a light breakfast, they got ready for the final part of the journey. They reached the main branch of the river and were carried by the current to the North, following the winding path of the waters under dozens of meters of rock.

After about one hour and a half of diving, Heinrich felt chilled to the bone and a slight dizziness. In front of him, Yussuf was clinging to the controls and tried to resist to the biting cold. Finally they realized with relief that the torpedo at the head of line was coming up slowly. The current became weaker and the water warmer as they were gradually rising. At last, they emerged in a narrow tunnel where the rock bore obvious signs of human labor.

They slid their crafts onto dry soil and warmed around a makeshift fire, burning pieces of old wooden beams from the mine. Everyone felt relieved, and a hot meal and dry clothes seemed a dream after the long nightmare in the cold stream of the river.

After a few hours of rest, the group walked along the gallery, led by the merchant who consulted the map at each fork. Water dripped from the ceiling and descended in small ripples along the walls of the mine. As they climbed, the air grew warmer and dry and they began to strip off their heavier clothes.

The merchant led them in a direction opposite the entrance to the mine and ventured with great caution into a maze of rotten tunnels which belonged to the oldest part of the mine and that crossed the mountain from side to side. They had to get around obstacles and landslides that had partially blocked the old steps marked on the map, but in the end, the darkness of the tunnel began to thin out. It was a clear sign that, not far away, there was an exit into the open air.

The merchant made them stop to take a rest. He walked away in exploration together with the other man and when they came back he had a radiant expression on his face.

"The exit is nearby. And it seems that there are no visitors on this side. The entrance is practically invisible from the outside, unless one knows its existence. It is going to get dark soon and we will take advantage of it and take a breath of fresh air without being seen. The temperature outside is still high and it will take several hours before the desert cools down to the point that our hot bodies could be seen by the infrared sensors."

After half an hour, Heinrich and Irina could finally see again the stars and enjoy a light breeze that had risen from the East.

The merchant began fiddling with an object no bigger than a walnut. He connected it to a small portable power generator that had been taken from the submersible. From a waterproof bag he pulled out a handheld computer and connected it to the object. Heinrich, intrigued, approached him. It looked like a big bug, a sort of bluish-black beetle, with long and semi-transparent wings.

"This toy," said the merchant, "is the modern version of a carrier pigeon. It will bring our message to the target, and no one will be able to intercept it. It can travel undisturbed for about fifty kilometers by calculating and comparing in real time its route to the destination with its present location. It uses a fairly common satellite positioning system, like the one that can be found in all wristwatches. No noise – other than the hum of an insect – and invisible to the infrared as well as to radar. It is a perfect messenger. Now I connect it to the computer and download which path it should follow. "

Heinrich was fascinated by the technology of the time, so far ahead of anything he had seen before and he wished to remain at the side of the merchant while he was instructing the electronic insect. But he understood that it would be best to leave him alone. And so he did, reluctantly, like a curious boy being refused an explanation by an adult just because he is a boy.

Once the preparations were finished, the merchant called Heinrich and freed the insect under his eyes. It began to hum, hovered for a moment above the two of them and disappeared very fast through the narrow opening in the rock. Heinrich was stunned.

"It is time to move. We have about three hours to get away from here. Then we will have to stop in a place sheltered from above, otherwise they will locate us with the infrared."

The group marched warily, edging forward in the moonless night. They moved on a rough terrain, but could see exactly where they trod thanks to night vision goggles that the merchant had distributed to all. It was still warm outside and Irina felt her legs as heavy as lead.

By scanning the horizon in the direction of the entrance of the mine with a powerful telescope for the night vision, the merchant had seen the silhouettes of the helicopters hidden under camouflage tarpaulins.

"I was not mistaken. The bastards were waiting for us!"

They crossed the ridge and disappeared from the sight of the mine to the great relief of all. Then they headed north for about three hours until they saw a rocky plateau full of ravines, large enough to make them invisible from the satellite and to screen them from the sun during the day. They camped under a rocky ledge and allowed themselves a few hours of sleep. The merchant and Yussuf took shifts at guard duty.

Irina and Heinrich were exhausted. They fell immediately into a deep sleep and awoke only when the sun was high and the heat had become unbearable. Protected by the shadow of the rock, they had to wait for the sunset before continuing their journey.

The night was clear and full of stars. Heinrich could not help but remember other nights and other stars of the past that now seemed so far away. Irina had resumed her strength and was marching briskly. At that moment, any pain was acceptable to her in comparison with the nightmare of the endless journey into the darkness of the cold river. So much better than fearing that the thin stream of air which had irritated her throat and lungs would suddenly run out and everything would end up in the darkness, the light of the sun never to be seen again.

She shuddered at that frightening memory and inhaled the desert air with delight. A light breeze was blowing a thousand different scents, reminiscent of minute traces of life, of small flowers grown in the shade of a rock and never seen by human eyes. She wondered if it was something real or just her imagination.

Anyway, now she was breathing good air and she felt alive. She was taken by the strange feeling of freedom that the desert gave.

"The desert makes you feel free," she thought, "even though, in reality, you are inside a prison with no walls."

She looked up and embraced the stars that were filling the sky.

They continued their journey for two days until the wilderness of the rocks and stones gave way to sand and dunes shaped by the wind. The merchant was the first one to see the little caravan that awaited for them under the shelter of a rock at the far end of the stretch of sand. Irina realized that Heinrich looked worried at the sight of the camels and gave him a mocking smile.

"Here they are! Our comfortable carriages!"

"Again those damned beasts? I'd rather go on foot," moaned Heinrich, foreseeing the pains that he would have to endure again.

The leader of the caravan exchanged courteous greetings with the merchant and offered a strong and hot tea, flavored with mint. They talked for a long time in their incomprehensible dialect and in the end the merchant explained that they were only one day distant from Baralla, the nearest town.

The caravan made a long detour, visiting a few villages to the West, so that their itinerary would look, to those who watched them from above, quite natural for a caravan.

The long line of camels was marching along. They traveled, taking many stops and avoiding the hottest hours without trying to hide their presence. After a day or so of travel, they saw in the distance the minarets of old Baralla, a town of low houses, flat-roofed, whitewashed. They avoided the downtown traffic – a chaotic bustle of cars and people – taking a half turn around the old city walls. Finally, they reached a secluded villa surrounded by tall palm trees on the eastern side of the city and the caravan of camels pitched into the large courtyard.

***

"Do you think they drowned like rats down there?" asked Rajiv in a cautious tone of voice.

"I don't think so. They have done the same trip before, therefore they know how to survive. But too much time has elapsed: they will not show up at the old mine."

The pipe was off again. The boss was upset.

"Had they gone somewhere else, we would have seen them from the satellite."

"It depends. If they are smart enough and traveled in the desert during the early hours after sunset it is difficult to locate them. Show me again the infrared pictures of the last three days."

On the screen appeared the false-color images of the mine with the date and time overlay.

"Make it go quicker, sixty to one at least."

In this way, one hour of recording took just about one minute to be displayed and one could see on the screen trajectories of red fire drawn by the movement of the warm bodies of the soldiers guarding the entrance of the mine.

Rekindled his pipe, the boss carefully studied the recordings, magnifying more and more distant areas from time to time.

"There, look there!" suddenly shouted to Rajiv, who was distracted and bored.

"When the ground has sufficiently cooled down, we can distinguish pretty well the movements of warm-blooded animals, even small ones like that…" Vincent pointed on the screen to a zigzag trajectory between the bushes, probably of a small desert rat.

"But if I look at the records of a few hours before…" he touched a button and the screen got filled with a bright red uniform color,"the contrast between body heat and the terrain is too low. If we apply an appropriate filter, with a window around the temperature of a human being, we may hope to improve things a little bit. Let's try… "

The image now showed some structure mottled with lighter and darker colors, but it was virtually impossible to make any sense out of it.

"There. What is that?… Zoom it out."

Rajiv pressed the button to zoom out and the picture showed a larger area, still covered with patches of lighter and darker colors.

"Squeeze the filter."

Now the screen had become dark gray, but clearer specks had appeared. With a little bit of imagination, they could be merged together to form a continuous line.

A powerful smoke broadside swept Rajiv.

"Bingo! Overlay the topographic map and increase the contrast."

The image now showed a continuous red line that the computer had traced by interpolation, starting from a series of bright red spots. The background in false colors showed a topographical map of the area with the height profiles.

"Look there, Rajiv! They have escaped under our nose on the opposite side of the mountain, a few miles away from where we were waiting for them. There must be a tunnel with a secondary exit from the mine."

"But, again, we checked the maps and all the exits were guarded."

"This mine is a maze of tunnels, some of which were carved centuries ago. Who told you that our maps are accurate? That part of the mountain opposite the main entrance is in fact the oldest part of the mine. It is obvious that they know it better than us."

"Damn it!" swore Rajiv. "And now how are we going to catch them?"

"We will try to locate the signal. Now that they are in the open, the bug that we have hidden in the woman's body should be traceable."

"We have not received any signal yet."

"It means that they have already gone too far. Define a grid search fifty miles wide and send our flight-spy birds. Let's hope they do not shoot them down as they did before."

Rajiv hastened to follow the orders and soon the desert sky was populated by hawks with great wings (and long antennas) that hovered slowly in wide turns above the dried ground.

***

The elevator descended three floors below. Oleg waited patiently while the system of access control to the laboratory identified him. Finally, a steel door slowly slid open on a hallway from which he entered a small cleanroom. There, with meticulous care, he put on a sterile suit, gloves, and helmet. He checked the intercom and verified that the suit was completely sealed. Then he pushed a button and unlocked the door to the main clean-room. Inside, a console was flashing of red green and yellow lights, topped by a row of monitors that showed data and multi-colored curves.

The man sitting at the console stood up to greet him. Oleg soon recognized his worried expression, barely concealed behind the visor of the suit.

"What's wrong?" he asked.

"It's too fast. He can't make it."

"Is he still alive?"

"Yes. But his temperature is dropping and his vital signs are weakening."

"Always the same story," Oleg thought "There's no chance. The brain of a human cannot be emptied or filled like a bottle."

Once a direct connection was established with the brain of another individual in a state of general anesthesia, the data flow was controlled by the brain of the recipient, which began a series of complex modifications of its neural network to replicate the deeper structure of the mind of the donor. To stimulate this process and make it reasonably fast, they had tried various methods, among which the most promising seemed to be the dispensing of biochemicals that acted directly on the neuro-transmitters. The assay was done by means of actuators of microscopic size, implanted in vivo and controlled by an interface with a computer.

But it was not as simple as copying data from one computer to another. The process of modifying the brain structure was highly critical and no matter how one tried to control it, the result was a stage of overexertion of the neural network, which was followed by an inflammatory phase with fever and convulsions, and finally by a degenerative stage leading, at best, to almost complete dementia or, at worst, to death.

"Did you try to lengthen the time above the millisecond?"

"No, not so slow. We went faster: 10 kHz. However, had it worked, it would have been so slow as to take several years to transfer everything. We are off by at least three orders of magnitude."

"There must be a way, damn it!" Oleg swore to himself.

They had an encouraging partial success, but only at the price of extremely slow transfer rates. Some memories of the donor were indeed implanted in the mind of the recipient and he recognized them as his own, even if this had often caused a state of confusion that created conflicts with previous memories. In these experiments, the 'contact' between the two minds had lasted less than two hours and the transfer rate was so low that the amount of data actually copied from one brain to another was less than one per thousand.

In reality, 'copy' was not an appropriate term to describe the entire procedure under the complete control of the receiving brain. Often, irreversible changes were induced in the brain of the donor. In a word, the poor man forgot almost everything he 'donated' to the other. Almost a century of unsuccessful attempts had shown that it was not possible to carry out the process bypassing the control of the receiver brain, which – via the interface – was 'seeing' the brain structure of the other as an extension of its own and, because of this, it could 'move' the data, reorganizing neural networks of both brains.

For a moment, Oleg's attention focused on the unfortunate 'voluntary' provided by the organization. He wondered if a violent, but quick death (that would surely have been dispensed in normal circumstances by his henchmen) would have been preferable for him.

"In any case he was a dead man," he thought, fighting against a sense of tiredness and an overwhelming sense of guilt. He stared at the man on the console who looked definitely uncomfortable.

"How many volunteers are left?"

"Three."

"Okay. Let's start over with another patient. This time at 1 kHz, and reduce by 20% the administration of NGF-4000. Let's see if we can get at least three hours."

"It will be done."

Oleg spun around and headed for the hallway. He avoided looking in the direction of the room where the two 'volunteers,' lying on two small beds at walking distance from each other, were slowly melting their brains in an exchange of memories completely alien to the one and irretrievably lost for the other.

***

The camels were resting under the palm trees of the villa. They turned their necks as if to shake something off when the first compact swarm of bees flew overhead. Released from the belly of the birds – that had quickly abandoned the field to avoid being shot down after having identified the villa – the electronic bees lowered to the ground level sniffing a weak signal, like bees in search of pollen. The signal came from an underground shielded bunker, where Irina and Heinrich were taken in custody since their arrival.

Now the signal was compared with the codes and identified. The spy-bees relayed the confirmation of their verdict. This triggered a complex military operation, which began by devoting to Baralla the discreet attentions of a pair of satellites equipped with SAR radars that could penetrate the soil in depth.

As the night approached on the city, the special forces took place in the vicinity of the house and waited for complete nightfall. The news of the operation came quickly to the long ears of Albert, through his well-paid informants. The temporary pause to wait for complete darkness gave him time to organize a plan and he immediately flew with his men in the direction of Baralla.

Inside the bunker the atmosphere was very tense. Yussuf was reporting what had happened in the cave, the aggression against Irina and the death of his companions. A tribunal, composed of five members and chaired by an old man with a long gray beard, was considering the responsibility of the merchant and the accusation that Irina and Heinrich were spies. Yussuf tried to defend his boss and to charge all liability on the two foreigners.

"It was all arranged. These two must have been in constant contact with the military. Thanks to them, they have followed up to the wadi and now the passage is compromised. I expect them to come here at any moment."

The merchant listened silently: he knew what awaited him. In any case, he was responsible for the failure of the mission and the loss of his men and of an asset of strategic importance that had not been challenged for years.

For him, there could be some kind of sympathy, but certainly no mercy.

"I think the two foreigners have no responsibility," he said in a firm voice. "Probably some new type of detector had been implanted, without their knowledge, on their body. The scan that we did before we left the village did not find any trace of electronic bugs."

"Do you think they will find us here?" asked the old man.

"I hope not. Ever since the mine, we have taken every precaution, but those bastards have a high level of technology on their side. I think it would be prudent to evacuate the men at the earliest opportunity."

"What makes you think that these two are innocent?"

"It is hard to explain. On many occasions they acted as if they were completely unaware of many things."

"I do not follow you. What do you mean?"

"In my long experience, I have seen at work professionals of simulation, but they behaved differently. I mean, they may have been perfectly trained, I know, but in certain unforeseen situations, it is the training itself that leads one to react automatically and this sometimes betrays him or her. These two instead…"

"Instead?"

"I don't know how to explain it. Sometimes they behave like children. There are too many things that they do not know. I mean, trivial things that relate to today's technologies. Things that a ten-year-old boy knows and is able to use without the help of an adult. And it's hard to believe that they are so good at pretending. It's like… they had grown up in the middle of the jungle. I do not know why they do it, but that's what it is."

"That's all?"

"Yes. I have no direct evidence of their innocence, or that they are involved in this story. I am deeply disappointed in myself for falling into this trap and to have served our cause so badly. I have nothing to say in my defense except that I acted in good faith. I know what awaits me and I accept it."

The old man nodded and stood up, leaving the room followed by the other councilors.

According to the provisions of the court, Yussuf was left free, while the other three were locked up in the bunker awaiting execution. A thin crescent moon appeared, pale in the sky, as sharp as the blade that would fall on their necks at sunrise.

***

The city of Baralla was borderland. On the one hand the desert and on the other the 'wall,' separated the town from a backward world, enclosed in itself and anchored to old traditions. The ancient walls of the old city reflected the bond with the past with the traffic of caravans, the bright colors of the suk and the dazzling white of the whitewashed houses. On the opposite side, the 'new Baralla' was an outpost of western civilization with gleaming skyscrapers and a huge urban traffic flowing quiet and orderly. On the highway that connected to the coast, darting cars arranged in long rows, ran fast and silent, kept at a safe distance from each other by a satellite guidance system. Yet, the minarets of the old Baralla continued to soar in the sky and kept their ancient charm intact. The old traditions of the place took a foothold in the new quarters, where a cosmopolitan population thronged the streets and the shopping centers. However, most of the local people were deserting the western fast foods, preferring instead the spicy flavors of the local cuisine.

Albert landed at the civil airport not to attract attention. He immediately debarked from his helicopter and headed quickly to the South.

"When they will block all flights," he thought, "the helicopter will be of little help."

He boarded one of the jeeps that were waiting outside the airport and the two vehicles headed for the old town while the first stars were beginning to sprout in the night sky.

On the other side of the city, Rajiv and his boss had landed at the military airport about twenty kilometers far from the villa. They directed the operations in person from the small control room, crammed with instruments and monitors, housed in the fuselage of the airplane. Black and bristling with antennas, it looked like a sea urchin.

Rajiv was frenetic and his eyes were red from lack of sleep and the smoke of the damn pipe of his boss. The radio announced that a blackout of the electricity grid was imminent and, a little later, the old Baralla plunged into almost complete darkness while the new town was glittering faintly in the distance, kept alive by emergency generators.

In the almost total darkness that now surrounded the villa, the special forces moved like cats thanks to their night vision equipment. They approached the house from multiple directions and placed explosive charges at various points along the wall.

Irina and Heinrich heard a series of loud explosions within walking distance of each other, followed by bursts of automatic weapons, shouts and the sound of a siren. The occupants of the house had armed a minefield in the courtyard in anticipation of a possible attack. This cost the lives of many soldiers. From the roof, a stream of fire poured on the attackers who had to retreat. In return they tortured the building with shots of grenades. The defense of the villa was assigned to a bunch of men: most of the others had been evacuated in small groups and had dispersed in the alleys of the old city.

An explosion stronger than the others tore the wall behind the villa. A commando penetrated into the breach and began to climb the roof without noticing a smaller group of soldiers who wore their same uniforms. Sneaking through the gate they headed for the bunker. Calmly and professionally, they systematically eliminated the guards and blew up the door of the cell. The three prisoners were taken out of the prison under the cover of four men armed to the teeth.

One of them was hit from above and fell to the ground. Without stopping to help him, the small group gained ground. They encountered a group of assailants who came from the opposite direction to give a hand to the others. They exchanged a quick salute and each pulled straight on his way.

Irina felt her heart pounding in her throat. The hours of anguish in the bunker, awaiting their execution, had exhausted her. Now she was running, scared, weary, and tired.

Suddenly she felt a sharp sting in her right thigh, like a bite of an insect. She stopped to check if she had been hit, but a soldier who ran beside jerked her violently, putting her in gear again. The man wore the insignia of lieutenant and kept up with her for a while. Later on, he slowed his pace, lagging behind the group. When sure to be unnoticed, he cut through the woods and circled back, heading again in the direction of the villa.

At the end of a grueling race, Irina and the others arrived at a clearing where two jeeps were guarded by men lurking behind a hedge. They had available firepower at the ready that would have been enough to hold off an entire battalion. One of them, his face hidden by a black ski mask, pushed both Irina and Heinrich inside one of the two vehicles. The merchant was lifted off the ground by force and thrown unceremoniously into the other vehicle which immediately set off in a cloud of dust.

The upper floor of the villa was on fire now and the crackle of automatic weapons continued unabated. The two cars made their way at full speed towards the coast using unpaved dirt roads full of potholes.

After an hour and a half of frantic ride in the darkness, broken only by the powerful headlights of the two jeeps, they saw a weak flickering of lights from a small harbor.

A slender crescent moon reflected on the sea.

Irina was sick and she was fighting hard against her urge to vomit.

The two vehicles arrived at a narrow dock and, after climbing a steep metal ramp, they embarked on a fishing boat that rushed on to weigh anchor. Once set sail, the crew turned off all the lights on board and sailed into the darkness relying only on their radar.

The man at the helm of the team took off his mask and, visibly pleased, introduced himself to the three with a dazzling smile.

"My name is Albert. Welcome aboard, ladies and gentlemen. Unfortunately, the airways are under tight control tonight and we will enjoy a nice trip at sea."

A few hours later, the vessel reached the cargo port of Bandar Abbas where the three were transferred to a container ship. At dawn, the vessel weighed anchor and headed West.

***

The Bretigny villa stood in the middle of a large estate surrounded by a park of not less than ten hectares about an hour outside Paris. Built by an Italian architect, the villa was not very large, but it featured an uncommon elegance with a triple staircase reminiscent of the late Sicilian Baroque churches of Noto.

Oleg had bought it from a noble family who had built it at the beginning of the eighteenth century. The ancient trees of the park surrounding the villa could not hide the dizzy heights of the skyscrapers at the outskirts of the capital reflecting the golden light of the early afternoon.

After receiving a call from Albert and learning the good news, Oleg had immediately mobilized all the employees of the villa to get the hunting house ready for Irina. It was a tiny architectural gem that overlooked a small artificial lake covered with water lilies, at short distance from the villa. The gossips said that it had been often used by the Count of Bretigny to host his many lovers. Oleg thought that for Irina it would be a great place, so similar to the stately homes of her time and almost completely isolated from the bustle of the modern world.

Albert informed him that, in addition to that dude he had seen pictured with Irina when they had been fished out of the ocean, also an Arabian merchant had been freed along with them. Without thinking twice, Oleg ordered the two taken to the laboratory where they would start the complex neurological and clinical analyses that preceded their use as 'volunteers' in the experiments.

Inspecting the hunting lodge, tastefully furnished and carefully prepared according to its provisions, Oleg could not help but rewinding the memories of his love affair with Irina and wonder what kind of reaction she would have when they would meet again.

He did not expect anything good. What kind of relationship linked Irina to that guy who was with her? And as for himself, how could he explain why he had abandoned her without uttering a word? After all he had done, surely Irina would not trust him at all. And this could be a big problem because he definitely needed her to retrieve the wooden crate.

With a cramp in his stomach, he imagined that the case had been destroyed during one of the many wars that had been fought since his departure. In that case, nothing else would be left for him than to wait for a few years, finish the experiments and eventually transfer his mind into the body of the young clone.

"I wonder how Irina managed to find the magic box," he asked himself, "She must have taken care to hide it in a safe place before making use of it."

He cursed himself for not having done the same. Actually, he had thought about this possibility long ago and had formulated a plan to hide the crate before his departure. But he had the police after him and not enough time for that.

Now the best strategy would be to pretend to be still in love with Irina and to try to re-establish a relationship of trust as they had when they were together.

It would not be easy. But he thought he knew what to do with her.

***

This time the roles were in reverse order.

Rajiv was standing quiet, lying on a chair placed in a strategic position under the blades of the fan that hung over his head from the ceiling. He enjoyed the air flow and the calm that followed the disappointment of the defeat. The breath of the air cooled his skin, seeping into his nostrils, fresh and odor-free. This just because the boss was so frustrated that he did not have any inclination to light his pipe.

"They escaped from under our nose! So much for our special forces."

Rajiv nodded.

"The Arabian guy who accompanied them could have been a mine of information. And I had not finished yet with those two!"

"At least we have found the passage under the wall and got rid of quite a number of those bastards," ventured Rajiv.

"We should have captured at least one alive. Most of them escaped free before the attack. Those who defended the villa to the end were all killed or committed suicide before being captured: too bad."

Rajiv looked up to the heavens and judged wise not to open his mouth. Then he said, "If it were not for that traitor…"

"Where is he now?"

"Under arrest, waiting for the court martial. He is in poor conditions after a little… busy interview."

"Unbelievable. A lieutenant of the special forces who has been corrupted not by only one, but even by two separate organizations apparently unrelated to each other."

"They offered him a lot of money. Flesh is weak."

"Have you found out who he is?"

"Yes and no. We know that he sold the identification codes of the bug that we had implanted on the woman to a certain guy known as Albert. He is a professional, a man without scruples who sells to the highest bidder. But he does his job well. We have placed an alert on the global research network, but I am ready to eat my hat if they can find him."

"And the others? Who are they?"

"I would like to know. The mode of contact, the method of payment and other details that have emerged from the interrogation, everything suggests that it must be a civilian, some kind of amateur. Well loaded with money."

"But for what purpose? Why so much interest in those three?"

"About that the lieutenant knows absolutely nothing. And I am inclined to believe him because in the last part of his interrogation he looked quite willing to tell anything. He was eager to end it…"

"You are always the same rude villain."

Rajiv shrugged and smirked, flattered.

"Can we track them down?"

"No, we can't. By this time Albert has deactivated the buzzer. But… "

"But what?"

"The lieutenant told us he used a sting to place a new bug on the woman as per the orders of the second contractor."

"Which, of course, was smart enough not to provide him the codes."

"Of course."

"Not bad for an amateur. This means that they are able to track them down, while we are out of the game."

Rajiv did not find anything intelligent to argue and devoted himself to improve his position on the chair, adding a pillow under his back.

***

The cars arrived in Bretigny at around two in the morning.

Irina passed a quiet night thanks to a sedative and woke up when the sun was already high. A soft light filtered through the linen curtains that surrounded her four-poster bed. She pulled them just enough to peep out and began to study the room.

Illuminated by two large checkered windows painted in white and separated by an elegant fireplace of pink granite, the room was furnished in the late eighteenth century style with a large golden mirror directly opposite the bed. For a moment Irina had the illusion of having rejoined her old days, but the distant sight of the gleaming skyscrapers through the window left no doubt about it. She vaguely remembered having dumped herself on the bed soon after her arrival, drained off of all energies. But now she could not locate the long tunic she had tugged off on the carpet the night before, the same one she was wearing in Baralla. Maybe someone had taken it away. Would she find something to get dressed?

She looked around, suspicious and uncertain about what to do. Then she took courage and slipped out from the protective curtains of the bed and ventured into the bathroom which could be accessed from inside the room, a small door being well disguised on the wall at the head of the bed. She locked herself inside and relaxed for a long time under the warm water of the shower. Feeling dry and clean after the refreshing bath, she observed her slender body reflected at various angles by the mirrors of the bathroom with a critical eye.

She then studied the wide assortment of cosmetics that were waiting for her, aligned in neat rows on a bean-shaped dressing table covered with lace and gauze and equipped with a concave mirror for makeup. Not at all satisfied by her face that looked tired and dehydrated, she was disappointed in discovering new tiny wrinkles here and there. Annoyed, she engaged in a work of careful restoration that took her almost half an hour. Inside a drawer in the bedroom, she found what she was looking for. She was surprised to find underwear of her size and an assortment of clothes in the closet. She chose a tailleur of modern cut, simple, no frills, and put it on. It fitted as if it had been cut for her by a tailor: white with a stylish thin black edge that fringed an elegant jacket complemented by a knee-length skirt.

"A little too short," she thought looking at the skirt and starting a thorough inspection of the others available. Eventually, she gave up and decided for the one she had chosen first, since they were all more or less cut the same way: too short for her tastes. Then she lingered for a long while in the choice of the shoes. She tried them all and found that only in one case they were slightly wide, perfectly fitting otherwise. She discarded those with too high heels and eventually she decided on a pair that matched well with the dress. She approved the final result in the large mirror and decided to leave.

She cautiously pulled the door of the bedroom ajar and peered out. A long corridor led to a well-lit large lounge from which she could hear what sounded like masculine voices. She took her courage in both hands and walked on tiptoe to the hall where a round table tastefully adorned with elegant bouquets of assorted flowers had been prepared for breakfast.

Albert, with his enhanced sensitivity gained after years of training, became immediately aware that someone was coming along and stepped forward to meet her, smiling.

"Good morning, madam. Did you sleep well?"

The other man, tall and raven-haired, was looking in the opposite direction and she could see him only from behind. When he slowly turned his head, Irina let out a cry of astonishment.

"Oleg, you... here?"

"Welcome, Irina. I've been waiting long for you."

***

Heinrich's awakening was not as comfortable. Still groggy from the sedatives they had administered to him the night before and afflicted by a severe headache, he found himself in a very narrow room with no windows that reminded him of a hospital. In fact, a dominant white color was shared by the walls, the furniture and even by the security door. The latter lacked the traditional peephole that had been replaced by a system of micro-cameras embedded in the ceiling and impossible to reach. Heinrich looked around unhappy, his empty stomach rumbling.

Half an hour later, the door opened and two strong individuals wearing green nursing gowns entered the room. Without saying a word they waved him to follow them and led him to a treatment room where a doctor was waiting.

"Good morning, Herr Mayer," he greeted him in German with a strong French accent.

"Where am I? Who are you?" replied Heinrich in the same language.

The other one did not flinch at all and continued the conversation in German in a calm voice showing a good proficiency of the language, though with a terrible accent.

"I am here to help you. I'm sorry we have to hold your breakfast, because first we have to do some medical analysis. It will take a short time. After, I promise you that you will have a hearty breakfast."

"Medical tests? Why? I'm fine."

"Sure. That's just what we want to check. In your own interest. Now if you will…" And he shook in his hand a tourniquet for a blood test. Heinrich let him do it and patiently endured a series of exams.

They laid him on a bed that slid slowly into the belly of a complicated machinery of a cylindrical shape that buzzed lazily. The scan lasted only a few minutes and he did not feel any pain. Then they fit his head into a kind of helmet connected to a machine and asked him to recognize images and sounds. They also asked him to make an effort to remember the face of his mother, the church where he went to mass as a child, the voice of his kindergarten teacher.

Finally, they brought him back to his room where a small white cart was waiting for him with a very generous breakfast.

Heinrich thought he had been taken in custody by a military unit and was being held in one of their bases for the necessary examinations. He felt restless at being separated from Irina and distressed about what they could do to both. He asked several times about Irina and the merchant, but he was given no answer, no explanation. They just told him that he had to press a button to call the nurse when he needed the bathroom. They brought books and magazines and regularly served decent meals.

The speakers on the ceiling were broadcasting music all the time, mostly classical music. The volume was too high and it bothered him. He asked the nurse several times to lower it, but to no avail. A particularly disturbing fact was that, at times, he seemed to hear lamentations or even cries of pain coming from a room nearby.

The following day the doctor came back. He reassured him by saying that the medical tests were good, but that soon he would have to undergo a minor surgery, under local anesthesia, to remove the electronic bug that had been implanted into his body. No need to worry.

Despite the doctor's take-it-easy advice, during the night, Heinrich had a strange dream. Irina was walking dangerously close to a precipice without being in the least aware of the danger and oblivious to the warnings of Heinrich. For some reason, despite his best efforts, something was holding him and prevented him from grabbing Irina while she mocked him, laughing merrily while getting closer and closer to the edge of the ravine. Heinrich awoke with a start, soaked in sweat, and he thought he had heard a scream. He listened, and listened again.

The music was turned off.

Shortly after, he heard muffled groans, as if someone was in delirium. Later, he heard hurried footsteps in the hallway and people bustling in the nearby room for about an hour. Then, the creak of a metal cart being slid away.

Silence.

Heinrich spent the rest of the night guessing what had happened. As sleep refused to come, he started thinking about his whereabouts and what the future held for him and Irina.

That night he could not sleep at all.

***

Oleg was now in front of her. Irina studied him with a critical eye. He looked more mature, more confident of himself, which made him even more fascinating than she remembered. His eyes, of a deep blue, were the same, but now they had a look as hard as ice.

Albert took the hint that his presence was inopportune. With an excuse he departed reluctantly giving up the breakfast. Oleg and Irina sat down at the table in an awkward silence.

"You are more beautiful than ever," he said sincerely.

Irina replied with a cold smile. She sat without saying a word and taking no food.

"Let me tell you how you got here, Irina. I happened to see you in a magazine and learned that you had been fished up from the Indian Ocean. So I instructed Albert to find out where you ended up. He did his job well. If it was not for him, I'm afraid you'd have come to a bad end."

"Many thanks, Albert." Irina said flatly, her eyes focused on the cup. She filled it with milk, then added black coffee and a lump of sugar.

"I see you are in a bad mood with me."

Irina ignored him and devoted herself to slowly butter a slice of bread and cover it with a generous layer of blueberry jam. The stress of the last few days made her ravenous, but she controlled herself and just took more bread and a plate of fresh fruit.

"I left you for a reason."

"Oh, really? And that is?" Irina raised an eyebrow, her eyes kept focused on the systematic work she was busy at.

"I did not want to die in that ridiculous epoch. And it was too dangerous to take you with me."

She incinerated him with a glance. "As you can see, I am still in one piece. So it is not as dangerous as it may sound."

"How could I know?"

"Stop this nonsense, Oleg. You've tugged me down like an old blanket. You left me without a word, and you left me in big trouble with the police. Do you have any vague recollection of that picture of Breugel the Elder, which…"

"Yes, I do. I made a mistake. I just wanted to protect you with my disappearance. Which trouble? With the police?"

"Which trouble, he says. Just a few years in prison to begin with, and they would have been more if…" She bit her tongue, "if I someone had not helped me to escape."

"Who helped you? The guy you have been rescued with? Mayer, I'm told. Is he your new lover?"

"You seem well informed. His name is Heinrich and he is a good man. Quite the opposite of you who, so I'm told, are now in good company with mercenaries and killers. As for the last question, it is no longer your concern since a long time ago."

Oleg realized he had started on the wrong foot and tried to step back.

"You're right, I apologize," he said with a sad look and downcast eyes. "I could not imagine that you would have been involved in the story of the paintings. They must have reported you to the police. They were indeed dangerous people and they blackmailed me. Do you remember when burglars broke into our house and messed everything up? It was a warning. After that, I was really scared that they could kidnap and hurt you. I thought that once I had left they would leave you in peace. But probably they hoped that by reporting you to the police they could find a way to get the paintings back."

"What kind of people were you dealing with? And why?"

"They were from the underworld. I had commissioned them to carry out the theft of some famous paintings. I thought – and I was right about that – that by bringing the paintings with me I could make a fortune. I paid them as per our agreement, but their greed had no limit. They began to blackmail me. Later, they turned to threats. The day before my escape they had a silver bullet delivered to me: a rather explicit message. Believe me, Irina, I was terrified."

"Do not even think for a moment that I will buy this crap so easily. If things between us had gone as they used to in the past and you had told me everything I would have been so… so damned stupid as to help you, as I have done so many times. But, by that time you were no longer interested in me. You were seldom at home spending most of your time with your lovers."

"Nonsense. I spent most of my time with Anselmo. There was someone who repeatedly tried to get in touch with him and I have never understood…"

"I do *not* care a fig about that. You betrayed my trust and you were gone, knowing very well that I would never see you again. To me, you're as good as dead. I just regret to having suffered so long in jail thinking of you. It was absolutely not worth my while."

"Don't be unfair, Irina. How did you find the crate?"

Irina told him, omitting some details and without mentioning Fred at all.

"Where is it now?"

"I do not have the faintest idea. Maybe it has been disposed of as firewood. In prison it was bitterly cold."

Oleg shuddered.

"What's up, Oleg? Do you want to leave again?"

Her eyes blazed. All the love she had once for him had turned into resentment.

"Unfortunately I chose the wrong time to stop by. I had to go farther. Here I have no chance."

"Chance for what? To live longer and do harm to even more people? You spoilt your happiness and mine, you have missed the opportunity that life had given to you and me just to follow a mirage. Poor Oleg: I sincerely pity you."

A heavy silence fell between them. Oleg got up slowly and walked to a window where he kept staring at the horizon.

"I was hoping you would make things easier, Irina. But I see that there is no way to argue with you. So, we'll do it in another way. I need that box and you and your boyfriend will help me to find to it, whether you like it or not."

"Here you are. Now you dropped your mask, revealing your true face. I'll give you some advice, Oleg: do not lift a finger against Heinrich. Where are you keeping him?"

"You are definitely not in a position to dictate your conditions. Nor your friend. Do you want to see him? Milady will be immediately satisfied."

Oleg pressed a remote-control button and one of the paintings that adorned the salon changed its appearance. Instead of the image of a precious oil painting by Turner, the view of a cramped little room appeared on the screen showing a bed where a man was reading a book."

"There is your friend. Apparently he is killing his time going through some literature."

"You weird son of a bitch! What have you done to him?"

"For the moment, nothing. It depends on how much you choose to be cooperative."

Irina, furiously grabbed the nearest porcelain bowl and threw it in his direction aiming right at his face. She just missed him by a few inches.

"Oh, madame is warming up. When you do that, you look even more attractive."

Irina, baring her teeth, grabbed a knife, but Oleg grabbed her wrist and held her. With the result of getting a fierce bite in the back of his hand and a kick in the groin:

a self-defense counter-measure which apparently came naturally to Irina.

"Damn you!" cursed Oleg, curling up in pain. "You will pay dearly for this!"

Irina, in tears, resisted the urge to run away down the hall. She was afraid for Heinrich. They were in the hands of a monster who could do what he wished of them. How could she have loved him for so long? How could one be so blind?

"Oleg. Look. All this makes no sense: neither I nor Heinrich know where the box is now. Even if we wanted to, we could not help you."

"We'll see..." moaned Oleg with a thin voice.

***

Albert entered Oleg's office at NeuroTech with a smug air of himself. It was payday and Albert was going to leave that very night.

"You did a great job, Albert. Here's the receipt of the bank transfer to your account. You cost me a fortune!"

"Boss, I told you that I needed to grease the palms of a lot of people and, basically, what is left after deducting all expenses is by far less than my usual standards."

"Here we go," thought Oleg, who already imagined his next move.

"Spit it out, Albert. How much more do you want?"

"Nothing, boss. Only, I'd like you to notice that the Arabian guy is a great danger for you. Our friends would give an eye just to lay hands on him. It is a potential goldmine of information on the traffic through the wall and I think they're biting their hands for having allowed him to escape. I really hope they don't become aware that you are keeping him here."

Oleg read a veiled threat in Albert's words. He knew he would not hesitate a moment to betray him.

"Acute observation, dear Albert. However, it is better for you to go as soon as possible because I am sure that, by this time, they will know exactly who has messed them up and they will hunt him down."

"Right, boss. Precisely for this reason, I was wondering what could persuade them to settle down?"

"Trading you against the Arabian guy, for example? For them, he is by far more interesting than you are, so they could make a good deal and will leave you quiet."

"Exactly." Albert pointed out with a smirk.

"What guarantees can you give me, dear Albert, that later on you will not try to extort me with something else?"

"Just professional ethics, by God. Had I not learned yet when it's time to give up, I would not be still in one piece after all these years. Come on, boss. I do deserve just a bit of your trust!"

"We have a deal, then. You take away the Arabian guy and, after everything has settled down, you will get unlocked the second half of your payment," smiled Oleg.

"I see. We just can't trust anybody nowadays. The receipt looked authentic. Please explain to me how this magician's trick works."

"Everyone has his own professional secrets, Albert. But do not worry, half of the total amount is available as of now. Perhaps, though, you'd better make sure…"

"It is not necessary. I have good reasons to trust you."

He looked at him spelling an unspoken sentence that Oleg read, literally, as 'otherwise I'll kill you.'

"Well," concluded Oleg, standing up and shaking his hand, "the Arabian is ready in the hall near the main entrance and you can take him away at your convenience."

"So, you expected that, right? Old fox."

"Coming from your side, I consider that as a compliment. Good-bye, Albert. And keep your eyes open!"

Sometime later, a black van equipped with reflective glass hiding the interior of the vehicle pulled away from the main gate. The merchant was lying semi-unconscious in the rear of the van under the influence of a powerful sedative. A black sport car followed the van.

Albert was driving. Alone.

The two cars covered a stretch of road together, then Albert's car swerved in another direction, heading for the airport. On the runway a private plane was waiting for him. Once on board, it immediately took off in the direction of London.

***

Anxious to have a face-to-face meeting with him, Oleg called the lab on the intercom and ordered them to get

Mayer ready for the interview. He took his time and finished reading his e-mail. Then he entered the elevator to the underground lab.

Heinrich was in a small room, sitting on a multi-function chair. Everything around looked like the office of a dentist: the spotlight that shone mercilessly on his face, the smell of disinfectant, the console in front of him bristling with metal probes. It did not look very reassuring.

Immobilized in the uncomfortable position of someone who is going to a get a tooth drilling, Heinrich had both his wrists and ankles tied to the chair. Oleg, towering over him, studied his face for a long time without saying a word. Heinrich squinted to be able to see him, which was difficult because he was dazzled by the strong light.

"Dr. Mayer, I presume," Oleg finally said, in German, in a mocking tone. The strong French-Swiss accent from Geneva area was not unnoticed by Heinrich, who replied to him in French.

"To whom do I have the pleasure?"

"My name is Oleg," he replied in the same language, "and I am a good friend of Irina. You've no doubt heard of me."

"Oleg, the magician. Of course: I have heard a lot about you. Now, if you will oblige me so that I get rid of these bracelets, I will be happy to make your acquaintance."

"Unfortunately," grinned Oleg, "your impulsive nature prevents me from meeting your understandable desire. But please: relax. After all, these chairs automatically adapt to the body and are very comfortable."

"You have no right to keep me here as a prisoner."

"You should thank me, instead. If it were not for our intervention, I fear that you would not have your head still attached to the neck…"

"What did you do to Irina? What do you want from us?"

"Don't worry. Irina is my welcome guest in a lovely place. Fear not, she has everything to make herself comfortable. I am sorry for you that you do not find this workshop equally comfortable."

"Let's cut short with this pleasantry. Let's come to the point. Why do you keep me here?"

"Because I hope for your cooperation."

Oleg checked that all the microphones and the cameras were turned off. They were going to talk about things that nobody else, except Irina, should be aware of.

"Good. Here is the point. Where did you hide the wooden box?"

"Is that all?" asked Heinrich.

"That's all. I have no interest in keeping either you or Irina here. I need the box because I want to leave. Let's try to help each other…"

"Thank you for your frankness, but unfortunately it not so simple."

Heinrich told him how he happened to see the wooden case for the first time at Stahl's shop, how he met Irina in prison and organized her escape with the help of Fred.

"Who is this Friedrich?"

"One of my classmates and a skilled carver of precious stones."

He told him of the dissection of the small bluish sphere and its microscopic analysis.

Oleg listened in silence, clearly interested.

"What do you think? I know you are a man of science," said Oleg, with a voice less arrogant and more respectful.

"At the time, I did not understand any of it. Based, however, on what I have been able to learn about the progress of modern technology, I would say that it looks like a device based on high-definition opto-electronic circuits. But the substrate does not look like one of those that are normally used, such as silicon."

"In fact it is not." Oleg smiled for the first time. "It is more likely a material that does not exist in nature. It is obtained by assembling 'artificial atoms,' according to a very complex scheme. Such things are now perfectly possible, I mean, in the epoch in which we find ourselves."

"But who could be able to do these things at the time of the Roman Empire?"

The academic nature of Oleg took over and he told him of the excavation of Herculaneum and the mysterious discovery. All of it matched perfectly with what Heinrich had reconstructed by reading the notebooks that he had found in Vienna and that related to the archaeological campaign of Herculaneum.

"Did you find offerings nearby the skeletons?" asked Heinrich.

"Yes. Everything suggests that the two of them were worshipped as gods."

"I'm not surprised. Maybe sometimes they made their appearance using those tricks that you know quite well. In those days, much less would have been enough to be worshipped as gods. But, apparently, they were not, because they were caught by the eruption. The glowing cloud moved at an impressive speed down the flanks of Mount Vesuvius and it did not give them enough time to escape."

"Yes, I also think it happened that way. However, it remains a mystery who they were and how they could be in possession of a technology that, even at the present time, is still unknown."

"One more reason for you to try to move forward, to move to a more distant future. But may I ask you if this is the only reason?"

"No, it is not. The real reason is that death is something I refuse to accept without fighting against it. For thousands of years, humanity has been accustomed to consider their own end as natural, inevitable. Everyone feigns to ignore it or at least tries to think about it as little as possible. It's like... well, imagine, for instance, a very safe cruise ship where suddenly rumors are spread around, among the passengers, that the hull has been damaged and the ship is slowly sinking, but everyone ignores it convinced of the futility of any effort. They all continue undisturbed in their frivolous amusements, instead of trying to solve the problem all together."

"I agree with you. As you have seen, however, in the present time, science has made enormous progresses and people age so slowly that it is fair to affirm that the natural process of aging has, in fact, been disabled. A great achievement for humanity!"

"Unfortunately, their gene therapy would not work for us. We are already too old. No, their science cannot save me. But I'm willing to take the risk again."

"And you need the box. I understand. Unfortunately it is not easy to find. Only Fred could help. I have no idea where he decided to hide it."

"And I do not believe you. You're too smart not to have foreseen that maybe one day you would need to use it. You must have made an agreement with your friend that he would bury it somewhere. If you have chosen a suitable place that has remained unscathed through all these centuries, then the box with the plate is still there."

"I thought about this possibility many times and we discussed it at length with Fred," admitted Heinrich. "It is not so easy: there is basically no safe place that remains untouched for centuries. Burying the box is risky. Even the most carefully hidden Egyptians tombs were often looted and there is no guarantee that natural disasters or devastating wars, such as those of the twentieth century, can spare a seemingly safe hiding place. With Fred, we did not reach any conclusion and I do not know what happened to the box after our escape from prison. Irina and I have done some research, but we could not even find the death certificate of Friedrich. I do not know what happened to him, poor fellow. He was a good friend."

During the entire interview, Oleg had been comparing the story of Heinrich with what Irina had told him and he had found no contradictions. But it was not in his nature to give up so soon.

"Very touching. Then we will do it my way."

He explained what they were trying to do in the lab and announced that he would proceed to transfer Heinrich's memories into the mind of a volunteer. He omitted to add that the poor fellow had been promised to have his life spared if they were successful and if he would be able to remember information contained in Heinrich's head. Oleg explained, in great detail, the high risks of the procedure and that his memories would be cleared.

"We will proceed at very low speed. We recently attempted a partial transfer that worked well that way. The problem is that the amount of exchanged data is very low. I fear that it will take years before we succeed."

"You are a despicable character. I have no interest to prevent you from leaving this time. If I knew where the box is, I would tell you without hesitation, if only to get rid of you. The only reason I got involved in this adventure is because I promised that I would help Irina in finding you. But, I see that she made a big mistake…"

"How do you know? Instead be sure that, over time, she will become more docile and will eventually forget.

On the other hand, as of tomorrow, you will forget about her for sure," Oleg hissed.

Then he walked away. Before exiting, he turned his head and, with a mocking smile, added, "I wish you a good rest, Herr Mayer. Tomorrow we will start early morning and you have to be in top form."

***

The next morning, Oleg and Irina were again face-to-face. Oleg had refused to let her see Heinrich and Irina was desperate.

"I'm sure you guys know where to find the box. Your stubbornness gives me no choice: this morning Mayer will be subjected to the treatment."

And he explained what it was.

Irina, at first incredulous that Oleg could ever be capable of such a monstrosity, realized that he was really serious when he showed her on a monitor the images of the laboratory, where the preparations had already started in the early morning. At the sight of Heinrich being anesthetized, Irina burst into tears.

"Leave him alone! Oleg, *please*. Do it in the name of what once was between us. Take my brain and dry it however you like, but leave Heinrich. Please, do not spoil his beautiful mind and the memories of a lifetime. He does not deserve it. I am the only one responsible for the fact that he's here."

"Uhm… I see that it is really a serious matter between the two of you. Why did you drag him here?"

"To try to find a person. Someone whom I loved to the point of not realizing that he was a monster."

"Come on, Irina." Oleg came closer and brushed her hair. "Do not be unfair: you know I'm not like that. I never wished to hurt you."

Irina felt mounting inside herself a blind rage and the urge to jump to his neck and strangle him. But the most important thing now was to save Heinrich. She fought against herself to dominate her rage, while Oleg caressed her hair gently. She stood there, sobbing, while a wave of disgust shook her stomach at the touch of Oleg.

In the end, she could not make it any longer. She pulled away abruptly and ran down the hallway. She reached her room just in time before her stomach gave out.

Later, lying in bed, she cursed herself. "Perhaps," she thought, "I should have pretended to be still in love with him, to be more available…. Maybe if I call him now… I could ask him to stop it. Or I could pretend to know where that damn box is."

While she tortured herself in this way, she heard a light knock at the door. Imagining that it was Oleg, she wiped her tears with the back of her hand and straightened her hair, with a deep dislike of the image she saw reflected in the golden mirror. "Come in," she finally uttered with a voice that sounded to her different from her own. The voice of a prostitute.

The man who entered was not Oleg.

Irina, surprised and irritated, was about to yell at him to get out immediately, when she realized that the man was beckoning her to keep silent by pointing a vertical finger in front of his nose.

Irina looked at him better.

She could not suppress a cry of joy. She ran into his arms and hugged him tightly. The man smiled and returned her hug, gently pushing her into the bathroom, where he immediately opened the shower and all taps, without saying a single word.

"There may be hidden microphones in the room," he explained later, in a faint voice. "Here we should be safe."

"Oh, Friedrich. What a joy to see you again! But how is this possible? We thought a lot about you."

"Irina, I'm so glad I found you!" He hugged her again. "Let me explain. A few years after you left, I decided to follow you and asked Anselmo to anticipate my arrival by a few years. So I had time to prepare everything for your arrival. I knew the place and the time and I had arranged for your recovery at sea. But that day I arrived too late: a failure aboard our boat cost us five hours of delay and when we arrived on site, you had already been fished out. A terrible bad luck. Since then, I have tried by all means to know what happened to you… but I'll explain everything in detail at another time. Now we must act quickly to save Heinrich."

"How?"

"Contact Oleg immediately. Tell him you are willing to talk. Tell him where the box is."

"He will not believe me."

"Yes he will. Show him this."

Fred showed her a photo. It depicted an ugly ring with a large black stone that reflected a bluish glow.

"Oleg has still with him the ring that is the twin of this one. The photo shows that the ring is now in the same epoch where we are. The only ones who might have taken this picture are you or Heinrich. Or me. Tell him that the box is in Vienna. Take courage: you'll see that he will believe you."

"But Oleg wants to know exactly where the box is hidden."

"Tell him that I hid it in the cathedral of St. Stephen, inside the sarcophagus that holds the remains of Emperor Frederick III. If he will not free Heinrich immediately, I will destroy the box."

"He will try to stop you."

"Tell him that I can blow up the box at any time, simply by typing a message from my mobile phone. Explain also that I bribed one of his guys to let you get this phone and that I used it to communicate with you."

He handed her a satellite phone.

"I never imagined that I could instead manage to reach you in person, here in Bretigny."

"But how did you do it?"

"Money. You can do almost anything with money. I'll explain later. Now I have to disappear quickly, otherwise I risk being discovered. Go to him and tell him I want to hear the voice of Heinrich, free and in good health, by tonight. Otherwise the box will blow up in a thousand pieces. Oh, and… also tell him not to waste time trying to locate me through my satellite phone. I have means to become aware of that, at any time. In such a circumstance, he would get the same pyrotechnic result as before. I think that's all. See you soon, Irina. I will wait for you in Vienna in two days. Oleg can use the box as he desires and, in this way, we will get rid of him *forever*."

The threatening tone he used when he uttered 'forever' was not unnoticed by Irina.

Maybe it could work.

Now there was no time to waste.

***

In the heart of the old Vienna the colorful tiles on the roof of St. Stephen's Cathedral reflected the bright moonlight. The cafes and restaurants had closed some time earlier and the square – teeming with tourists during the day – was now completely deserted.

The huge dark mass of the cathedral with its towers soaring in the clear night sky was a large stain of black ink in a carpet of glittering stars. Irina felt a lump in her throat in front of the once familiar vision she had dreamed of for so long. Heinrich could read her emotions on her pale face while she was staring at the sight in front of her.

He took her hand and they walked to a side entrance hidden in the shadow of the cathedral. Oleg followed them, alone, with neither bodyguards nor any other potential witness, carrying an eye-catching shoulder backpack.

The door was ajar and the three of them stepped inside trying to make as little noise as possible. The echo of their soft footsteps broke the solemn silence of the huge empty space, a heavy silence that seemed to weigh on their heads. Inside, a metal framing formed an awkward sort of skeletal shape near the apse and projected long shadows on the walls in the light of the few votive candles burning near the entrance gate. The restoration work hid from the visitor the elegance of that happy mixture of Gothic and Romanesque architecture that raised toward the sky in a single dizzying leap of the three naves.

They walked cautiously to the altar, trying to peer into the threatening semi-darkness of the aisles. Suddenly, a hoist driven by an electric motor started a slow descent to the floor.

The three froze.

Oleg extracted a handgun from its holster and took off the safety. The hoist moved slowly down to the red marble sarcophagus of Frederick III and finally stopped.

Fred slipped out from behind the column that hid him from the sight of the three and walked in their direction. Heinrich hugged him, happy to have rejoined his friend.

Oleg pointed the gun at him.

"It's just a little precaution, Friedrich, I do not really want to use it. I trust you. Let's try to end this business quickly," explained Oleg, keeping the gun pointed at him.

Aided by Heinrich, Fred harnessed the heavy lid of the marble sarcophagus and maneuvered the hoist. For quite a while, everything remained still, the taut straps creaking on their supports. Then the eight-ton tombstone lifted up by millimeters and slid painfully slowly to the side. Fred deftly maneuvered the hoist and finally placed it on the floor next to the sarcophagus.

Oleg jumped forward and peered inside. Then he turned to Fred, a look of bewilderment on his face. Behind him a shadow had emerged suddenly from the darkness and now Fred had a second gun pointed at his head.

A familiar voice spoke to Oleg, his tone calm and reassuring.

"Put it down to the ground, dear Oleg… slowly… and kick it in my direction. If you follow my advice you will see that everything will be fine."

"Albert! What are you doing here?" asked Oleg while reluctantly dropping his gun.

"It was not an appropriate move for a gentleman, dear Oleg, to conceal from a friend the most interesting part of the business. The old man that you know of is apparently not happy at all about you…"

"That rogue, do you work for him now? If so, then you are in deep trouble, dear Albert. Those are people who do not mess around."

"True. In fact, the old man is *very* disappointed and wants to see you soon."

As he spoke, he made him back away.
Slowly.

Finally, he picked up Oleg's gun.

"And now let's see what we have got here."

He leaned his head over the high sarcophagus and peered inside, illuminating it with a flashlight.

Surprise and disappointment.

Albert could not help but take a second look. That moment of distraction was fatal to him as it was long enough to allow Oleg to pounce on him. Albert's automatic gun, equipped with a silencer, fired two muffled shots.

Oleg slumped on his side, clutching his leg and screaming in pain. But it was too late: Heinrich and Fred had also attacked Albert and were struggling to restrain him.

Albert was well trained and defended himself like a lion. In the melee that followed, they rolled along the floor of the cathedral in a jumble of tangled bodies. Albert was hitting both very hard and was likely to win the game, when Oleg, dragging his injured leg, grabbed a heavy metal candlestick and joined the fray using it like a mace. Fred quickly ducked to dodge the deadly blow he saw out of the corner of his eye coming in their direction. Albert instead was hit in full and collapsed to the ground, his skull smashed.

Oleg, exhausted, collapsed to the floor, a visible patch of blood spreading on his pants. Irina ran to his aid, let him lie on the floor and bared his leg. She was relieved to see that the bullet had gone through Oleg's thigh without severing the femoral artery. Using what she could find inside Oleg's backpack, she made a tight bandage that stopped the bleeding.

"You cheated me," complained Oleg, gritting his teeth in pain.

"Not really," explained Fred. "I came here, removed the case from the sarcophagus and moved it to a safer place. It was only a small precaution. Don't blame me for that. In the grave there are only the remains of the emperor."

"Let's get out of here quickly," Oleg hissed. "It looks as though Albert came here alone, but not far away there could be a bunch of henchmen of the old rogue. Give me a hand to get up."

Heinrich and Fred helped him get up and they slowly reached the exit.

Not far from the cathedral, Fred had parked a van that carried the banner of the company in charge of the restoration work. Oleg was complaining about the terrible pain in his leg. They shoved him quickly inside the vehicle and drove away in the direction of the outskirts of the town.

***

Glued to the window, Heinrich began to orient himself only after the countryside had taken over the maze of glass and steel that had spread, over the centuries, like wildfire around the old town. Under the bright moonlight, the irrigation channels had turned into long silver strips of molten metal breaking the darkness of the cultivated fields and alternating with the dark shadows of the woods or the dim lights of small groups of houses. Slowly, the landscape turned into something vaguely familiar to Heinrich's eyes.

Fred smirked when the van stopped in front of a brick cottage covered with ivy and now standing in place of the old hunting lodge demolished centuries before. Heinrich gave no sign of having recognized the place and looked amazed at Fred.

"A nice surprise, no? The old pavilion is gone. Instead, here is this charming cottage. It was for sale, and then I thought…"

Irina squeezed her hand into Heinrich's.

"It's wonderful!" she exclaimed. She could not take her eyes from the lovely garden, the windows framed by flower pots. Maybe, she thought, they had finally reached the end of their journey. Perhaps, in a house like that, she would age beside Heinrich together with their children.

She wished nothing more.

Inside, another surprise was awaiting for them. A young woman ran into Fred's hug and kissed him passionately, her arms around his neck

"Let me introduce Uma, my wife," said Fred, beaming with happiness, when he had recovered his breath.

"Bravo, Fred, I see you've been busy at work!" Heinrich complimented him, smiling and winking in the direction of Uma whose silhouette clearly showed a rotundity that she could no longer hide.

"And you have dared to leave this lovely creature alone and in that state to come and look for us? You're a real monster, dear Fred," Irina scolded him, with a forgiving smile.

She had already decided that Uma looked nice to her and the two women, as magnetized by a mutual attraction, soon got busy in a tight conversation, while the men helped Oleg to lie on a cot.

Heinrich inspected Oleg's naked leg. The bullet had left a clean wound, but it was still bleeding. They carefully disinfected the wound and administered an injection of a powerful antibiotic. Then they called Irina for help because they did not know what else had to be done.

Almost annoyed at being interrupted in her conversation with the pregnant young lady, Irina looked at the wound with a detached and professional attitude.

"Nothing serious. The bullet came out in one piece. You just need a couple of stitches," she said, looking straight into Oleg's eyes.

"Yes, stitches that I would have gladly applied without anesthesia…" she added with a vindictive smile, as she pulled out a bottle from the first-aid kit, "but fortunately for you in this highly civilized time it will be sufficient to spread this kind of glue on the two edges of the wound and it will heal quickly and without pain. Tonight though, you will get a high fever. But tomorrow you will be able to stand up."

"Thanks, Irina," Oleg whimpered, his eyes glued to the floor. "I hope I can make it. We must not stay here too long, otherwise the old man's people will find us. When you came to Bretigny I disabled the bug that Albert implanted in your leg, so they cannot track us. This will make them waste time, but we are probably not more than a few hours ahead of them."

Irina ignored him and continued to do her job on the wound.

"Tomorrow early morning we will leave this house and I will bring you to the place where I hid the box. I do not think they will be able to find out easily where we are. At least, not tonight," said Fred.

"But the problem must be resolved once and for all," said Oleg. "The old rogue will not give up until he puts his dirty hands on me. I cannot let you get hurt after I am gone. It is a matter between me and him. And I have a pretty good idea of how to settle this matter once for all."

"Maybe it's the same idea that has occurred to me…" Fred smiled.

"We will send him a gift," said Oleg. "I'll talk about that with Anselmo. I know the coordinates of the villa and it should be just a breeze for Anselmo to deliver the parcel."

Fred nodded and the two exchanged a knowing smile.

Overnight, Oleg's pain became unbearable. He had a high fever and was drenched with sweat.

Irina got out of bed to assist him.

She was cooling his forehead with a wet cloth when Oleg reached out to grab her wrist.

She pulled her hand right away.

"Oleg, we have nothing more to say to each other. I just hope that tomorrow you will feel better and be gone."

"I'm so sorry, Irina. You have all the reasons to hate me for what I did to you."

Irina nodded, but her resentment had given way to an expression in her face that Oleg knew very well. She was studying him. Now it was up to him to try to convince her of his feelings.

"Irina, I know very well that I cannot help but leave. This time it'll be fine. Please come away with me. Let's start it all over again. Together we can still build a new life and I'm sure there we will be time to forget… time to forgive…"

"It's too late, Oleg. For you, the life I dreamed for us was just too small a thing. Simply not enough for you. You knew it would end too soon and you could not resign to it. For me it is different. Life – as my father would say – is made of small things: what matters is the intensity with which you live, not how long. It is a great effort, life, and an extraordinarily long one must really be worth it, otherwise it can become an unbearable burden. Are you sure you want it?"

"Yes, Irina. I do. It is what I have always hoped for."

"Life runs too fast," he added. "Worse, over the years my perception of time has changed. Now I am sure time does not run at a constant speed. It runs increasingly faster with age, like hailstones that start falling on your head one by one, then faster and faster until they hit you as a fierce cascade. Life is a like a meat grinder: you grow, you die, and in the meantime you live at a pace that you cannot control. I cannot accept this. I saw with my own eyes that, in the time where we are now, mankind has been able to escape this merciless mechanism. So, I was not mistaken."

"Yes, you are right. Here people live much longer and without the slow decline of age. But do you think they are happier?"

"What is happiness for you?"

"It's a difficult question. When one tries to remember the most important things of one's life we always focus on some special events (like the day you graduated, a wedding, a birth) and we tend to forget those of minor relevance, those rare but lucky moments when we have been able, just for a moment, to slow down the pace of time or even to stop it. It is perhaps only in one of those moments – suspended in a time bubble where the strokes of time are frozen – that we can happen to grasp the sublime beauty of a light ray refracted by a drop of dew, the elegance in the movement of a swallow, the harmony of shapes, colors and sounds, whether by nature or by human expression. It is perhaps only in one of those rare moments that we feel amazement for what we usually neglect, all taken as we are by the relentless pace of our lives. By the pace of the meat grinder, as you would say.

"I do not believe in beauty, elegance, harmony as absolute categories. I simply rely on my perceptions. If, for a few grains of rice, the smile of a hungry child is able to slow down the hands of my clock in the same way as a Vermeer's painting does, well, that's *my* time, the time of my perception. Nothing absolute. And that's why it is even rarer to share these moments with another person."

"But we did it. Sometimes."

"Yes we did, Oleg. We did it. And it was beautiful. A piece of our lives is enclosed in those moments. No one can take them away. Neither can I, even if I wished to. But now that time has gone."

"I've lost you and it hurts. You will never forgive me, will you?"

Irina did not answer.

"Tomorrow I'll be gone," Oleg cleared his throat, "and I have no idea what will happen to me. Maybe I will smash into a thousand pieces against a solid body or perhaps I will find a civilization destroyed by some war. Who can predict the fate of humanity? But I want to know. I want to take that risk. I cannot sit here with my hands in my lap…"

"I know. You told me so many times, Oleg. I wish that this long life of yours will not become a conviction. I've already forgiven you."

Their eyes met and Irina recognized in Oleg's something that reminded her of a time long gone.

"I do want you to be happy, Irina. There is not much I can do for you… but in some sense I believe I have already done it. Before leaving, I told my lawyers… you know, the villa of Bretigny… is yours and also…"

"I do not care for your money," Irina interrupted him dryly. Her voice had become hard again.

"Please do accept this gift. You may need it one day. Do it for your children… for those that will come, I mean."

"You have a high fever, Oleg. Sleep now. Tomorrow it will be a long day for you."

***

As Irina had predicted, the next morning Oleg's fever was over. He got out of bed, pale, stubble faced and ravenous. He limped slightly, but he made it to the kitchen where he ate such a huge amount of food leaving everybody bewildered. All but Irina, who knew him quite well.

Wasting no more time, the five of them took place in the van and left the cottage, heading South. They drove on back tracks through the woods, avoiding as much as possible the main roads and the villages. It was a beautiful summer day; the sun was high and shone strong in a cloudless clear sky. The air was getting cool and crisp as they climbed higher, among the fir trees. It was a moment of great hope and all the suffering and anguish of the previous weeks seemed to belong to the past.

Oleg looked more relaxed and did not seem concerned at all about what awaited him. He was sitting in front, next to Fred who was driving the van. He watched the green mountain landscape that developed before his eyes without uttering a word until he suddenly realized where they were directed. He started laughing.

"You do not want to bring me back to the same place where I started?"

"Why not?" Fred smiled, amused.

"It could be embarrassing. When I left that dingy little hotel, I think I... neglected to pay the bill. I prefer not to take the risk they still remember it."

Everyone laughed, except Irina.

Indeed there was no reason to worry: the hotel no longer existed. In its place, a series of villas had been built with a magnificent view of the lake. Children were playing on the lake shore and their shrieks and laughter could be heard at a distance.

After the village, the car left the highway and turned onto a dirt road. Fred drove slowly along the steep and narrow path that climbed uphill. Fortunately Uma did not suffer from car sickness and she felt comfortable enough despite the hairpin bends. They reached a clearing where they could see the whole valley. Below, the lake sparkled with golden patches of light. The air was crystal clear.

"From here on we will have to go on foot," announced Fred. "The hut is not far. Only a short walking distance. Uma will have a chance to stretch her legs a bit."

The small hut was built with wooden logs and was little more than a tool shed.

"Heinrich, please come in and give me a hand to carry out the box," Fred invited him.

They looked as if setting the table for a barbecue, but Oleg was already searching the nearby ground area for something suitable to his purpose. Eventually he found a large square stone partially buried on the ground. They pulled it out and it was so heavy that two of them could hardly manage to move it. They rolled it near the wooden case that they had placed under a tree.

"It looks something in between a picnic and a funeral," said Oleg, in a good mood, pointing to the box.

"We shall first take care of the old man and deliver the gift we have prepared for him," he added, casting a knowing glance to Fred.

"Maybe we are overreacting," warned Heinrich. "That stone looks a bit too big."

"Better not to take any chance," Oleg said curtly,"I've been told that the old man never leaves the villa. We will get him for sure. If you consider that I almost managed to knock down a brick wall simply using a coin, then with this sweet cake… I think that very little will be left of that dirty murderer. I only regret for the stupendous artworks in the living room."

Fred passed him the ring and the earring. Then he waited until Oleg opened his eyes again after his contact with Anselmo.

"Anselmo was annoyed. He says it is in the human nature to identify immediately in any new technology the way to transform it into a lethal weapon. He says that we are a primitive race."

"So did he refuse to do it?"

"Yes. But I ordered him to do it anyway. After all, he is nothing but a machine and he has been programmed to obey orders. Come on, give me a hand to ship this jolly package…"

Only with the considerable effort of three people they were able to slowly lay down the stone inside the case. Then they closed the lid. Oleg placed his hand on the plate and closed his eyes.

"Done!" he exclaimed shortly after with a broad smile of satisfaction on his lips.

"I regret for the evil I did to those poor people who were used as guinea pigs. I should not have allowed that, but the old madman forced me to do it. He would have killed them anyway. Now at least they have their revenge. I did track down their families and they too will receive a pack, but this time of a different nature. It will help them to live with dignity."

At that precise moment – as it was reported on the next day in the London morning newspapers – a powerful explosion literally blew a secluded villa in the green Essex countryside up into pieces. There was a rumor that it was the result of a settling of scores, as it was known that the house was frequented by people of ill repute. Only two oil paintings had emerged intact from the smoking ruins, by sheer miracle, as someone said. One turned out to be a famous painting by Breugel the Elder, stolen centuries before in Vienna. It had reappeared later in London where it had been sold at an auction at Sotheby's and purchased by an anonymous buyer for a staggering figure. It was said that the painting would be returned to the city of Vienna and displayed along with other works by the same painter in the Kunsthistorisches Museum.

"Now it's my turn," said Oleg, looking at the bottom of the case, now empty.

They helped him to wear a neoprene wetsuit and a life jacket.

"What time at destination did you choose?" asked Irina.

"It took me a while to figure it out. My guess is that a couple of hundred years should be enough. I do not trust to go beyond. I fear that, sooner or later, mankind will meet a sad end."

They had already discussed what to do with the case.

"As the box has been reactivated, I'm sure someone has already taken notice of it and will try to get it back. All you need to do is to move it as soon as possible from here. You'd better return the case to the cathedral. It is a good hiding place and, one day, you may change your mind and decide to use it for yourself or for your children."

Irina nodded.

She was well aware that Oleg wished to be sure to know where he might eventually find it, just in case he would need it again. But Irina thought otherwise. She was determined to get rid of it forever and prevent anybody from using it.

For this reason she had lied to Oleg. They would simply hide the case inside the shed and just leave. That's all. She did not want to take the risk that someone might chase her for the box. If one day they would come, well, let the damn box be theirs and let her alone in peace!

She looked at Oleg for the first time with indulgence.

Soon he would be gone.

Forever.

She was overwhelmed by the memories of her time with him and she knew very well how much she had loved him.

She considered that, at all times in history, there are men and women who cannot resign themselves to their fate. Without those navigators of the unknown we would never have discovered the new lands hidden across the ocean, nor the planets hidden in deep space beyond the sun.

Oleg was one of them.

His horizon was the human lifespan.

His barrier was the wall of time.

Now he was going to cross the barrier again and nobody except Irina, perhaps, could prevent him from doing that. But she had decided to let him go. They were too different: she had realized it too late.

Now Irina had before her an entire new life.

It was just one, and it would not last long.

But she was determined not to waste a single drop of it.

And that was enough for her.

Author's Note

The "Villa dei Papiri" in Herculaneum

The "Villa dei Papiri," a sumptuous Roman villa, was discovered in the Bourbon period in Herculaneum. It probably belonged to Lucius Calpurnius Piso Cesonino, father-in-law of Julius Caesar and consul in 58 BC.

The villa was initially explored from 1750 to 1765 through a network of tunnels that were dug in a compact layer of solidified mud lava about twenty meters deep. The excavations, carried out under the supervision of the Swiss engineer Karl Jakob Weber, led to the creation of a map of the villa. The first excavations allowed access to a rich library in which 1826 papyrus scrolls were found. The villa was named after them.

The huge villa is spread over multiple levels along a side parallel to the sea stretching for about 250 meters from an elegant round lookout. Continuing eastward, a large peristyle with 25 columns on the long sides, almost 100 meters long and with a central ornamental pool (*natatio*), was linked to a smaller peristyle of square shape via an room identified as *tablinium* (archive room). The eastern building hosting the accommodation facilities contained the library.

As of today, a large part of the villa is still buried and not completely explored.

The library

Filodemo of Gadara, refined poet, author of elegant epigrams and philosopher of the Epicurean school, had arrived in Italy from Athens in the late first century BC and he had strong personal friendships with Piso Cesonino.

In the villa at Herculaneum, Filodemo had collected an impressive library with copies of his innumerable works, transcribed on papyrus scrolls, and writings of the masters of philosophical schools and of Epicureanism opponents. The alleged intention of Filodemo was to create a center of diffusion of the Epicurean philosophy in the context of an ideal refoundation in Italy of the Garden of Epicurus in Athens. In the elegant surroundings of the villa, Filodemo met with his friends in a cenaculum where they used to discuss the philosophy of Epicurus and to read his works.

The papyri

In the tunnels dug into the archeological site of the Villa of the Pisoni family, in addition to numerous sculptures of marble and bronze, the Bourbon excavators found blackened cylinder-shaped objects that looked like pieces of coal. Their first reaction was to throw them away as debris of no interest or as the remains of wooden structures. Fortunately, in a few broken rolls appeared traces of writing that revealed their nature of ancient books, transcribed on papyrus scrolls.

After the first trials to unroll the scrolls with disastrous results, various techniques were envisaged that have evolved to the present day. The method known as "scorzatura" consisted in wetting the rolls with hydro-alcoholic solutions, solvents and glutinous substances and then cut them into two semi-cylinders. The inner surface of the two portions was scratched to reveal a portion of readable text that was transcribed and then destroyed so to be able to uncover the underlying sheet. Only the outer layers of the two semi-cylinders, known as "peels" were preserved pasting them on a sheet of canvas or paper.

In 1753, father Antonio Piaggio invented a machine to unroll the papyri that has been in use until the early twentieth century. A portion of the outer surface of the papyrus was smeared with glue and a sheet of membrane, obtained from animal intestines, was connected with silk threads. The machine slowly exerted a gradual pull on the roll thanks to a series of keys to which the silk threads were connected.

A more modern method, dating back to the eighties, is based instead on the use of a paste of gelatin and acetic acid of varying proportions in relation to the degree of carbonization of the papyrus. The several phases of the operation are accompanied by a photographic documentation of the original position of the pieces.

In addition to the writings of Filodemo, the recovered rolls have unveiled important Greek texts such as the famous work of Epicurus, *The Nature,* and the works of other Epicurean philosophers as Demetrius Laco, Polystrate, Carneisco, Colotes and Metrodorus both from Lampsacus, and the stoic Chrysippus. There are few works in Latin, including comedies, historical works, political and legal texts.

Acknowledgements

I would like to express my most sincere thanks to the many friends who encouraged me to translate this book into English from its original Italian version. In particular I would like to thank Prof. Martin Israel and his wife Margaret for their careful reading of the manuscript and patient correction of the many language imperfections therein.

Many, but not all, of my early readers are physicists like me and my wife Agnese. They share with us a real passion for the old good books of science fiction (ranging from the classics, as for instance "*The Time Machine*" by H. G. Wells, to the more modern works known today under the collective name of "hard sci-fi") and also for a branch of literature that cannot be strictly categorized as science fiction, but rather as highly imaginative fiction (e.g., *El Aleph* by J. L. Borges).

My wife and my daughter Alessandra had to endure a severe strain test as this book was mainly written during the summer holidays. It owes its existence to their remarkable patience.

I would also like to thank my early readers who gave me advice on several aspects of the story and suggested that I should consider writing a sequel of Oleg's wanderings in a more distant future.